ANGEL OF THE ABYSS

Stella Drexler

An imprint of Diogenes Club Press

Worldly, Whimsical, and Weird Books

www.diogenesclubpress.com

Dallas, TX

DC Dreams, an imprint of Diogenes Club Press
8619 Reva St. Dallas, TX 74227
www.diogenesclubpress.com

The characters and events in this book are fictional. Any similarity to real persons, living or dead, is coincidental and not intended by the author.

ISBN: 9781622010073
Library of Congress Control Number: 2017955900

CHAPTER ONE

*D*usk descended upon the capital city of Zooni, on the west side of Varuna in the shadow of the widely venerated Queens's majestic palace. The glittering glass and gold tents of the Carnivale of Magic and Mysterie glinted in the last rays of the setting sun against a sky emblazoned a dazzling scarlet. They nearly blinded Jila as she moved through the jubilant crowd still cascading into the streets at the end of their business or market day to catch a glimpse of the revered spectacle of the travelling circus. Laughter and shrieks of excitement, fear and delight filled the air.

A small troupe of acrobats in metallic blue and silver costumes bounded through the delighted crowd, cutting a line through the centre. They leapt up and down. They whirled in the air and tumbled all over each other. Men and women with copper and blue, pink, red and gold masques dressed in elegant, lush liveries wandered the crowd. Ribbons flowed from their elaborate headdresses. They were indistinguishable as the carnival players or Varunians. On this magical evening, they were all the same. Jila was among the Varunians disguised. The masque that covered her pale, distinct features was copper and metallic pink, glinting in the last rays of the falling sun. Her long, black hair flowed like liquid to her waist. She felt light and liberated and exhilarated by the cries of her people around her, united in exhibition.

Under one of the of the sparkling glass domes, an Abyssal marionette puppet show was in full swing. Children gathered around the stage to watch the funny little automatons act out their maniacal scene. A short man with a large, red painted nose in a pointed hat and brown coattails shouted to the crowd, directing them to the show and collecting their money. Drums and pan pipes punctuated the strange, unnatural movements of Mr. Punch and the Minstrel. The marionettes possessed an uncanny sentience, moving without the direction of a puppeteer. Their voices seemed to issue from somewhere within them, as if they had tiny voice boxes inside their bellies.

The Abyssal puppets did not hold Jila's attention for long. She had seen such a thing many times before. Six clowns in shiny costumes, as huge as giants and giggling like mad, juggled huge, ominously sharp bronze knives that caught the dazzling, multi-coloured lights of the circus on their surface. The knives emitted a shower of sparks when they collided in the air. Jila passed the clowns, smiling at their comically painted faces--comedy, tragedy, anger, surprise, confusion, laughter--and pushed through the group of young men and women dancing in the streets. In the centre of the dancers was a large, glowing blue globe that spun in dizzying patterns. Music rose from the globe: a quick, spirited and ecstatic melody. The dancers spun and leaped and twirled in time.

Jila ducked as lightning arced from the globe, causing the hair on her arms to stand straight up and the dancers to shriek and laugh as it struck them. Perhaps it gave them a small jolt, a thrill, spurring them to faster, wilder steps. Jila laughed in delight, pausing only a moment to watch the young people before moving forwards, through the throng of animals from lands both near and foreign. Some were familiar and plain, with long trunks and huge bellies. Others were strange and exotic with metallic skins and brass armour.

A fire-breather spat streams of flame into the crowd. Above their heads, in the darkening sky, fire-works popped, sending sparks cascading over the pointed tips of the circus tents, turning to oddly sweetly scented ash before floating down on top of the crowd. The air practically crackled with Abyssal energy, smelling faintly of the sea where the Abyssium was buried in the darkest caverns of the deep.

Jila's ladies-in-waiting trailed several paces behind, keener to pause and view the spectacles than their mistress. She turned to call to them over her shoulder, bidding them join her before a small, glass and gold box. The Abyssal fortune-teller had been popular in the early days of the Carnivale. Now it was only a sentimentality, a relic of the days before the people required more thrilling, imaginative displays. Jila stood behind a mother and her young daughter, whose face was painted with garish flowers and butterflies. Clutching her money in her hand, Jila felt once again like a young, innocent princess, enjoying the Abyssal circus for the first time under the watchful eye of her indulgent father.

When the young girl stepped away from the box, dragging her mother impatiently along towards more exciting fare, Jila stepped up to the gilded box. Her pulse leapt and her skin tingled slightly. A tarnished, gold placard on the base of the box read: Marjan, Mysteries and Fortunes. Jila did not turn to her ladies. If they had followed her to peer over her shoulder and hear her fortune, she did not notice them. Marjan was a small, delicate ivory and brass doll with long, curling blonde hair and the sweet face of a young girl. The little doll moved with slow, jerky movements in her enclosure. Its glittering green jewelled eyes spun towards Jila as if it could actually see her.

Jila slid her money into the small slot beneath the base of the box. It disappeared, as if snatched up by an invisible hand. Marjan leaned forwards with

4

a strange, eerie grace, as if to catch a better glimpse of her subject. When her voice issued from some hidden place, from some Abyssal core inside the tiny doll, it was high and sweet and piercing. It carried on the air with spine-chilling clarity.

"Queen Jila, you are in grave danger."

A murmur passed through the nearby crowd, carrying like a cry and spreading as quickly as a wild fire. "Her Highness!" "The Queen!" "Queen Jila!" "The Queen is here!"

A frisson of fear raced down her spine. Jila's guards, too, must have felt a ripple of indefinable apprehension. They appeared perplexedly, emerging from tents and the arms of beautiful circus performers in stunning, glittering costumes. The crowd parted as one, leaving her alone with her grim soothsayer in the centre of a teeming gauntlet. A startled shriek rent the suddenly still, eerily quiet night. Jila spun, in time to see light glint off the blade of a giggling clown's bronze knife as it hurtled through the air.

Fear seized her. The lights, the music and the spectacle of the carnival had surely weakened her wits, for she had not the sense to step from the path of her certain death. Time seemed to slow in the dread of the moment. She saw the flash of the blade. She saw the alarm on the faces of her people and her ladies. She experienced a moment of simple resignation. She closed her eyes, lifting her chin. She did not feel the blade. She did not feel the pierce of it through her skin or her heart.

Screams echoed through the crowd. When she opened her eyes, time snapped back to its former pace. A young, fair-haired boy in her guard's livery wobbled in front of her. He turned to her. His large, glittering green eyes were wide and supplicating. She stepped forward. She caught him as he collapsed to the cobblestone at her feet, clutching the hilt of the knife in his chest. It had sliced through him as if his skin were butter, piercing straight through his ribcage to his heart.

The young guard was dead almost before they reached the ground, sinking into a pool of his blood. She heard the last, soft murmur of his breath as he whispered her name. Jila did not notice as her guards surrounded her and the young man. His name was Jasper. He only just joined the palace guards. If they ran into the crowd to discover the assassin, she did not hear their shouts or their commands. Queen Jila exclaimed in shock and grief and deep, anguished outrage. His name was Jasper.

She ripped off her mask, tossing it to the ground where it was instantly soaked and stained with the young man's blood. Her long, black hair covered them like a veil, shielding them from the dazed and curious onlookers as she cradled his head in her lap. Her tears spilled onto his pale, frozen face. "Jasper, oh, my darling boy. You have done so well. So very well." She brushed a stray lock of his fair hair from his eyes. She smiled down at him. Her tears streaked unrestrained down her cheeks. They pooled in the blood at the corner of his mouth.

"My Queen, we must go. It is not safe here." Jila looked up, into the dark, tormented eyes of the tall guard leaning over her. Captain Jaime Rand looked as if he meant to drag her by the arm to her feet. Yet, he did not dare touch her without permission. "Your assassin may still be in the crowd, Your Highness."

"Take his body," she murmured, peering back down into the young face of her saviour. "Take him to his family."

"He has no family, Majesty."

Her deep, dark eyes were glittering with ferocity. "Then take him back to the palace! He will be honoured. He saved my life."

"Yes, my Queen."

Captain Rand stepped back and motioned to the guards around him. They lifted Jasper unceremoniously from the Queen's arms, hoisting him over the shoulder of the largest of her men. "Be careful with him."

The onlookers did not move as the procession passed, leading the Queen away from the carnival in painful silence. Murmurs spread through the stunned, terrified crowd. Mothers wept softly for the youth while their children sobbed in confusion at their sides. The laughter and crackle of excitement and pleasure in the air was quiet. The fires were tamped out. The Abyssal globe still spun. Its brilliant arcs of lightning struck out into the evening sky. The music seemed remote, distant and tinny. There was no one dancing.

The Queen's gilded airship was waiting on its landing strip. It seemed to glow in the dusk. Its sleek, globular body, a radiant, luminous ivory, was silhouetted against the purple sky. Jila watched as the guards lifted the young man carefully into the berth. Her heart ached for the loss of the brave guard's young life and the innocence of her childhood memories.

Captain Rand offered his hand to assist her into the ship. "Your Highness?"

She did not turn to peer back at the Carnivale of Magic and Mysterie. Her ladies-in-waiting surrounded her morosely as she took her cushioned ivory throne in the centre of the berth. The propellers kicked up dust as they whirred to life. The ship lifted gracefully, silently into the air and away from Zooni.

6

* * *

The sun rose slowly in the east. An angel cast a strange shadow over the quiet, morose funeral party. Beads of light, warm rain pelted the ladies' black parasols and the shining polished brass of Jasper's coffin as it was lowered unhurriedly into the grave. The soft, melodic drops punctuated the minister's final murmured prayer. Queen Jila sighed deeply. No parents or friends had come to mourn the young man who had sacrificed his life to save his queen. He had been an orphan, one of the city's lost boys. But he had died a hero. He would be honoured as a hero in Varuna for years to come.

Queen Jila turned decisively away from the grave. She led her ladies in waiting silently up the winding, overgrown path towards the sprawling palace. The gold and copper domes of the palace were just visible over the cemetery's spindly, black, claw-like, leaf-less trees. They sparkled in the early dawn sun. The domes seemed strangely out of place. They were offensively garishness against the forlorn place of fallen warriors, heroes, and the Queen's ancestors. This place had seen better days. It had seen sun and light and spirit. Today, on this dreary grey morning, it seemed a place of deepest gloom.

Crumbling black stone and metal angels loomed over the graves, casting shadows over them. They alone mourned the lost when no one else came. The dilapidated stone mausoleum through which their procession slowly passed was tarnished with age and neglect. The once lustrous tombs were decaying and lonely and despairing. The dreariness of the mausoleum clung to them as they emerged back onto the path towards the tall, rusted brass gate. It creaked in anguish when the Queen's escort pushed it open, gesturing her towards the sparkling, rambling palace courtyard.

Passing through the gate out of the wretched, murky cemetery was as if passing into another world. The early morning sun shone brightly over the blooming spring garden, brilliant with roses of white, red and gold. Perfectly manicured bushes and gleaming bronze statues, a superior depiction of the lost interred in the graves behind them, lined their cobblestone path. The Queen sighed softy in relief. The vestiges of depression and morbidity left her as she left young Jasper, her fallen hero. The shadow over her pale, brazen features passed. She turned her face up towards the sun for a brief, indulgent moment.

Queen Jila was not to linger long in indulgence. In her chambers, she removed the funeral veil from her carefully plaited hair and tossed it atop the rich, scarlet brocade of the counterpane. She yanked decisively on a large, brass bell on the pull chain beside the bed. She had only reached her office before her tall, thin major-domo appeared at her door. His steel grey hair was combed as

7

meticulously as ever it was. His black suit was crisp and pristine. He wore an expression of complete compliance on his dark, patrician features.

"Your Majesty?" Abraham asked, bowing deeply.

Jila strode to meet him in the doorway. Her sad, weeping mien of mourning was gone, replaced with a cold, indomitable resolve. "Abraham, there has been an attempt on my life."

Abraham's face did not reveal any sentiment. He raised his thick, black eyebrows impassively. "Your Majesty?"

"It is time for Kai Vale to return to the palace."

He inclined his head. "Yes, my Queen. Right away." He spun on his heel and was gone with the sharp, quick click of shining black heels.

Jila sighed, pinching the bridge of her nose in consternation. There was little choice in the matter. She could allow no one else to die in her place.

* * *

Kai raced past the rickety, wooden storefronts. Her boots kicked up dust as they pounded the well-worn dirt road through the sad, lonely town. The people of the nameless, faceless, inconsequential little town ducked into their homes as soon as they saw her. They peered cagily through the drab curtains of dirty windows to watch the pursuit, fearful to rouse the interest of the woman and the angry cadre on her heels.

Kai tucked the small, bronze sea horse into a pocket on her thigh, barely chancing a glance behind her. She did not pull her guns. Beams of deadly light rushed past her ear, crackling and humming in the charged air before they were drowned by the shouts of the thieves at her back. A glass street light above her head shattered. She ducked, dodging to the left to avoid it. She was obliged to dodge again, to the right, as one of the thieves' miscalculated shots struck the dilapidated roof of the suddenly quiet, breathless saloon. The remnants of the roof sprinkled the ground in a shower of sharp, jagged splinters and dusty plaster.

She burst through the gauntlet of the main thoroughfare, reaching the edges of the terrified town. Even the horses seemed to sense the trouble. They pawed restlessly at the ground as if they wanted to flee or join the chase. They snorted and whinnied. They shied away as the group of men reached them, shouting orders and curses and threats.

Kai did not pause to reply to her cross pursuers or to select a mount upon which to escape them.

Ahead, just beyond the borders of the town where weeds sprung up through the loose, dusty earth, her flyer waited, practically humming in the brilliant afternoon sun. She did not chance a glance behind her. She yanked down the goggles from the top of her head to shield her eyes from the sun and the swirling dirt. She leapt upon the flat, tarnished brass body of the flyer and yanked up on the arched, copper steering bar. She did not sit upon the worn, dusty brown leather seat. She swayed slightly as the flyer lifted abruptly in the air. The propellers stirred the dust beneath her, concealing her in the sudden storm.

Kai cackled, pushing the tiller forwards sharply. The long, skeletal copper wings flapped wildly. The flyer shot quickly towards the sun. She could hear the whirring of wings and propellers behind her. The thieves must have caught her up, pursuing her on their own Abyssal machine. She glanced over her shoulder. Their flyer was tarnished and ancient. It was not as sleek and fast as her own.

The men were heavier than she. Their machine appeared scarcely able to support the weight of them all. It was larger than hers, though, and meaner. They remained in pursuit behind her, shouting and firing their guns into the air between their machines. Kai tilted the flyer sharply to evade their fire. She threw her head back and laughed in delight. Her long, moonlight pale hair streamed out behind her, lifting in the wind. She crouched low as a streak of deadly energy flew over her head. It barely missed her.

Inside the bottom pocket of her soft, calfskin pants, a tiny chirping noise interrupted her laughter. Kai sighed deeply, bending down to yank the small, brass compact from the pocket. Her flyer dipped alarmingly as she did. Another blast of Abyssal fire whizzed over her head, crackling in the air around her. She flipped open the compact, scowling when she saw the dark, narrow features and perfectly combed, steel-grey of the man on the screen.

She pressed the huge, glowing white button beneath his image with a sigh. The image spoke. "Hello, Kai."

"What do you want, Abraham? I am somewhat preoccupied at the moment." "Not anymore. Your services are required at home. Her majesty, Queen Jila, requests you return to the palace at once."

Her face twisted sourly. "Right. I'll be there in just a tick." She jabbed at the button irritably. Abraham's image disappeared. "Right." She stamped a small, brass lever at her feet, engaging the auto-pilot. She spun, yanking the guns from the holsters on her belt.

Behind her, the thieves had nearly caught her up. She raised her guns, firing a single shot from each simultaneously. She heard a soft, subtle hum from each of the long, glass barrels. Then they exploded in her hands, kicking her slightly backwards. The wings of the thieves' flyer lit up a garish, poisonous red. The men reacted with confusion, firing their weapons into the air and hurrying towards their tiller. Then their flyer was plummeting down, spinning wildly towards the ground. The men's shouts of panic carried up to her in the rushing wind.

She spun back to the tiller. She kicked the lever back into place and dropped onto the soft, worn cushioned seat. She heard one loud, terrible splash beneath her. Then she heard three quieter, more satisfying splashes. She smirked and steered the flyer up, into the sky towards Zooni.

CHAPTER TWO

*T*he Queen's private chambers were as large and grand as Kai remembered. Queen Jila sat at a polished gold vanity, plaiting her long, dark hair into a thick braid. There was no expression on her face. Electricity crackled in her dark eyes when they met Kai's in the mirror behind her. "Ah. Kai."

Jila stood to embrace the tall, pale woman, but she drew up short when she saw the state of her. Kai looked weather worn. Her black, leather suit was dusty. Her long, pale blonde hair was a mass of filthy tangles. Her face was streaked with dirt. Despite her atrocious appearance, Kai dipped a low, graceful bow to the queen. "Your Highness."

Jila eyed her in distaste. "Where have you been?"

"The Outerlands."

Jila scowled. Kai did not seem concerned by her monarch's disapproval. "What were you doing there?"

Kai lifted her shoulders casually. "I was hired to recover a priceless artefact for one of the nobles." She ignored Jila's imperious snort. "It was stolen by a band of thieves."

Jila was unimpressed. "I am pleased you have made it home at last. It appears to have been a long time since you have experienced the comforts of running water."

Kai snorted, crossing her arms over her chest. "Is there something you require of me, or have you simply called me here to make discourteous remarks regarding my appearance?"

Jila lifted her chin haughtily. Her eyes twinkled in merriment. "Need I remind you that I am your Queen, Kai?"

Kai rolled her eyes. "That has not escaped my memory, despite my time away from Varuna, Your Majesty."

Jila shook her head. She gestured towards the sitting room. She changed her mind moments later, remembering the condition of her guest. "Perhaps you should visit your chambers before our audience. I will send Elita to attend you."

Kai held up her hand. Her lips twisted in aversion. "I hardly think I require one of your ladies to attend me. I have been minding my own toilette these last thirty years and have not found it to be outside my particular capabilities."

Jila was sceptical. "Thirty?"

Kai smirked as she sunk into a deep, exaggerated bow. "My Queen," she said obsequiously. She straightened and spun on her heel to stride abruptly from the room.

When Kai returned several moments later, Jila was dressed in a lovely scarlet gown and a stiff, black lace corset that held her upright upon the sitting room stool on which she awaited her audience. Jila's long, dark hair was drawn back from her bold, striking features into an elegant bun. It shone like ebony as it caught the light. She did not rise as Kai entered to join her in the sitting room.

Jila's guest was now a different woman than had first appeared in her chambers, gnarled and windswept from her adventures. The filthy, pragmatic leather suit was, Jila hoped, a thing that would never again disgrace her chambers. The young woman was washed and appropriately adorned in her usual palace attire. Despite the Queen's leaning towards tradition, Kai preferred serviceable garments. Her own corset was soft, brown leather. Her calfskin pants tucked into tall boots with large, brass buttons up the side, and her long, pale hair was braided into a simple plait.

Jila smiled. "Ah, a much more appropriate mien in which to meet your Queen. I am highly gratified." She gestured towards the seat beside her. "Please, Kaia, sit. Would you care for tea?"

Kai's brow furrowed slightly. She sat, eyeing the elaborate tea service between them ravenously. Despite her hunger, she sipped her tea primly and nibbled at the corner of a scone with the grace of a nobler woman. After several long moments, she asked with deceptive nonchalance, "Consequently, Jila, what has happened that requires my immediate return and interference?"

Jila met her gaze over the top of a delicate ivory china teacup. She sighed and returned the cup to its saucer with a careful hand. "I was attending the circus in Zooni."

Kai raised her eyebrows. "The circus?"

Jila's deep amber eyes sparkled, sliding away as if peering at something very far off. "Yes. Oh, the sights I saw. Lightning and fire and animals of all colours and shapes and foreign lands." Kai waved her hand impatiently. Jila's face grew serious and grave. "I was attacked when my identity was revealed by an Abyssal fortune teller."

Kai frowned censoriously. "A fortune teller, Jila?"

Jila sighed. Her eyes grew wistful again. "When I was young, Father took me to a carnival in Tyr, and I had my fortune read." She smiled wryly. "Perhaps I was feeling sentimental."

"What did the Abyssal tell you?"

"That I would grow up to be a noble and venerated ruler."

Kai rolled her eyes. "Not when you were a child. In Zooni, when it revealed your identity."

"That I was in grave danger, and of that I am certain. A young guard, an orphan child called Jasper, was killed in my stead." Jila looked down at her hands, as if the youth's blood were there. "He received a hero's burial, but it was small consolation."

"Someone tried to assassinate you?"

Jila lifted her head. "It is the only explanation. I do not believe it was an accident, though the culprit could not be discovered."

Kai's eyes were sharp and watchful. "You expect treachery."

"Yes, of course."

"One of our people?"

The queen sighed deeply and shook her head. "If only it were so straightforward, my friend. No, I expect it is far graver a crisis than a disgruntled nobleman or merchant dissatisfied with my rule. Our people are content."

"How can you be certain?"

Jila's lips turned up slightly at the corners. "My flies and my people in the cities are listening all the time for signs of treason. The Hive has not revealed any indications that our people are involved."

"You have spies all over the city?" Kai's expression was blank, but her voice was incredulous.

Now Jila smirked. "I have flies on every wall. Including this one. They all report back to me." She held up her hand. From the corner of her eye, Kai caught a flash of metal. She swivelled her head to watch the tiny, gold fly zoom across the room. It buzzed for a moment around the Queen's fingertips. A faint, purring hum emitted from inside its Abyssal body before it darted away.

Kai's jaw dropped in pique. "Jila!"

"Oh, don't sound so scandalized, Kai. How else do you think I maintain the serenity in the country? Signs of treachery are dealt with promptly and silently." Her smile was slightly dry. "You, yourself, have helped me with this."

For a moment, Kai's eyes slid away, remembering the people she had seized from their beds in the darkest hour of night to face the Queen's guards. Sometimes, in the case of an eminent noble or distinguished merchant, the Queen herself brought to bear her terrible wrath. Kai had seen these people afterwards at court or in the taverns along the main drags in town, for they were neither gaoled nor executed. They never looked the same, not quite. They all looked at her as if they had never glimpsed her before.

Kai's face remained impassive. She pushed the thoughts aside, for she desired not to know any more about such things than already she did. She inclined her head. She knew that Jila prized her most highly for her inclination to ask no questions. "If it is not a prominent noble, who do you suspect is behind the assassination attempt?"

Jila stood, pacing to the large picture window on the far wall. She drew aside the scarlet drapery abruptly, casting the room in sudden, brilliant sunlight. Below, the tops of Zooni's tallest glass and copper buildings glittered on the horizon. The queen seemed not to see them. "It is most upsetting to contemplate, Kai, but I am convinced," she said in a low voice and spun back to face her friend. "Julian, the Duke of Tyr, is an excessive and foolish ruler, full of more greed than morals. He has nearly depleted Tyr's oceans' supplies of Abyssium since he took the throne, and there is precious little left in the caves and mines. He is deeply in debt to Varuna, and he has refused to pay his debt to us."

Kai considered this. Abyssium, the primary energy source used to power the cities, homes and Abyssal machines, was an extremely valuable and not inexhaustible resource. Nations had gone to war over far less. "The Duke has been importing Abyssium from us and Leza in almost ludicrous quantities," Jila continued, returning to her seat beside Kai. "Yet his people are poor, underfed and without the resource."

"He's taking it for himself?"

"For his own pleasure, his home, to augment his own army of guards and Abyssal machines," Jila agreed. "He himself has become so intoxicated by the augmentations, he is practically half Abyssal construct himself."

"You think he means to invade Varuna and seize our supplies?"

The Queen shook her head. "Perhaps. Or perhaps he merely wants his debt dissolved. If he does mean to seize our supplies, he cannot do it without seizing our oceans. Our entire empire."

"You."

"Me." Jila sighed. "I knew there would soon come a time when the Duke's excesses would lead to his ruin. He is surely behind this. Perhaps he believes his debt can be settled if I am out of the way. Or that Varuna would be weaker without their leader."

"Why not simply declare war upon Tyr if you believe him guilty of this treachery?"

The queen's expression was rueful. "There has been peace among our two countries and Leza on our other side for generations. There is no telling how King Silas of Leza will respond if all out war is declared among Varuna and Tyr. The Varunian army can defeat Julian's, even with his augmented soldiers and Abyssal machines. But we cannot defeat Julian if Silas decides to take his side. Varuna lies between them; we cannot protect both sides of the country at once. We are not equipped for such a war."

Kai's eyes narrowed. "You think Silas will join Julian in the war?"

Jila lifted her shoulders delicately. "I know not what Silas will do. He himself is in debt to us, though his supply of Abyssium remains robust. Still, I do not know what he will decide. He may join Julian if our country is to be divided between them. It has been long since Silas and I were well-acquainted. He has always been honourable, but a man changes over time. Julian's greed may persuade him."

"What can I do to help you, my Queen?"

Jila's eyes burned. She clutched Kai's hands between them. "I must know if it was the Duke who orchestrated this treachery and if he will persist now that the attack has failed. If it is him, the road ahead is troubled indeed. I must know the truth so that I may begin to plan how to retaliate or guard against him."

Kai inclined her head. "Of course, Jila."

"Locate the evidence I require. I must see proof he is responsible. I must see proof of what he is planning."

Kai was silent a long moment. Her mind worked like a ticking clockwork. She nodded decisively to Jila. "Yes, Your Majesty."

Jila did not smile. Her eyes shone in satisfaction. "Report back when you have completed the task."

Kai rose and bowed low to her queen. "Of course."

Jila called to her as she neared the tall, arched door leading from the chamber. "Kai?" Kai half turned her head, waiting for her Queen's words. "Please be cautious. The Duke is not someone with whom to trifle. He will not be merciful if your deception is exposed. You must remain judicious, and you must remain unrecognized."

Kai nodded shortly. "Yes, of course."

"Abraham will provide you with all that you require."

Kai did not turn. Her lips twisted in a smirk. "I already have everything I require."

* * *

The Ducal Palace in the capital city of Tyr was immense and majestic. It was gilded in gold, silver, copper and sparkling jewels that glittered in the descending sun. On the vast, brightly flowered lawn, fire breathers spewed flames into the purple sky. The firelight glinted off the metallic costumes of the tumblers contorting on the grass. The Duke's guests were equally garish in their finery, dressed in bright, frilly gowns with enormous skirts of layered lace and suits trimmed in gold or dazzling with gems. Trinkets twinkled on their wrists, necks and in their hair. They were spun into each headdress and ribbon.

The valets and augmented ducal soldiers stood guard on the pathways and at the palace gates. The guards were like silent, motionless sentinels. The Abyssium crackled in the air around them. They all showed various signs of Abyssal augmentation. Some had brass plates concealing half their faces, others hands that formed the barrels of enormous brass cannons. Their skin glowed translucent, electric blue where the Abyss seeped through their skin from the inside. Their augmented Abyssal organs pumped and worked better than any normal, human organs. They would probably continue to work long after the human fleshed had shrivelled and died.

Many of the soldiers had hardly human flesh left at all. They were almost fully construct. Their eyes showed the bright, glowing blue of the Abyss that controlled them. They did not speak, these Abyssal atrocities. They did not move. There was no intelligence in their deep, blue eyes. The Abyss may have made their bodies strong and powerful and nearly indestructible, but the glowing rock would seep into their brains eventually. They would be rendered mad or senseless or even catatonic.

Kai had witnessed what extended exposure to Abyss could do to a human

man. She had seen the madness of the Abyssium miners who dove deep under the ocean day after day to harvest the valuable, powerful rock. The Abyss miners were among the strongest, most dangerous of all the cities' dwellers, half-mad from Abyss exposure and powerfully augmented to withstand the depths of water.

For a moment, staring at the brilliant blue eyes of the huge, motionless man with thick, brass forearms and shining gold hands beside her, Kai imagined the deep, dark blue sea. She could smell the salt in the air of the ocean shores bleeding from his pores, could see the brilliant colours at the bottom of the ocean floor. She remembered the glowing Abyss within the mines, the beautiful, sapphire blue stalactites that jutted out from the cave walls. Deep sadness filled her. She touched her chest instinctively, gasping for a moment as if she could feel the press of the water all around her.

Kai shook herself from her thoughts as she reached the tall, arched palace gates where a solitary soldier guarded the opening to the palace courtyard. He was dressed in the Duke's traditional blue and silver livery. His ageless face was so unnaturally beautiful, unlined and oddly sculpted, it might have been carved from stone or ivory. His deep, luminous blue eyes swept her from head to toe. There was no response, no reaction in them. He paused for a moment without seeing her, as if listening to something she couldn't hear.

She lifted her chin. Her breath caught in her throat. Then the guard bowed slightly to her, gesturing her inside the gates. She released her breath silently and smiled. She curtsied primly at him. His gaze had already left her, inspecting the next guests in the queue. She did not waste a moment in contemplating her good fortune. She made haste through the gates where a procession of gold and white carriages waited to chauffer the guests along the winding pathway towards the palace.

Massive, gleaming ebony and bronze Abyssal horses drew the carriages. They stood uncannily still as they waited in a queue for their passengers. Their red jewelled eyes did not spin or glance towards the guests. Their long, sparkling silver manes did not move in the slight, warm breeze, though they appeared as fine and soft as silk. The Duke had spared no expense on his splendid conveyances.

The Duke's extravagances did not occupy her thoughts for long. On the path towards the carriages, Kai near drew up short. She met a tall, well-built man in a smart, olive green uniform with squared, sharp shoulders and shiny black boots up to the knees. When the man turned to her, an excess of bronze medals gleamed on his jacket, which was buttoned up to the tall, square collar with eight polished bronze buttons. The medals distinguished him as a man of consequence despite his apparent youth. She did not know him.

The soldier's features were carved and as curiously striking as the Abyssal guard's had been. His smile was brilliantly white. His eyes were dark and alert. They held not a even hint of the mad blue glow of Abyss saturation. He was pure human. His hair was shoulder-length, jet black, and combed neatly back from his smooth forehead. It shone in the fading light of the setting sun.

His gaze swept over her in frank, guileless interest, taking in her opulent scarlet finery and painstakingly coiffed, moonlight pale hair. She met his gaze just as brazenly. She did not return his smile. Instead, she watched him guardedly as he bent in an elegant bow and offered his hand to assist her into the waiting carriage. "My lady."

His voice was low and deep. It carried with effortless, confident clarity. She smiled demurely. She accepted his hand and stepped up into the stage. She did not recognize the others seated primly on the lushly cushioned seats. The men wore uniforms alike to her gallant soldier's. They were not so highly decorated. They possessed little of his grace. The women beside them were of varying ages and diverse degrees of beauty and plainness, but they were all dressed in rich, charming gowns.

She knew the men at once as the palace guards of King Silas of Leza. As she sat in the empty space across from him, a middle-aged soldier smiled at her with straight, perfect teeth. He was yet still strapping at his advanced age and very capable-looking. He had shortly cropped, steel-grey hair and ruddy, finely-lined features. When he spoke, it was in a deep, lilting Lezan accent. "Who have you brought to us, Lockley?"

The black-haired soldier climbed into the carriage. He dropped into the seat beside Kai. He smiled at her. His gaze was ingenuous and inquisitive. "I don't know. She appeared, as out of the fire and the moonlight."

The older soldier laughed. His dark eyes danced in the light of the small, glowing torch on the side of the carriage wall. "She does look like a moonbeam, Commander." Kai's smile was diminutive and tight-lipped. She folded her hands in her lap. Her decorum drew another chuckle from the grey-haired man. "Are you a shy one, little moonbeam?"

Kai glanced at the man the older had called Commander. Her face was carefully expressionless. His smile was kind. There was no guile or cunning in his expression. He was peering back at her with frank curiosity. "This is Colonel Darius Grimes," he told her, indicating the teasing soldier across from her. "He intends no harm."

"I did not feel myself threatened," Kai told him in an even tone. Grimes' grin widened in a wolfish way that was nevertheless unsuccessful in rousing a stir of unease within her.

The Commander laughed heartily. "See that, Colonel? Even the ladies are unmoved by your jostling." Colonel Grimes merely waved his hand glibly. "I am Commander Draven Lockley of the Lezan guard." He made introductions round the carriage. Kai paid little attention. The Lezan guards and their women were of no significance. She inclined her head to them politely in turn. She forgot each of them directly.

Grimes grinned and leaned back in his seat as if to make himself comfortable for the proceedings. "And you, lady? From where do you hail?" He narrowed his dark eyes at her as if to study her. "You're not a Tyran, surely. You are much too refined for a lady of Tyr." When she merely smiled at him, he glanced at his friend. "What do you think, Draven? Is she Lezan?"

Commander Lockley's sculpted mouth turned up in a teasing smile. "Could it be she is one of ours and we've never noticed her before?"

"I suspect you would have noticed her, were she ours, would you not, Draven?" Grimes smirked.

On his left, the young, pretty, dark-haired woman in a bright yellow gown seemed suddenly interested in the conversation. Lockley had called her Marina. Her large, pale green eyes narrowed at Kai in appraisal. Kai returned her scrutiny levelly. The men seemed not to notice the women's silent consideration. "Surely, she's Varunian," the young woman interposed. There was a faint note of distaste in her voice.

Grimes raised his eyebrows, glancing at the woman in yellow. Despite her provocative timbre, he did not seem to consider this a grave failing. "Is that so? Are you Varunian, little Luna?"

Kai's mouth turned up in an involuntary smile. "Little Luna?"

"Ah, yes, she is a Varunian. You don't like our name for you, Luna Varunian?"

"Actually, I think I like it very much."

Grimes smiled brilliantly. "Then that is what we shall call you. We will see much of you this evening, we hope?"

They would not. Nevertheless, Kai inclined her head graciously. "Perhaps."

"Have you come in your Queen's stead? I heard she is unable to attend the festivities this evening. An accident at the carnival in Zooni? Have you heard of this, Luna?"

Her face remained impassive. "I might have heard something of the sort."

Grimes looked amused. "You aren't much of a conversationalist, are you?"

Kai smiled. "I am when I am required to be."

"And you do not feel now is a time that you might employ your craft?"

"Leave her alone, Darius," Lockley scolded. "You come on too strong. You're upsetting her."

Kai glanced at him. "I am not upset."

Lockley smiled at her. The look he furnished Grimes was reproachful. "Then you are upsetting me, Darius, and I will not stand for it. You leave Luna alone."

"You are very gallant, Commander."

He smiled. "Come now, Luna. We are somewhat acquainted. We may dispense with the formality. I am just Lockley. And what, may I ask, is truly your name?"

Her smile was gentle. "I rather think I prefer Luna, if it's all the same."

He chuckled. "As you wish. Far be it from me to refuse a lady what she desires."

Kai turned away from his twinkling dark eyes to peer out the window beside her. The courtyard was passing quickly outside, and the sprawling palace loomed nearer. She was not the only one who had taken an interest in reaching their destination. "Oh, we're here," Marina announced with pleasure. "I'm looking forwards to the dancing." She turned back to the party in the carriage. "Lockley, will you be dancing?"

Lockley smirked. "Perhaps. If the mood takes me."

Grimes seemed disinclined to remain excluded from this change in the conversation. His eyes gleamed. His mouth curved up. "Or if there is a fine enough woman who will have you?"

Lockley did not take offence. He laughed. "Just so, Colonel."

The horse pulled to a graceful stop, barely jarring its passengers. The men alighted first from the carriage to escort the ladies to the polished marble steps leading to the magnificent palace. Kai remained in her seat while Lockley offered his hand to assist Marina out of the carriage. Despite the expectant expression on her face when she landed safely on her high-heeled feet, however, he did not present his arm to her. He peered back into the carriage, proffering his hand to Kai.

"Lady Luna?"

Kai hesitated an ephemeral instant. She rose, accepting the Commander's hand. As she alit from the carriage, careful not to snag the preposterously ample skirt of her scarlet silk gown on the step, Lockley caught her around the waist, drawing her nearer him. For a moment, he peered down at her with a rapt, serious expression in his dark eyes. Kai had seen that expression before. She knew what an expression such as that meant. Commander Draven Lockley of the Lezan palace guard, however, was not her intended object for the evening.

She drew back, pressing her hands to his chest to gently nudge him away from her. His fingers clenched fleetingly on her waist as if he meant to tug her back, but he released her. A small, wry smile twisted his sensual mouth. "Will we see more of you this evening, lovely Luna?" Grimes asked again, pausing on the path with his wife on his arm. His eyes glinted with an amused sort of gratification.

Kai stepped away from Lockley without meeting his gaze. She smiled at Grimes. "Perhaps," she repeated intractably.

Grimes watched after her as she strode away ahead of them, her long, full skirts swirling around her. Grimes clapped his younger Commander on the shoulder with a grin. "Ah, young Lockley, it is women like pretty Luna who stop the world spinning on its axis and shatter the hearts and minds of men." He winked at his tall, slender, pretty wife, who waited patiently for his return. "Take it from a man who married one. Do not trouble yourself over her."

Lockley did not glance at his friend. His gaze followed the luminous woman in red as she strode unaccompanied towards the palace. A small, wistful smile danced upon his lips. "Perhaps, my friend, it is just such sort of trouble my life has been lacking."

CHAPTER THREE

The Duke's ballroom was as brazen and flamboyant as the Duke himself, who held court at the front of the room in a garish black and sapphire velvet suit. His long, curling, caramel-coloured hair was combed back from an unexpectedly fine, handsome face. He appeared far younger than the years for which he was known. His eyes were the same glowing blue as an Abyssium miner's. Kai suspected the slight lustre of his skin was born of exposure to the rock rather than a luminous inner beauty.

Duke Julian moved with the natural vigour and carefree grace of a large feline. Even from her position near the doorway, Kai recognized the manifestations of his Abyssal nature. He was taller than a normal man by nearly a foot. His powerful body was thick with flat, brawny muscle. His features, ageless and beautiful in a strange, synthetic sort of way, were unnaturally animated. His smile was slightly fixed, as if it were difficult to move the muscles of his face or alter the sentiment upon it.

His right hand moved as sinuously as a human hand, but it was shiny, metallic copper. He displayed his singular hand unabashedly, waving it about as he spoke as if to display its greatest advantage in the brilliant firelight. Though it was slender and oddly delicate, Kai suspected it possessed the strength of a machine.

Like the Duke, the melody lilting through the ballroom was ostensibly exquisite and striking. Its insidious, lurid cadence seemed to sink into her skin and straight into her bones. Even at the early hour of evening, there were already several couples on the floor, spinning together to the supple melody. They stared into each other's eyes intensely, as if the music itself was an aphrodisiac or elixir.

In a corner of the room set aside from the dancing, the country's most inspired and innovative inventions were dazzlingly displayed for the guests to admire. Kai drifted through the crowd towards them. They were only the usual sort of Abyssal machines. Prominently displayed was a pair of wide, sleek, silver wings that purportedly fitted over the arms of a man and eliminated the necessity of a flying machine. Kai suspected they were less for actual human use than tawdry pageantry.

There was a small, bulbous carriage encrusted with dazzling red and white jewels which held only a single passenger. Its expense likely outweighed its efficacy. It was remarkable only in that it was autonomous, drawn without the additional requirement of an Abyssal horse. She did not linger long in the perusal of the innovations as she might normally have done, most notably in the inspection of the weapons. She held a particular interest in weapons. The inventions were as flash and overstated as Julian. They appeared nothing more than the products of his pure excess.

She did not speak to anyone as she wandered the sparkling, polished ballroom. She felt the probing stares of the other guests as she passed. The gentlemen and some of the ladies scrutinized her in interest. Others eyed her in mistrust, as if they sensed she was not among the welcomed company in this gilded cage. She recognized some of Varuna's nobles in their meticulous plumage. She avoided them. She understood that, were they to catch sight of her, they would not remember her face. They never remembered her face.

A young, rosy-cheeked, boyish man dressed in the livery of the Lezan guard obstructed her path. Though she tried to slip past him, he bowed courteously when he spied her. His smile was as perfectly brilliant as his superiors'. The Lezans surely bred their soldiers well. "May I have the honour of this dance, my lady?"

Kai ignored his extended hand. She smiled. "I am sorry, but I must decline." Her gaze flitted across the room. "I have promised this dance to another."

She did not linger to consider the young man's expression. She moved promptly onwards. She took a flute of sparkling, bright pink wine from a short, youthful waiter in a sleek, gold tuxedo as he passed. It tasted like honey on her tongue. She sipped it meditatively. For a moment, she watched the Duke. She did not move immediately towards him. Instead, she cast her dark, midnight blue eyes around her, seeking an exit from the bright, crowded ballroom.

On the far side of the room, crossways from the display of Tyr's most impressive inventions, was a pair of tall, gleaming ivory doors with polished brass trim. They were closed tight against the crowd. They possessed no lock that might hinder their opening. She moved slowly towards them. A powerful sensation of watchful eyes weighed heavily upon her. A frisson of unease travelled down her spine.

She glanced back into the crowd. She met Commander Lockley's dark eyes. She held his gaze for a passing moment. When he smiled, she turned away from him. The ivory doors lay ahead. The Duke was in her sight. It was not the time for diversion.

* * *

"Where is our mysterious Varunian heading, I wonder?"

Lockley peered at his friend. He had not realised Grimes was watching him and had discerned the direction of his gaze. "Perhaps she is in search of the loo."

"My boy, I see stars in your eyes. Or is it moonbeams?" Grimes smirked. "Perhaps she is here to steal national secrets from the Duke. Perhaps she is a Varunian spy."

Lockley laughed. "Now, Darius you are painting fantasies. She is nothing of the sort. She is only a woman."

"No woman is only a woman, particularly not a beautiful one. She is a good deal more than a woman."

Lockley's eyes slid away, towards the tall, ivory doors and the pale woman in red. "Yes, she is."

"Do not allow your wits to be lost so early in the evening, my friend."

He was not paying attention to his older companion's wisdom. One of the ducal guards had caught the Varunian woman as she attempted to slip from the ballroom. The guard steered her firmly back towards the crowd. The guard's expression was eerily vacant. "Perhaps she did not find what she was seeking."

Grimes grinned. "Or she is to be thrown with haste into the dungeon for her treason."

Lockley laughed. "Enough, Grimes."

"Leave the Varunian alone. Come. There are young ladies of our most particular caste who are very anxious to dance with you."

Lockley sighed. Nevertheless, he permitted his friend to conduct him away.

* * *

"Nothing to be sought there, my lady. You must have gotten turned around."

The Ducal guard's voice was low and gruff. His ageless, waxen face did not move, nor did his eyes seek hers. Nevertheless, Kai smiled up at him. "Surely I must have. I am much obliged, sir, for your timely intervention."

He inclined his head. She sighed as he moved back to his post beside the doors. She had not anticipated the interference of the guard. She felt more acutely now the allure of the barrier. The Duke, so much taller than those flanking him, was of nothing to trace again. She began her measured advancement towards him once again. As she did, she took another glass of the sweet, sparkling wine. It had not yet gone to her head, but perhaps the luxury was ill-advised. She reluctantly resolved to limit further indulgence.

She caught the gaze of a distinguished older gentleman with fine, patrician features. He was dressed in the rich, extravagant finery of the aristocracy. She knew him at once to be of Tyran birth by his curling golden hair and the synthetic flawlessness of his glowing skin. He bowed to her. H offered his hand as the young Lezan had done. "My lady, may I have this dance?"

Her eyes sought the Duke. She found him near, on the very edge of the dance floor as if awaiting a suitable partner to appear in his view. Though she meant to catch the Duke's attention, she curtsied primly to the Tyran. She took his hand. "Thank you, sir, I would be most delighted."

She did not know the Tyran's name though he had spoken it to her the moment he had drawn her into his arms. He maintained an unremitting flow of prattle as he swayed her skilfully to the pleasant melody. He did not seem to mind her silence. He did not, evidently, require her to respond. When he asked her for her name she was obliged to return her attention to him and smile. "Luna."

He closed the space between their bodies. His voice was a low, sensual purr. "Luna. It's very pretty. It becomes you."

She lowered her gaze demurely. She peered through her lowered lashes towards the Duke. She caught his gaze. She raised her head to meet it squarely. His brilliant blue eyes were glowing with intensity. Her lips curved into a coy smile. The contact of their eyes was broken, however, when her partner spun her abruptly. Her skirt swirled. She clung to his shoulders to steady herself. The Tyran's expression was arctic.

When the music stopped, he bowed to her curtly then spun on his heel. He disappeared into the crowd without thanking her for the dance. Had she indignation, it was short-lived. When she turned, the Duke was before her. His hand was extended. He bowed to her. Even as he was bent, he was taller than she by nearly a head. "My lady. May I have this dance?" His voice was a deep, husky purr. It resonated as if it were projected from deep inside his Abyssal belly.

Her lips curled up. She lowered her gaze with practiced politesse. "I would be honoured, Your Grace."

Despite his enormity, the Duke was lithe and eerily graceful. He did not speak to her as he moved her to the insidious melody. He stared down into her eyes with an unwavering intentness. His full, plump lips were curled in a small, cunning smile. His right hand curved around her left. Somehow, despite

25

the sleek, metallic sheen, it was smooth and silky to the touch, like an infant's flawless, unblemished skin. It seemed made of nothing resembling human flesh.

It was strong, too, unnaturally strong. He slipped it abruptly around her waist, drawing her against him so there was little more than a breath between their bodies. Kai met his intense gaze steadily. She smiled up at him. She slithered against him, into him, allowing him to feel the length and shape of her figure in her crimson dress. His hand clenched on her lower back. He raised an eyebrow. "What is your name?"

"Luna."

"Luna," he repeated in a distant voice. She wondered if he had truly heard her at all. He was preoccupied. She knew it little mattered whether she spoke again. He was not listening. His hands slid over the silken fabric of her dress, over the curves of her waist and hips. His gaze was narrow and focussed intently upon her. She did not recoil or demure when his hands stroked down her arms and encircled her waist to guide her provocatively against his massive, powerful body. She sighed, melting unresistingly into his touch. She could feel every artificial muscle and sinew of his Abyssal form.

The melody faded on a low, tinkling note. Even as the song ended, the Duke did not relax his hold on her. "I am feeling slightly faint, Your Grace," she murmured breathlessly. She did not attempt to draw away from him. She fanned her hand in front of her. "Would you mind terribly if I took a moment to myself?"

He smiled. "All alone? Perhaps I might accompany you."

She inclined her head. "Of course."

For a moment, her gaze drifted across the ballroom, as if her eyes had designs quite their own. Commander Lockley was dancing with a very beautiful young, black-haired woman with deep, mocha coloured skin and eyes like flecks of onyx. Her simple, sapphire blue sheath dress and glittering diamond jewels marked her as a Lezan noblewoman, though her colouring was exotic. Kai wondered for a moment how the lovely woman had come to be a Lezan. Then she caught the clear, dark and oddly intent gaze of the woman's dance partner. She forgot the mystery of the woman's origins directly.

Her eyes met Lockley's. For a moment, she found herself quite captivated by the openness of his stare. The Duke's hand tightened upon her lower back, drawing her attention back to him. She looked up at her dance partner with a luminous smile. He leaned down, near her ear, and spoke in a husky purr.

"Lovely Luna, perhaps you would prefer to lie down?"

His connotation was not unclear. She did not recoil from him. Her smile was coy. "Sir, I am a respectable lady."

Duke Julian's expression was unconvincingly innocent. The look in his glowing blue eyes was unmistakable. "Dear Luna, I meant no offence. I merely mean to make you as comfortable as possible. My palace offers...many comforts indeed."

"I do not doubt it, my lord. Thank you. However can I refuse you?"

He smirked. "You cannot."

* * *

"See there, Draven, your moonbeam's gone off with the Duke." Grimes smirked, resting a hand on his young friend's shoulder. "A social climber, then, eh?"

Draven bowed to the Lady Lorelei and spun to face his friend with a dark expression. "No, I don't think so."

"Ah, worse, then, perhaps? Perhaps she is a lady of the night."

Draven's expression sharpened. "Don't talk about her that way, Darius."

Grimes snorted. "Forget her. They are all alike, beautiful women."

"No, I don't think so. There is something about her. Something different."

"Well, she's gone now. No need to continue mooning over her, then." Grimes raised his eyebrows. His friend was peering at the door through which the woman had disappeared. "Perhaps when the Duke is finished with her, she'll have something left in her for you." Draven's dark eyes snapped back to him. For a moment, the Colonel looked startled. He held up his hands. "All right, all right. I'm sorry. I hadn't realized you were sincere in your fancy. I was merely having a laugh."

"I do not have a fancy. I hardly spoke to the woman. She hardly spoke." Lockley sighed. "There is just something about her. She has a strange sort of draw to her."

"Hm." Grimes sounded disapproving. If Lockley heard him, he did not respond.

Lockley lifted a drink from a passing waiter's tray and spun away from the door. He tilted the glass back and finished it off it in a single swallow.

* * *

The Ducal palace was as large and impressive inside as it had appeared from the courtyard, as gilded and ornate as the Duke's accoutrements, the lavish carriages and the impossible inventions. Julian conducted her to a moving walkway which travelled through the richly carpeted and sumptuously festooned corridors to a pair of carved ivory doors in the furthest annex of the palace. He pushed them open. Kai suspected their immensity might have been impossible for a normal man to manage alone. Julian, of course, was not a normal man. He moved the heavy ivory with ease.

She stepped inside the room, finding herself in an opulent sitting room with pairs of doors leading deeper into the Duke's more private chambers. Her eyes darted quickly about the room, finding only comfortable furniture in which the Duke might entertain a favoured friend or foreign dignitary. If evidence of the Duke's treachery lay in this room, it was well-hidden from the accidental observer.

Julian did not seem concerned with entertaining her in the traditional sense, nor apparently did his designs involve her respite. He was suddenly upon her, kissing her, his plump lips pressing against hers. Before she recovered her breath, his tongue plunged insistently into her mouth. Kai shuddered involuntarily in intense antipathy. Julian was encouraged, as though he'd perceived her tremor as a passionate response.

He pulled her to him, lifting her as easily as if she were a child. He dropped her hastily on the surface of a nearby tea table. His lips and tongue and teeth tore ravenously across her throat, shoulders and mouth. His hands balled on the layers of her silk skirt, bunching them at her waist so he could slide his fingers across the garters on her thighs. Julian's hands were powerful, inhumanly strong. She did not fight him. She responded to his touch. She ignored the rising revulsion in the back of her throat.

Julian worked his fingers under the fabric of her skirts, between her legs. She turned her head away from him, closing her eyes. He kissed her neck, her ear, and yanked down on the thin, silk chemise across her legs. It tore with a soft, whispering sigh. Fabric fluttered slowly to the ground. His powerful right hand groped at her bodice, cupping her left breast and squeezing almost painfully. His erection was unnaturally large. It jutted between her legs, pressing closer and closer as if he would take her through the layers of his elegant clothing. His free hand fumbled urgently at his belt.

The door of the sitting room burst open with a loud bang. Julian's livid gaze snapped to the offending guard at the door. Kai sighed heavily in relief. She was, for the moment, forgotten. "Your Grace," said the guard urgently.

Julian spun away from Kai, advancing angrily upon his guard. "What is it?" he barked harshly. "As you see, I am busy!"

"There is a quandary downstairs, Your Grace."

"Can it wait?"

"No, Your Highness, it requires your personal attention. Quite directly."

Julian sighed, turning his head to look at the woman perched on the corner of the tea table. His voice did not brook argument. "Do not move, Luna."

Kai nodded, casting her eyes to the floor and straightening her skirts in a show of delicate modesty. When the Duke strode out of the room behind his guard, however, she sprung into action. She hopped off the table and hurried towards a set of lovely glass and gold doors through which she glimpsed rows of books and a large, polished ebony writing desk.

The desk was stacked with disorderly piles of parchment. Droplets of ink stained the surface of the blotter. It appeared as if Julian had lately scribed and discarded several editions of a missive. The final rendering was carefully folded and tucked inside an envelope bearing the Duke's waxen seal. She glanced up once towards the door and broke the scarcely hardened seal with a flick of her fingernail.

Dearest Silas,

As we discussed at length upon our last audience, Jila refuses to dissolve our debts to her. She continues to hold them and threatens to charge an exorbitant fee should we fail to pay them promptly and in full. I fear there is no other alternative. I regret that the Queen no longer seems in control of herself or her precious resources. I feel most strongly that our direct intervention may be in order, no, absolutely essential in order to maintain continuing peace and prosperity among our countries.

Jila has resources we desperately require, and her country prospers while ours fall further into debt. I know you, Your Highness, are quite in agreement over the necessity of peace and harmony. I implore you, aid me in convincing the good Queen, whether through convention or force, to see things our way. The tenuous hold we have over our own countries may be shattered when Jila finally sets her mind to moving her Abyssals against us.

My sources tell me she has been gathering an army of soldiers and machines, the like of

29

which our people have never seen...

It would be sufficient to satisfy Jila. Kai looked up sharply as the door in the chamber beyond swung open with a delicate bang. "Luna?"

She cursed under her breath and folded the letter swiftly. She slid it into the bottom of her corset. "Luna?" Julian strode into the room. When he saw her, his expression hardened. "What are you doing in here?" His eyes narrowed upon her hands. She had not hidden the missive quickly enough. He strode forwards. "What is that? What have you taken from me?" He was upon her in an instant, catching her wrist ferociously. "I knew you must be a thief! What have you taken?"

He yanked her up against him, his free hand groping at her waist. A strange, soft whirring noise from her free wrist startled him. Before he had the chance to thrust her from him, a small, brass wand shot out from the sleeve of her gown. The Duke had little time to reconcile the nature of the object, so caught up was he in the blind rage of her betrayal. He understood only in the split second before lightning arced from the wand and jolted through his entire body.

The Duke fell forwards. Kai took a quick step back, her eyes narrowed as she watched his luminous blue eyes roll back and finally close. She prodded his solid, bulky arm with the pointed toe of her boot. Though he did not stir, she angled the wand towards him again, sending a bolt of Abyssal energy pulsing through him a second time. It would do little to halt him for long, she knew, as large and engorged by the Abyss as he was. She spun from his prone form quickly. She raced through the doors of his chambers into the corridors.

The hour had grown late as she had entertained the Duke. When she returned to the ballroom, most of the revellers had begun to move towards the flourishing courtyard. She joined them, as if she had been amongst them the entire time. They paid her little mind. They glowed with spirits and the elation of the evening's festivities. The flood of bodies pressed her out onto the thick, plush green lawn. They gathered there. They stared up, riveted, into the darkened sky.

The Duke's midnight display of pyrotechnics illuminated the atmosphere, casting shadows and eerie light across the faces of the revellers. They exclaimed in delight and astonishment. Their eyes followed the dancers that contorted to the rhythm of the music booming from a large orb in the centre of the guests. Streaks of lightning burst from the orb, crackling in the night air and setting the hairs on the arms of those closest to it on end.

Kai pushed through the crowd. She ignored the indignant admonishments and protestations from the jostled revellers interrupted in their rapture. Her eyes were riveted, not on the display despite its beauty, but on the guards who stood among the crowd. The guards' attention, like the guests', was directed at the sky and the dancers. Their eyes reflected none of the enchantment of the crowd.

Quite suddenly, however, they all paused and snapped to attention. They were little more than automatons, activated in a simultaneous instant. Their dull, empty blue eyes glowed ominously. They swept the crowd in calculated, clockwork ticks. Oh, no. Duke Julian must have awakened sooner than she had expected. He had surely already called upon his Abyssal army. The Ducal guards did not shout. They did not have to. They seemed to share a collective consciousness or, at least, internal communication devices that allowed them to hear and speak to their master without alerting those around them. The guards sprung into action. They struck out into the crowd in search of Kai.

Her Abyssal flyer was outside the gates upon the palace air strip. It was an agonizing carriage ride from the palace. Kai took a very long, deep breath, filling her augmented lungs with the clean, crackling night air. In a swift, fluid move, she ripped the long, voluminous skirt and bustle from her legs so she could run, unencumbered, in the remnants of her black, lacy petticoats. Shouts of indignation and shock rippled through the party. She could not be certain if they came from the guests jostled by the teeming, excited crowd or the modest ladies catching sight of her disreputable dress.

It wasn't the time to worry over such things. It was not her way to worry over such things, in any event. The Abyss pulsing through her veins ensured she could run long distances without tiring and at an almost supernatural speed. The guards spotted her breaking free from the crowd. They were nearly as quick, despite her head start. She was relieved the ostentatious pyrotechnics distracted the party. She did not have luxury to think of them now, to wonder if any of her people or the nobles and soldiers of Tyr or Leza had noticed her escape or her dogged pursuers.

At the palace gates, the tall, handsome, blue-eyed Abyssal guard she had met upon her gate-crash still waited. She wondered if the internal communication between the guards was limited to inside the gates. He was standing completely, eerily still, as if he had been switched off to await further orders. Kai did not wait to see if he would activate upon spotting her. She brandished the small, brass wand in her sleeve. The guard dropped heavily to the ground. He was, most certainly, only briefly stunned by the bolt of dazzling blue light.

Kai's flyer was several paces away, among the rows of vessels silently grounded for the remainder of the night's festivities. Though she darted quickly through the labyrinth, her flyer might have been leagues away. The guard had reactivated behind her. He was closing in with such determined alacrity, she felt a fleeting frisson of alarm frisk down her spine. The blonde guard was not so far behind he could not catch her up. If he did, it was only a matter of time before she was overcome by his comrades and the wrathful Duke himself.

She heard the hum of an engine and the whispered whir of wings ahead. Her gaze snapped wildly to the active flyer. It was only a few rows away. The small, sleek machine bore an insignia on its pale, olive green canopy. Her racing, agitated mind recognized it instantly as the Lezan coat of arms. Behind her, the Abyssal guard was so close, she could nearly feel his breath. She could feel the air stir as he reached in vain for her, scant inches from seizing her long, pale hair. She crouched, barely evading his grasping fingers. She leapt straight up in the same moment the Lezan flyer lifted gracefully off the ground.

The flyer lurched with her sudden weight as she caught herself on the edge of the flat, polished floor of the its deck. Kai glanced down at the guard below in the ephemeral instant before the machine bore her away. He still groped desperately in the air as if he might yet catch her up. Then she was dragged fully into the flyer and through the torn, fluttering canopy that had screened the passengers from her view.

Had she seen them, perhaps, she might not have been so rash.

CHAPTER FOUR

"Good god, woman," Commander Draven Lockley exclaimed, lifting her hastily to her feet. He guided her to sit on a padded bench across from Colonel Grimes, whose hand had stilled upon the helm of the ship.

"Luna?" Grimes' face was frozen in astonishment. "What on earth are you doing leaping onto our air ship?"

She eyed them both carefully. She momentarily considered stunning them and shoving them out into the night sky. She might overpower one of them, eventually, but there were two of them. They were likely very quick and skilled fighters. She would only be able to stun one of them before it came to blows. Lockley kneeled in front of her. His eyebrows knitted together in uncertainty and concern. His breath was shallow and quick. She realized that her own breathing was slow and even.

This isn't going well. She sucked in a rapid, shuddering breath. She let it out again in a quiet sob. She hoped they hadn't noticed the delay. Grimes did not seem to. Lockley's eyes narrowed slightly. He seemed preoccupied by more pressing matters at the moment, however. "What has happened to you, Luna? What has happened to your dress?" he asked. His tone was quiet and carefully gentle. He peered at her as though he feared a burst of manly vigour might startle her. Inspiration struck her.

Kai burst into tears. The men recoiled from her as though she'd struck out at them. Realizing they were, as any other man, terrified in the presence of a weeping woman, she sobbed desperately for a few moments before turning her watery, luminous eyes to Lockley. "The Duke..."

It was all she needed say. The words had an instant, startling effect. Lockley shot to his feet. His eyes flashed dangerously. "The Duke did this? Did he hurt you?"

The Commander exchanged a look with his companion. Grimes' face was as white as marble. He nodded kindly towards Kai. Then he conspicuously turned his back on them and moved behind the canopy to escape her outburst. Kai watched him go from beneath her tear-soaked lashes. She swivelled her gaze back to Lockley. He kneeled in front of her and grasped her hands in his own.

"Tell me what happened, Luna." Concern, confusion and indignation smouldered in his eyes and turned down the corners of his mouth. Then he paused. He lifted an eyebrow. He actually smirked. "That isn't your real name, is it?"

"It was your friend who gave me that name. You never asked it." She met his dark gaze squarely. She heaved a deep sigh.

"I did ask it. You would not give it to me. I am certain you spent the evening evading me."

She turned her head away from him. "It's Kaia."

He moved to sit beside her. He wrapped a warm, comforting arm around her shoulders. She did not shrug him off. She did tense slightly. As if he sensed her trepidation, he drew his arm away. He turned to face her. "What happened to you, Kaia? What did the Duke do to you?"

"He deceived me..." Her mind raced. The lies poured from her lips in a soft, tremulous voice before she had even fully formed them. "He asked me to dance with him. I was very flattered. I'm a travelling circus performer, you see."

"A circus performer?" he repeated in bemusement.

She winced imperceptibly. It was the first thing that had popped into her mind. Now it was too late to retract the idiotic declaration. She soldiered on. "Yes. I'm an aerialist. I have never received such exalted attention. I was quite taken in. The Duke told me he had..." She sucked in a shuddering breath. She flicked a covert glance at Lockley's face. His brow was furrowed. His expression darkened as she spoke.

"Go on," he urged in a gentle voice.

"It was foolish, really. I shouldn't have believed him, but he told me he had a collection of art by the great Dray Ozell."

"Dray Ozell?"

She didn't pause. "Yes. He was a great artist who illustrated the old carnivals and circuses. I was very interested to see his work. I had only heard of it before; he's been dead many years, you see, and his work has been all but lost. It's legendary among my comrades."

"He did not have such a collection," Lockley surmised. His voice was low and level. She studied his face carefully. She had laid it on rather thick. She would be lucky indeed if he had not already seen through the flimsy deception. Perhaps she could toss Lockley off the side of the vessel before his companion even noticed anything had happened.

"When I arrived in his private chambers, it was to find it was merely a tactic to seduce me...he..." She took another deep, racking breath. She looked away from him. Beside her, Lockley shifted. This time, he wrapped his arm firmly around her shoulders and drew her against him. She sniffled and spoke into the warm, solid expanse of his decorated chest. Men, she decided, were fools. "I refused him, but he is so big, so strong...he tried to force himself on me, and when I struggled, he threatened to lock me in his dungeon, to do terrible things to me..."

She was rambling. Lockley shushed her gently. "It's all right now, Kaia. You don't have to explain it to me. I understand." He sighed heavily. He stroked a hand tenderly over her long, dishevelled hair. "What did you do? How did you get away from him?"

This time her voice was level. She might as well tell the truth. "I stunned him. I am a woman alone, Commander Lockley. I have to take care of myself." She raised her arm. A smooth, metallic whirr preceded the snick of her retracted lightning wand.

Lockley eyed the small, brass weapon in interest. He nodded gravely. "I stunned him, and I ran," she continued in a low voice. She looked down. She covered her wrist with her hand as she slid her sleeve over the stunner to conceal it once more. "But he is so strong; it did not stop him for long. He sent his guards after me. I wasn't able to make it to my own airship before his man caught me up. I panicked and jumped into the first ascending flyer I saw." She looked up to meet his intent gaze. "I'm sorry. I didn't mean to..."

Lockley shook his head earnestly. "No, Kaia, you did the right thing."

Colonel Grimes poked his head into the deck from behind the torn canopy. He exchanged a look with Lockley, who nodded and stood to speak to him in hushed tones. Grimes glanced at Kai over the commander's shoulder. His brows knitted together in a concerned expression. Kai lowered her gaze. She sniffled softly into her sleeve as she listened to Lockley's murmured words.

"The Duke attempted to force himself on her. She stunned him and barely escaped."

Grimes' expression changed. His eyebrows rose in interest. "That's very impressive." He leaned towards Lockley, speaking as though Kai were not in the small ship and could not hear them over the hum of the engine and the flapping of the wings. "But, good god, man, what are we to do with her?"

35

Lockley glanced over his shoulder. Kai wiped her eyes theatrically. She turned a brave look upon him. "We cannot allow this to go unpunished. Kaia, where can we take you?"

Her eyes narrowed for an ephemeral instant. "To Queen Jila."

"Yes. Yes, of course," Grimes said, nodding vigorously as if the matter had finally reached a satisfactory conclusion. "This is an international matter for the Queen to sort out. She will decide how to deal with Julian. We will take her home to Varuna straight away. It is on the path, after all."

Kai sighed heavily in relief. If they suspected there was anything amiss with her story, their expressions did not reveal it. She smiled meekly at them both in turn. "Thank you, Colonel. Commander."

Grimes nodded brusquely. He returned to the helm, as if relieved to be away from the weepy, distressed woman. Lockley sat across from her upon the bench. He watched her quietly, as if awaiting signs of a renewed onslaught of tears. Kai gave him a wavering smile. Then she swept the small ship with a narrow, wary gaze.

"Where are your women?"

Lockley blinked. "Pardon?"

She realized she had spoken in a tone that might have been considered slightly sharper and sterner than was appropriate to her imagined predicament. It would little do to be too terse towards her saviour at such a crucial juncture. She ducked her head demurely. "I'm sorry. It's just that Mrs. Grimes and your companions are not travelling with you."

"The Colonel and I received instructions from our King to return to the palace in Leza at once. There is a matter that requires our immediate attention. Mrs. Grimes and the others did not wish to leave the palace before the pyrotechnics display and will return in Lady Lorelei's airship."

Kai did not reply to this. She was silent for a long moment, staring down at her hands. She felt Lockley shift abruptly. He moved to sit beside her on the padded bench. He draped an arm around her shoulders once more. This time, she flinched. The commander pulled away from her instantly. He returned quickly to the seat across from her. There was a sheepish expression on his sculpted features.

"I am sorry," he told her in a low voice. "I won't touch you again. I was mistaken in thinking you might require comfort."

Kai stared at him. Her eyes narrowed thoughtfully. A woman in her wildly imagined situation might require comfort, she mused. Still, she ought not to allow the commander of an enemy country's royal army to take liberties with her, even if Leza was only a potential enemy at the moment.

As if he sensed the sudden tension in the hull, Grimes peered through the canopy to rejoin the conversation. His voice was light, as though he were attempting to distract them from the awkwardness of the moment. "Did I hear right, moonbeam? You're a circus performer?" Grimes asked. There was a definite note of amusement in his voice.

Kai's head snapped up. She eyed both the soldiers carefully. There seemed to be no suspicion of her deception in their gazes. In fact, they looked quite keen on the idea. If she was going to continue the charade, she may as well make it good. "Yes, sir. I was raised in the circus. My parents, they were performers, as well." She lowered her head. She dropped her voice to a sad, hushed murmur. "They died many years ago. I was brought up by my troupe. We have been travelling all over the world together as long as I can remember."

"What were you doing at the palace?" It was Lockley who asked this. He wore the same frank, trusting expression with which he had gazed at her upon their first meeting. For a moment, Kai was astonished at the Lezan guards' credulity. Leza bred them handsomely, but it didn't seem to breed them clever.

She hesitated a theatrical moment. "Gate crashing," she admitted finally with a snuffling laugh. "My troupe hasn't performed many shows lately, and I heard about the party. I thought...perhaps it would be a ripping good time. A nice distraction." She sighed deeply. "It was not what I had hoped."

Grimes' voice was gruff. "This would never have happened in Leza. Duke Julian is an awful cad."

Kai smiled wanly. "It would never have happened at home, either."

Lockley shot to his feet. His features were closed and dark. He paced towards the front of the ship. He peered out of the canopy into the night sky. "I see the Scyllan Sea below," he murmured in a low, husky voice. "We are nearing Zooni and Queen Jila's palace."

Kai touched her waist subconsciously. She felt the parchment there, still safe despite her daring escape. She sighed softly in relief.

She felt Lockley's eyes upon her. She folded her hands in her lap. "Shall we call your Queen?" he asked. "We should inform her of your arrival."

She smiled at him. "Yes, please. I would be most grateful."

Lockley glanced at his colonel. Grimes was already punching coordinates on the large, round numbers stamped upon the long, skeletal brass keys of his console. The incandescent glass mounted on the console upon a thick, brass easel began to shimmer and glow a pale, milky blue. After several long moments, a dark, patrician face appeared on the screen. His expression was perfectly gracious, despite the late hour of the call.

"Yes?" Abraham asked courteously. His dark, almond shaped eyes swept the interior of the airship. When they found Kai, his expression remained as politely neutral as ever. Their eyes met briefly. She thought she saw a very slight waver upon his lips, as if he were suppressing a smirk. "Can I help you?"

Lockley stepped in front of the screen. His back was so perfectly straight, he might have been carved of marble. "I am Commander Lockley of the Lezan Imperial Army. I regret to inform you that one of your citizens has been the victim of a terrible crime."

Abraham's expression now revealed his surprise. His eyebrows knit together in confusion. "In Leza?"

Grimes's voice was gruff with indignation. "No. In Tyr."

Abraham's gaze flicked to Kai. She gave him a small, tight smirk behind the soldiers' back. Abraham nodded curtly. "I will call the Queen directly."

For a moment, the screen swirled again. Then Queen Jila's face appeared. She looked slightly harassed, as though nothing could be more inconvenient than a late call from the guards. Kai did not doubt Abraham had warned the Queen of her predicament on the other side of the glass. Jila's long, dark hair was braided down her back. She still wore the smart, grey day dress in which she'd conducted her daily audiences, despite the lateness of the hour. She had, of course, been anticipating Kai's return and had yet to retire for the evening. Kai doubted she had expected this particular turn of events.

To the Queen's credit, her face did not alter even slightly when her gaze found Kai, sitting meekly on the bench behind Commander Lockley's erect figure. If she was irritated or amused by the situation, her expression did not reveal it. Kai wondered what sort of reception she would endure when she arrived at the palace. "Commander?" Jila asked in an authoritative voice. "What is the meaning of this? My major-domo tells me one of my people has been the victim of a crime."

"Yes, Your Majesty."

Jila's eyes flicked to Kai. If they revealed more interest than concern, the

Lezan guards did not seem to notice. "What sort of crime?"

"A violent crime, I believe, Your Majesty."

Kai met her Queen's eyes. Jila looked grave. "I see. Yes, that is dreadful, indeed. I wish to speak to her at once to ascertain the details of the transgression. Please, bring her to my airstrip straight away."

Lockley bent in a curt bow. "Yes, Your Majesty, as you command."

Jila appraised him sombrely. Her eyes flicked back to Kai. "Commander, I thank you for bringing my subject home safely. How did you come to be in her company?"

Lockley smiled. Jila's elegant eyebrows rose ever slightly. "She found us, Your Highness, and requested our assistance in fleeing Tyr. We could not refuse a lady."

Jila inclined her head. "Of course. Thank you. I will have someone waiting at the airstrip to collect her." Her head lowered, as if she were reaching for the console. She lifted her gaze abruptly to Lockley once again. Her voice was perfectly even. "Is there a reward you would request for your service?"

Lockley glanced over his shoulder at Kai, who gave him a small, wavering smile. "No, Your Majesty. Her safe return is all I require. It is our duty to protect the weaker sex."

Jila's lips turned up in a smirk. She did not respond to this proclamation. Her screen swirled. Her image disappeared, leaving the glass blank once again. As he returned to her side, Kai smiled at Lockley. "Thank you, Commander. I am in your debt."

He sat beside her. As if he sensed the strengthening of her spirit by the appearance of her Queen and the promise of her safety, he wrapped an arm loosely around her shoulders. She did not flinch this time. "No, Kaia, it is all I can do. You have had a very dreadful experience. I would wish to do more for you, if only I knew what I might do."

Grimes rolled his eyes at his superior officer over his shoulder. He returned his attention to the helm, spinning it smoothly onto the course towards Zooni. Kai smiled shyly at Lockley. "You have done quite enough, Commander. More than I could ever ask or deserve." She looked down at her hands. "Certainly more than I deserve."

CHAPTER FIVE

*T*he Queen's airstrip sparkled with small, blue lights. As the airship descended with a soft, metallic clatter upon the polished glass floor, Lockley rose to his feet, offering his hand to Kai. She hesitated a brief moment. Then she took it, allowing him to assist her to her feet. He smiled encouragingly. Grimes approached her gingerly. He took her free hand and bowed low to her.

"My lady, I pray if I see you again, you are in higher spirits," he said gallantly.

"Thank you, Colonel, for your quick rescue. I can never repay you. I am in your debt."

"No, lady. I wish you well."

She smiled luminously at him. She turned back towards Lockley. He assisted her down from the deck, holding her waist carefully. For a moment, she balked. As he held her gaze a long moment, she realized he had not discovered the roll of parchment in her waistband. His brilliant dark eyes were blazing. His hands slid slowly down to her hips. She pressed her palms to his chest to give him a gentle shove. His expression cleared. He stepped away from her abruptly. His eyebrows knit together guiltily.

Abraham strode towards them with a brisk gate that caused his polished, pointed boots to click smartly against the glass floor. His eyes darted between Kai and the Commander. His expression was impassive. "This is the young lady, I presume?" Abraham asked pointedly.

"Yes, sir. This is Kaia." Lockley pushed Kai gently towards the major-domo, as if presenting her in her tattered condition.

Abraham blinked. His eyes flicked to Kai. If he had been surprised that the Commander seemed in possession of information she rarely, if ever, shared, it did not show on his deadpan face. He raised a single, bushy black eyebrow as Kai turned to look back at Commander Lockley. Abraham stepped away from them diplomatically. "I will allow you a moment."

Kai shot him a mercury scowl. It was gone when she met Lockley's gaze. "Thank you, Commander," she said in hushed tones. She glanced askance at Abraham to ensure he could not overhear the embarrassing exchange. There was a shrewd glint in his dark eyes that Kai did not like.

40

Lockley smiled. His eyes looked slightly sad, as if this parting were significant. "Come now, Kaia. We have been through much together, have we not? I insist you call me Draven." He bent over her hand, pressing a soft kiss to her knuckles. "It was a pleasure meeting you, despite the dire circumstances. It is my hope that one day we will meet again, under happier ones."

Her smile wavered. There was a strange, unfamiliar roiling in her belly. She considered herself incapable of guilt and wondered if the strange, pink sparkling wine had affected her more than she had realized. "I hope the same, Draven."

He gave her an affectionate smile and stepped away from her. He watched as she turned from him. She strode towards Abraham, who advanced forwards to meet her. Abraham saluted Lockley briskly and laid a firm hand on the small of Kai's back to lead her to the awaiting carriage at the end of the strip. As Abraham assisted her into the carriage, Kai glanced back towards Lockley. She met his dark, disturbing eyes. She smiled. She gave him a small, meek wave before the door closed and she lost sight of him.

The door closed on her. Her expression changed instantly. She shrugged off the vestiges of feminine weakness. She turned to Abraham with icy, vacant eyes. She was surprised to find him peering at her anxiously. He looked genuinely concerned. "What happened, Kai?" he asked gently, laying his long, slender fingers lightly on her shoulder in an oddly paternal gesture of comfort. "Were you hurt?"

Kai looked at him incredulously. She shrugged him off. "Get your hands off me. Of course I wasn't hurt." She crossed her arms over her chest. She smirked at his piqued expression. "Just take me to Jila. I have some very interesting information."

* * *

Jila rushed out to meet Kai as soon as Abraham ushered her into the Queen's sitting room. Jila caught Kai's shoulders. She looked her up and down with a slight frown. "Oh, what happened? What happened to your dress?"

Abraham cleared his throat irritably. He strode brusquely from the room. He closed the door on the two women with unnecessary force. Jila raised her eyebrows. She turned to her friend in interest. "What is the matter with my major-domo?"

Kai smirked. "I might have hurt his feelings."

Jila looked at her sternly. Kai squared her shoulders and slipped the parchment from the bottom of her corset. It was slightly crinkled. She shook it

41

out with a flourish and handed it to the Queen.

Jila scanned the missive quickly. Her expression changed from irritation to dismay in a breath. She looked up at Kai. "How did you manage to get away with this?"

"I hitched a ride with the Lezan Imperial Army."

Jila shook her head. "Yes, so I saw." She chuckled. "Truly, Kai, even after all this time, you impress me with your gall."

"I am impressive."

"Did you suffering terribly?" Jila's voice was teasing. Kai smirked.

"I did not suffer. But I suspect the Duke did, a bit. Have you seen him? He's enormous."

Jila chuckled, gesturing her to sit across from her in one of the audience chairs. "Yes, I know. He's completely ridiculous. He's so addled by the Abyss, he's practically mad."

"I had to stun him."

Jila looked interested. "Did it work?"

"Well, not very well. He activated his guards. One of them barely caught me. It was all I could do to escape on the Lezan airship."

The Queen's expression fell. She no longer seemed interested in light banter. Her eyes dropped back to the missive. She sighed heavily. "This is quite unequivocal. It very much seems as if Julian is attempting to induce Silas to invade Varuna. To surround us on all sides." She rose to her feet. She paced smartly across the carpet in her small, dainty slippers. "The situation is desperate, indeed." She paused. She hung her head sadly. "There may be no choice but to go to war."

Kai sat back in her chair and watched her friend pace distractedly. "You could implore the King yourself, Jila. All hope is not lost. The missive did not reach Silas; I've ensured that."

Jila was surprised by Kai's reasonable tone. She shook her head. "It is only a matter of time. I do not believe for one moment the loss of the missive will affect his determination." She spun on Kai. Her expression was sharp. Her amber eyes were piercing. "He did catch you with it, didn't he?"

"Obviously."

"Does he know who you are?"

"No. I did not tell anyone who I am."

Jila looked at her shrewdly. "Not even the Commander?"

"Of course not; we cannot be certain of anyone's loyalties. I did not risk yours and our nation's security over the whims of a fine-looking man."

Jila smirked. The expression did not last long. "Then we have a bit of time before Julian realizes I am aware of his plans."

"Perhaps Silas can be persuaded to our side. You could appeal to him. Surely you and Varuna have more to offer than the Duke."

Jila paused to consider this. "Yes. Perhaps I could appeal to Silas myself. But I fear attempting to fight Julian will only worsen matters."

Kai's expression was sceptical. "It cannot get worse, my Queen, surely. You cannot allow the Duke to persuade him to attack without offering an alternative."

Jila nodded thoughtfully. "Even if he does not agree to go to war on our behalf, at least he may agree to remain neutral on his side of our country. He might be persuaded not to involve himself with the Duke..." She looked at Kai with narrowed eyes. "But I must first discover if he already intends to side with the Duke. The content of the letter intimates they have already spoken regarding me and our countries. If he intends to go to war and I reveal my hand too soon, Silas may be prepared for an attack."

Kai sighed deeply. She recognized the calculating expression in her friend's dark eyes. Draven's face flashed unbidden in her mind. She scowled and thrust the unwanted image away forcefully. Her stomach churned. She squirmed uncomfortably under her Queen's gaze.

"Kai," Jila began firmly. "You know what it is I need you to do."

"I barely managed to escape this time," Kai complained.

Jila smirked. "Does that mean you are losing your mettle? I needn't remind you, if you have lost your touch, you have lost your usefulness to me."

Kai rolled her eyes. "Rubbish. If not for me, you would not have anyone around who would treat you like a normal person."

This did not amuse Jila. Instead, the Queen sighed. She looked slightly sad. "Yes, this is true." She looked at Kai. This time her expression brooked no argument. "You must go to Leza."

Kai sighed. She flicked her fingers across her brow. She was perturbed. She wasn't accustomed to the feeling. She didn't like it. "I told the Commander and the Colonel a very intricate lie in order to preserve my safety. They will surely be in attendance if I am to go to Silas' palace."

Jila raised her eyebrows. "What sort of lie?"

Kai hesitated. "I told them I am a circus performer."

The Queen's lips quivered, as if she were suppressing a smile. "A circus performer?"

"An aerialist, actually."

Jila burst into peals of laughter. "Oh, Kai, why did you not simply tell them you're a miner?"

Kai's mouth tightened. Her ominous expression did nothing to silence her Queen. "Well, I mean..." she said with a hint of discomfiture. "The truth just did not occur to me."

"It did not occur to you that you might have to face the lie?"

"Well, I did not have a lot of time, Jila! It was the first thing I thought of."

"I would think someone in your profession would have cover stories planned for this sort of situation."

"Well, I do, normally, but none of them made any sense at the time, and they were looking at me, and it just came out!"

Jila laughed. "Well, then, my dear friend, you shall be an aerialist."

Kai sighed deeply. "I was hoping you wouldn't say that."

"Have you not always wanted to try it? It looks very flash and exciting."

"Not especially," Kai replied resentfully. "I have plenty of excitement in other forms."

"Well, get used to the idea."

"How in the bloody hell am I supposed to pretend to be an aerialist?"

"Well, you are rather spry. I'm sure your Abyssal augmentations will help."

"That is not what I meant."

"It is most convenient that the Carnivale will be in Leza soon. I believe I can persuade them to include you in their tour." Jila smiled. "But you'd better start practicing and straight away. You wouldn't want to make a complete fool of yourself."

"I think it's a bit too late for that, don't you?"

* * *

The Carnivale of Magic and Mysterie was as alive with activity and energy on the sprawling courtyard of King Silas' palace in Leza as it had been in Zooni several days past. The Lezan people were turned out in their finest dresses to enjoy the debacle and forget themselves in the magic of the illusionists, the Abyssal puppet shows and the silliness of the clowns, jugglers and tumblers. The crowd was thick with delighted revellers. The performers were as enthusiastic as they had been on the day the Queen had escaped her death.

Commander Draven Lockley, dressed in a slim black civilian waistcoat for his day off-duty, strode comfortably through the crowd. He chewed a slab of tender, sweet meat on a long, pointed spear with the air of one who was prepared to enjoy himself under any circumstance. He smiled as a cluster of small children in shabby clothes pelted past him. They giggled and shouted as they chased a small, strange, hairy creature of which Lockley had never before seen the like. The little creature paused long enough for the children to grasp at its long, fluffy, silken tail then darted away again, as quick and nimble as a fox.

Draven drew up short before a small huddle of revellers. They exclaimed and murmured excitedly as they gathered around one of the shining brass and glass tents. Interested, he ducked inside. He wove through the crowd to see the act. Suspended from the centre of the room, surrounded by the rapt audience, was a woman. She dangled from a thick, braided, copper-coloured silk rope. Draven pushed forward to the very edge of the crowd to see her better. His pulse leapt briefly before settling into a brisk, anxious thump.

She was dressed in skin-tight, metallic pink and copper leather. Her long, moonlight pale hair was unmistakable. She twisted and contorted in strange, sinuous formations. Her movements were odd and so unnatural, she might have had no bones at all in her body. The music reached a loud, pulsating crescendo. The aerialist spun in dizzying circles on the chain. Her audience below was almost hypnotized by the rapid, confusing contortions. A loud, startling Pop! Pop! Pop! filled the air. Fireworks sparked around her, as if she were tossing the sparks and flames from her fingers and toes, as though she were breathing fire.

Draven stood spellbound in the crowd. He tilted his head back. The aerialist wrapped the cord around her body in midair. She inched slowly upwards, puzzlingly, barely moving her arms and legs as she rose towards the frosted glass ceiling of the tent. When she reached the very top, she let go. She spun dizzily out of the twisted cord. The crowd exclaimed in shouts of surprise and fear. She caught herself abruptly at the bottom of the cord and lowered herself slowly to the ground.

She held up her hands theatrically. She beamed at the applause erupting around her. She bowed low and swept her hands across the floor. Then she was moving suddenly away, towards a shimmering gold curtain near the back of the tent.

"Kaia! Wait!" Draven pushed through the crowd to follow her. He darted across the empty stage after her. A circus security guard, an enormous, Abyssal man in plain, grey coveralls met him halfway. The construct pressed a single, ominous palm against his chest. His face was featureless and impassive. He exuded danger. The aerialist was disappearing through the curtain. Draven called to her again. "Kaia!"

She paused and spun around. She smiled when she saw him. Her face was painted with metallic pink and copper swirls like a masquerade mask. He still knew her instantly. Her dark, glacial pool eyes and wide, expressive smile were inimitable. "Commander Lockley," she exclaimed. She moved forwards to lay a gentle hand on the Abyssal guard's arm. "Pyo, let him through, please."

Draven smiled at her. He flicked his eyes to Pyo. The construct stepped back. He cast an arctic, threatening look towards the solider as if to caution him to mind his manners. Draven ignored the Abyssal. He stepped past him to peer down into Kaia's face. "I did not think I would see you again so soon. Are you well?"

She smiled shyly. She fluttered a hand across her brow. "Yes, I'm very well now, thanks to you, Draven."

"You did not mention you would soon be in Leza."

She looked away sheepishly. She took his arm and led him towards the shimmering curtain. Behind it was a simple dressing room with a tall, glittering mirror and a collection of cosmetics scattered across a vanity. "I did not know. I just joined the Carnivale, you see. I did not know where they planned to be next."

She sat on the stiff, brass chair before the vanity. She gestured him to take a seat on a small, threadbare pouf beside her. He eyed it dubiously. He perched instead on the edge of her vanity. "You were amazing."

She smiled. She shrugged in a pretty display of coyness. "Thank you."

"I mean..." He paused. He peered at her silently for a long moment. "I'm glad to see you here, in Leza."

"So am I glad to be here now." She held his gaze for a moment. She dropped it demurely. Her fingers fluttered over a small, fluffy pink wash cloth. "I had better get out of this costume. It's not..."

He shook his head earnestly. "It's lovely."

She laughed. "You are very gallant."

"King Silas is having a ball this evening," he said abruptly. "Were you planning to gate crash it?"

Her smile was slightly brittle. "It did not go well for me the last time I did that. I thought perhaps I would renounce my gate crashing ways this evening."

"No, don't," Draven blurted, startling them both. "What I mean is, would you like to attend? As a guest this time, not an interloper." He smiled wolfishly. "Not that beautiful women are ever unwelcome at Silas' palace." She laughed. He leaned towards her. "As my guest, I mean."

She appeared to consider this uncertainly for a moment. She smiled up at him. "All right, yes. That would be very nice."

He grinned and rose to his feet. "I will have a carriage awaiting you at half six. Does this suit you, my lady?"

She covered her giggle with her hand. "Yes. That suits me very well, thank you, sir."

He bowed low over her hand. When he looked back up into her eyes, he wore a radiant, mischievous smile. "I shall see you again very soon, Kaia."

He turned from her and slipped back through the curtain. Kai spun back to the mirror. She squared her shoulders smartly and smirked at her reflection.

CHAPTER SIX

Kai listened to the soft plod of Abyssal horse hooves from inside the large, ornate copper carriage as it travelled the smooth, polished pathway towards King Silas' palace. The path was alight with sparkling silver lights that guided the uncannily sentient horse without need of a driver. Kai slid her hands across the soft, silky emerald green cushion beneath her. She idly wondered how many women Draven had summoned to the palace in the same luxurious carriage.

How many women had the Commander impressed with his good looks, his gallantry, his position and power in the kingdom? Scores, surely, for a man such as Draven Lockley must draw many women to him. Kai, however, would not be drawn in by his stirring guile. She was, after all, on the job. There was little time for diversions or carousing.

The carriage pulled to a smooth, gentle stop at the large, ornately carved gold doors that lead into the King's palace. Before she had time to push the handle, the door opened. The cool night air swirled into the interior. It rustled her skirts. Draven Lockley held his hand to her to assist her down. She took it. She answered his tranquil, enchanting smile with a radiant beam.

She pressed her palms to Draven's shoulders. She allowed him to assist her lightly to the ground. Her high heels clicked softly on the polished marble step. She peered up into his brilliant gaze for a moment before stepping away. Draven folded her hand over his arm to escort her inside. "Hello, Kaia. You look lovely this evening."

She nudged him gently with her shoulder. "Thank you. You are quite dashing yourself, Commander." He laughed. She looked up at him with a mischievous sparkle in her dark blue eyes. He really was quite dashing, she decided. He wore a black Imperial uniform for the King's ball. It better suited his long, lean form and black hair than had the drab olive green he'd worn on the eve of their meeting. She wondered indolently what significance this slight alteration indicated. Did the Lezan guard have a uniform for a visit to Varuna, as well? Perhaps it was grey, she thought vaguely. Draven would probably be very well suited in grey.

King Silas' palace was not as gauche as Julian's, nor as grand and elegant as Jila's. It was magnificent in its simpler, singular beauty. It was carved of what looked like solid ivory, though surely it could not have been. She had little time to admire the exterior. Draven led her into the enormous, gilded hall. His mood was light. He chattered excitedly as they walked, regaling her with tales of the sights he'd seen that day at the Carnivale. She had been there, of course. She had been part of it. He seemed under the impression she regarded his praise of the circus as a compliment to herself.

It was sweet, really. She found herself drawn into the engaging animation of his tales. She found herself reluctantly picturing the small, furry Abyssal foxes as something cute and delightful, rather than the disgusting, glorified sewer rats she knew they were. His exhilaration was affective. She watched his full, sculpted mouth as he spoke. She discovered that she enjoyed the deep, rumbling tenor of his voice. He was a far more agreeable mark than had been Duke Julian of Tyr.

They entered the ballroom. It was as dimly lit as a sinister masquerade, illuminated only by small, open flame torches in the corners. The torches cast shadows across the faces of the dancers. It muted the thrilling jewel tones of their intricate livery. Indeed, some of the pairs of dancers already spinning together on the floor had gleefully donned the carved, ornate masques they had acquired at the Carnivale.

Draven gave her a charming smile. "You may seem more at home in the present atmosphere, yeah?"

She laughed. "It does look somewhat familiar. I am sure it has everything to do with the torches and the outlandishly posh gowns. They take me back."

He chuckled. "The King enjoyed the circus so much, he insisted the theme of the evening mirror it. Our people adopted the idea quite passionately."

"You, however, my dear, require no masque. Indeed, we would wish nothing less than for you to cover your lovely face." Draven spun her to face Colonel Grimes, who had approached them from behind. He beamed as he had when first they had made each other's acquaintance. He winked at his commanding officer. He bowed low to Kai. "Ah, my young friend, I see you have finally found your moonbeam."

Kai smiled. Her eyes slid to the stunning woman who joined them. The woman tucked her hand into Colonel Grimes' elbow. "You remember my wife, Yvette," Grimes continued without skipping a beat. "Yvette, surely you remember the lovely Luna. This is the young lady we have all been gossiping so much about."

Yvette Grimes smiled. She inclined her head to Kai. Kai raised her eyebrows uneasily. "I have heard much about you in the past days, Luna. All of it is quite fantastic. But that isn't your name, is it?"

Kai smiled. "No. It is Kaia."

Yvette's expression changed in the blink of an eye. She stepped away from her husband to lay a gentle hand on Kai's arm. "Are you quite all right, dear? I hear you have had quite an experience."

Kai bowed her head. She was slightly startled when Draven pulled her more tightly against his side. Though she required no comfort, for she felt no lingering agony over the fictitious assault, the nearness of his strong, sinuous form was oddly reassuring. She nodded. She smiled shyly up at Yvette from under her lashes. "I am quite all right now, I thank you. It is lucky your husband and the Commander were there to rescue me."

Yvette squeezed her arm. "Indeed. It was a stroke of great fortune." Her expression grew curious. "Is it true you leapt upon their airship just as it was taking flight?"

"I told you it was true, my dear," Grimes announced. He sounded slightly put out. "Do you never believe me?"

Yvette faced her husband unabashedly. "Well, it was rather fantastic. I wish to hear it from the lady's lips."

"It is true," Kai told her earnestly. "I did do that."

Yvette laughed. She clapped her hands together in delight. "How wonderful. Are you Abyssal?"

Despite the blithe tone of her voice, the small group fell deadly silent. Kai felt the weight of their eyes upon her. She considered for a fleeting instant telling them that yes, in fact, she was. "Yvette," Draven began tightly, "Kaia is an aerialist."

"Oh, are you?" Yvette seemed not to have noticed the charged pause. Her eyes twinkled merrily. "I saw a delightful aerialist at the Carnivale earlier today. Was it you?" Kai inclined her head demurely. "Oh, that's simply enchanting. No wonder you were able to accomplish such an extraordinary acrobatic feat." She leaned towards Kai conspiratorially. "My dear, you will find King Silas a much more hospitable and agreeable host, and he is quite taken with this wife, Leona. You will face no treachery here." She winked slyly at Draven. "Except, perhaps, at the hands of the Commander."

"Come now, Yvette, you know Draven is a proper gentleman. Don't scare the young lady away. He will cherish Miss Luna and treat her with the utmost respect and dignity."

Yvette laughed. "I do not doubt it for a moment, dear husband." She spun away from them abruptly. She clapped her hands as the band began to play a lively, festive tune. "Oh, darling, please let's dance."

Grimes sighed. "Women. They always want to parade you around as if you were a show pony."

"Well, you do look dashing in your uniform, my love."

Her husband was suitably won-over. He inclined his head and offered his arm. "All right. A dance for my wife." He grinned at Draven and Kai. "Will I see you pair out there soon?"

Draven smiled. "Perhaps. If the young lady will have me after your wife has slandered my good name."

Yvette waved over her shoulder at Kai. Kai watched the older couple go with a reluctant smile. When she turned back to Draven, he was peering down at her with an intent gaze that caused her stomach to roil uneasily. "Draven?"

He blinked. "Can I get you a drink?"

She smiled. She shook off the disquiet. "Yes, please. Thank you."

He led her towards a table draped with shimmering blue silk upon which a selection of fine Lezan and foreign hors d'oveurs was spread. Another table bore small, delicate gold plates and brass goblets filled with a sweet, smoky wine. Draven handed her a goblet that smouldered slightly and smelled faintly of fire. She sipped it slowly and closed her eyes in reverence. It seemed to evaporate in her mouth like puffs of sweet, tangy wood-smoke.

Watching the exultant expression on her face, Draven smiled. "It is a specialty of Leza. Do you like it?"

"Yes, very much."

"Perhaps it will convince you to visit our humble country more often."

"Do you wish me to visit more often?" She smiled coyly up at him from under her lashes. She batted them slightly. She stopped and straightened almost at once. Certainly, she needn't flirt so much, no matter how amenable she found him.

He didn't seem to notice her internal struggle at all. "We will see how the night progresses, and I shall tell you."

She laughed. She turned to sweep her gaze across the lively ballroom. King Silas was instantly recognizable in an elegant, black suit. His glittering golden crown perched jauntily on his head, as if he had jostled it in a dance. He was dancing still with a tall, lovely, willow-thin woman with long, snow white hair. It contrasted vividly with her curiously smooth, porcelain face. Kai was unable to determine the woman's age. Her pale, almost translucent green eyes glittered with intelligence. The curve of her lips was proud, confident and majestic .

She turned back to Draven to inquire if the woman was the Queen Leona. The intense scrutiny in his gaze caught her out. "Draven?"

He smiled. "I was just admiring your eyes." His voice was low, slightly husky. She lifted an eyebrow. "They're blue, not brown. I had thought they were brown."

She looked down. Unease shivered down her spine. Her eyes had been brown, long ago when she'd been an untouched and untainted child. Her exposure to the toxic Abyssium in the mines and in her own body had tinted them dark blue.

As if he sensed her discomfort, he smiled and offered his hand. "Would you dance with me?"

She hesitated a brief moment. She nodded. "Yes, I would like that."

Draven was an accomplished dancer. He moved with the easy grace of a large cat. He led her first into a simple, uncomplicated step. His arms around her were firm. He seemed braced to restrain her if she attempted to flee. She did not step back from him. The distance between them was slightly less than might be considered strictly proper by the discerning aristocracy. She did not widen it. The intensity of his gaze sent unfamiliar frissons down her spine. She wondered if, perhaps, the Lezan wine had been stronger than she had imagined.

When she looked into his clear dark eyes, she felt as if the air around them had thickened and warmed. She studied him intently for a moment. She was fascinated by how boldly he endured her stare. Her glacial scrutiny had been known to turn men's insides to liquid ice. "How is it you came to be a commander, Draven, when Grimes is only a colonel? You are very young to be the commander of the King's guard."

She had expected him to receive the impertinent question with as much amiability as he had born her gaze. It seemed she had introduced a sensitive topic. He averted his eyes for an ephemeral moment. She was confused by this. She realized she might have said something wrong. She sighed. "I'm sorry, Draven. I did not mean to pry. I should not have asked such a question."

He shook his head. He smiled tightly. "No. You may ask me anything you like. It is a fair question." He took a deep breath, as if he were preparing to impart a great burden. "It is true that I am much younger than Darius. However, I have been in the guard longer. My father was a nobleman, but he died when I was very young, and my mother sent me to the palace to enter the guards."

His tone was odd. She did not know him well. She could not tell at all what he was thinking. "Is that what you wanted to do?"

He shrugged. His eyes slid away again. "When I was young, when my father was still alive, I was interested in science and inventing Abyssal machines. My father was also interested in such things. He and I would tinker all day long in his workshop." He smiled. His dark eyes were wistful. "It drove my mother spare. When Father died, I was not given a choice."

"I'm sorry, Draven." There was pain in the depths of his eyes, as though it still hurt to remember it. She found, to her astonishment, that there was a part of her, deep down inside, that twisted in sympathy.

"I am content. I enjoy my position. I have come to regard this as my life's work. I was born to it, after all."

She nodded. Her eyes grew distant. "I, too, was born to my profession," she murmured. She thought perhaps it was one of the few true things she had ever said to him.

"We are very alike then."

The tone of his voice was lighter. She laughed. "Perhaps in that aspect we are. I suspect there are many ways in which we are very dissimilar."

"Perhaps. I would not mind finding out."

Kai pressed closer to him, closing the distance between their bodies. She peered up at him through hooded eyes. He took her intense gaze as encouragement. His hands slid slowly, suggestively, around her waist and over her hips. She shivered involuntarily. She rested her head on his shoulder. She nuzzled his neck with her soft, warm breath. His hands clenched on her hips. He drew her against him. Unexpectedly, she felt his lithe body go rigid.

His expression was grave as he tilted his head back to look down at her. "Are you all right, Kaia? After...what happened in Tyr, I mean. Is something to be done about the Duke?"

She sighed. "I am quite well. The Queen was very good to me. She was most empathetic. She did not share her plans for the Duke with me, however. Nor would she, I shouldn't wonder." She smiled wanly. "I am a circus performer, not a political emissary. In any case, I'm sure the matter will be handled appropriately." She smiled again. She slid her hand lightly over his arm. "And I am quite well. No lasting damage to body or soul."

His smile returned. It was slightly tighter than it had been when he had been charming her with his wit and vibrancy. "I am very pleased to hear you say so. I shouldn't like to think you were experiencing any lingering pain or fear."

Kai slid a hand around the nape of his neck. She leaned close to whisper in his ear. "No. No fears. None at all."

"I am very relieved." His voice was low and husky. He wrapped his arms more firmly around her waist. She rested her head on his shoulder. She enjoyed the music and the feel of Draven swaying her slowly to the enchanting melody. For a too fleeting moment, she allowed herself to feel contentment. When the song ended, she looked up at him with a sly smile. "I am feeling slightly flushed," she purred. "Would it be too much trouble to sit down a while?"

He looked vaguely disappointed, as if he too were enjoying their dance. "No. Of course. Anything you like."

She looked at him silently. That roiling, uncomfortable feeling gnawed at her belly. The Commander was quite taken with her. There was no mistaking the glint in his eyes. Her errand would be effortless. Yet there was no exhilaration at the prospect of a job completed with alacrity and zeal. She did feel something, though. It was dark and troubling.

Draven led her through the dancers. He wrapped his arm tightly around her shoulders as if he expected someone to try to snatch her away or feared she might flee. She did not. He nodded to his compatriots as he passed them. He smiled stiffly. He did not pause to speak to any of them. He acknowledged the Grimes' with only a brief, curt nod. The bench to which he led her was on the edge of the ballroom under a glowing torch that cast shadows across their faces

The bench was lined in deep, green velvet. The cushion was threadbare and stiff. Kai wondered if it had seen much use in the last several years. It was likely a relic of the Kings of ancient Leza, rather than a suitable seat for repose. Kai sat straight up in the seat, perched on the edge of the bench.

Draven's lips twisted into a smirk. "May I bring you another glass of wine?"

"Yes, please." She felt as if her voice sounded as stiff as her back. She wondered how long she could sit like that, without shifting, before her companion noticed her uncanny stillness. "You are quite an accommodating host."

He winked at her. "Not at all. I am merely attempting to ensure you don't get it into your mind to disappear from my life again."

She smiled. "I believe, Commander, I have no intention of disappearing any time soon." He sat beside her on the bench. He did not seem to notice the awkwardness of it. Perhaps his years in the service had accustomed him to uncomfortable conditions. "Do you live here, in the palace?"

He raised his eyebrows. "I wasn't expecting this to be quite that easy."

She laughed genuinely. "My intention was not to be forward, Commander."

He grinned. "I apologise for the misunderstanding. I did not mean to suggest you were anything but a lady of class, sophistication and virtue."

"Laying it on a bit thick, aren't you?"

"Probably. Is it working?"

"It is working a bit."

"Excellent. Yes, I have a room in the palace. As commander of the guards, I am often needed at inconvenient hours of the night and day. King Silas prefers to keep me close at hand. I have a small troupe of guards who live here with me in the palace, as well."

"Colonel Grimes?"

"No. Darius has a wife and children. He prefers to keep his home in the city."

She raised an eyebrow at him. "So, you have no wife and children?"

He laughed. "No, of course not. What sort of man do you think I am?"

She cocked her head to the side. She studied him with narrow eyes. "I really wouldn't know what sort of man you are, Commander."

"No? I would have thought I had highly recommended myself by my impeccable manners and gallant treatment of you so far."

"Oh, you are quite the gentleman. I find myself positively overwhelmed by your elegance and chivalry."

"I suspect you are teasing me slightly, Kaia."

"Perhaps slightly."

He smirked. He turned away from her to gaze out at the room. "I find myself thoroughly disinclined to enjoy the company of so many tiresome nobles and dreary soldiers with whom I already spend too much of my time. Would you care to go somewhere a bit more private?"

She smirked. "Are you attempting to take advantage of me, Commander?"

Draven looked startled. His brow furrowed. His back stiffened. "No, of course not. I would never."

She held up a hand to appease him. She slid her other hand into his. "It is all right. I am again only teasing you." She leaned towards him. She murmured in his ear. "I would like to go somewhere private with you. Yours is the only company I am inclined to enjoy."

He smiled and stood. He drew her to her feet and tucked her hand into the crook of his elbow. Without a further word, he led her out of the ballroom. The antechamber outside the hall was blessedly quiet. There were only a few people catching their breath or heading outside towards the courtyard for some fresh air. Draven turned towards the castle's main entrance. He steered her in the direction of the lovely, clear evening sky.

Kai resisted. She tugged gently on his arm. "Where are your chambers?"

Draven paused and looked down at her in surprise. "I did not expect you would be interested in seeing them quite so soon." She laughed. He relaxed. His sensual mouth twisted into a smirk. "They're upstairs. Would you like to see them?"

She hesitated for a brief moment, as if in reservation.

"I assure you, Kaia, your virtue is safe with me."

She eyed him suspiciously for a moment. Then she pressed closer against his side. "I am certain you will treat me right, Commander."

He smiled and spun her without further hesitation towards a large, winding staircase carved of smooth, polished ivory with ornate brass and glass banisters. At the end of the staircase was a set of gold doors embossed with the King's coat of arms. Though Draven was continuing down the corridor with single-minded determination, Kaia paused in front of the golden doors. She peered up at him.

"Do they lead to the King's chambers?"

He inclined his head. "Yes. Where he holds his summits. Beyond the meeting chamber are the King's and Queen's private rooms."

She peered up at him with bright, keen eyes. "Can I see them?"

Draven laughed. "Are you simply using me to get to the King?"

"That would be a very convoluted deception, were that my intention."

"Perhaps. Or perhaps you are merely very clever."

"I am not clever. I'm simply curious. I have only had occasion to see my Queen's chambers the night you rescued me from Tyr. They are magnificent. Gilded in gold and ebony. I have never seen the like of it in my life."

Draven raised an eyebrow at her. "You wish to compare?"

She lifted one shoulder in a delicate shrug. "I appreciate beauty."

"As do I." His brilliant dark eyes were glittering with intensity. Her breath caught as he leaned towards her.

He pushed the doors. They opened with a smooth, soundless grace, as if they weighed nothing at all. Their entry was not unnoticed. A sentinel stepped forwards as they entered the antechamber. He was more Abyss than man. He was as tall and huge as the Tyran guards. A spyglass extended from the socket in place of his left eye. His right glowed a gleaming, toxic blue. Though he wore a uniform similar to Draven's, a strange blue hose that embedded into the side of his neck ran down the collar of his crisp black jacket. Kaia could not see where it terminated, but the outline continued down the length of his torso and into his waistband.

When he saw Draven, his single blue eye flashed slightly in recognition. He stepped aside without a word. Once inside the summit chamber, Kaia looked around as if in awe. The ceiling was domed glass. The stars of the night sky twinkled above them, bathing the room in pale, eerie moonlight.

She exhaled in a soft, reverential sigh. "Oh, it is so lovely."

Draven smiled. He peered up at the ceiling. "Yes, it is beautiful at night. In the daytime, the ceiling is shuttered to keep out the sunlight, or it would become as warm as a greenhouse in here. Very uncomfortable. A bit like baking in an oven, I expect."

The ceiling was the room's singular opulence. It was otherwise well appointed and elegant, but utilitarian. It was very unlike Jila's audience chamber, which boasted tapestries and magnificent art. It was a room in which business was conducted efficiently. There was no need of flourish and fancy. Kaia's eyes narrowed single-mindedly upon the desk nestled in the back of the room. Its surface was so carefully polished that it perfectly reflected the stars above. It was covered in papers. It appeared oft used.

"Do you come here often?" she asked Draven. She peered up at him.

"Yes. Often enough."

"Do you ever get tired of looking at it?"

He dropped his head back to stare thoughtfully up at the sky. His gaze returned directly to her face. "No, I never do. Perhaps I can give you a tour of the rest of the chambers?"

"Won't the King mind?"

He smirked. "No. Silas understands what is required to impress a woman."

She laughed. "Are you trying to impress me?"

"Of course. Is it working?"

"It is beginning to."

"Come. I will show you the other rooms."

The sitting room was no less breathtaking than the summit. Though smaller, it boasted the same glittering ceiling. The furniture was plush and inviting, draped in rich silk and velvet brocades. Stunning, brilliantly coloured landscapes hung along the walls, each surely more valuable than anything she had ever owned. The room seemed also to function as the King's library, for there were rows and rows of books covering the length and width of the furthest wall.

Draven smiled down at her. His expression was expectant. "It is very beautiful," she told him. "But it all looks so sensible."

He laughed. "Sensible? You stand in the King of Leza's private entertaining room with the night sky above and the world's finest art around you, and you think to call it sensible?"

"Well, Queen Jila's chambers are so full of poufs and cushions and garishness. I was expecting something a bit more flash, I suppose. Perhaps it is the distinction between Kings and Queens."

He chuckled and tugged gently on her hand. The next door he opened lead to the King's and Queen's bedroom. "There is slightly more here." The four-poster bed was draped in heavy silk. It matched perfectly to the three wardrobes constructed of sleek, polished wood. Two vanity tables sat side by side, one each for the King and his Queen. The surfaces of the tables were covered in cosmetics and creams and ornately carved gold combs. They were all very fine and very lovely. The delicacy of the items belied their common use.

She smiled coyly at him. "Well, I suppose it depends entirely upon what is expected to be accomplished in this room."

He winked at her. "Perhaps it is not gentlemanly to show a woman a bedroom on your first encounter."

"Not our first. I think it could perhaps be considered our third, yes?"

"If you choose to consider it as such, it could be said to be our forth, counting this afternoon at the Carnivale."

"That seems enough encounters, don't you agree?"

He raised his eyebrows at the husky timbre of her voice. He did not resist when she turned him to face her. She caught the lapels of his jacket to tug him forwards. He met her halfway. He leaned down as she turned her face to him. When their mouths met, she moaned low in her throat. Draven wrapped an arm around her waist to draw her so tightly against him, she could barely catch her breath.

His hand slid softly over her cheek and into her hair. He cupped the nape of her neck to tilt her head back. His tongue dipped experimentally into her mouth. She wrapped her arms around his neck. She drew him nearer to deepen the kiss. Her fervent reaction was all he required. He lifted her easily with one arm. He moved her backwards towards a library table covered in books.

He swept the books aside. He dropped her on the edge of the table, which felt as solid as stone beneath her. He did not break the kiss. He leaned forwards, against her. She opened her legs brazenly to accommodate him. His arm supported her firmly as he pressed her back against the surface of the table. His body was hot against hers. It seared her through the layers of silk and wool and fabric that separated them. Her pulse leapt. She moaned guilelessly.

Draven groaned gruffly. He gripped her hips. He slid her abruptly to the edge of the table to meet his body. His arousal pressed against her. She moved restlessly against it. He tore his mouth from hers to press hot kisses down her throat. His breath was ragged. His body was rigid against her. Heat blossomed relentlessly inside her. She clutched him to her. She threaded her fingers into his silken black hair.

Her head fell back. She exhaled in a soft plaintive sigh. Draven cut her off. He pressed his mouth to hers again. His kisses were fervent and unrestrained. Kai allowed the kiss to go on for several long moments. She was enjoying the feel of his body beneath her hands and against her own hot, tingling skin. For an endless, irrational moment, her senses filled only with him.

Her fingers fluttered against his jacket fumbling with the large, gold buttons. He caught her hands before she had reached the third. He broke the kiss. He pulled back to look at her. His breath was shallow. The look in his dark eyes was sharp and focussed as they met hers. His voice was husky and ragged. It drew her sharply and reluctantly out of her throe. "I will not have you on a table in the King's library."

She laughed. He cut her off with a sound kiss on the mouth. "Come with me," he ordered in the same deep, tempestuous voice that had roused her senses once more. "To my chambers."

Kai nodded. She sat up as he stepped away from her. She allowed him to assist her to her feet. He took her hand to lead her out of the room. She paused and glanced sharply at the clock on the wall. It had begun to chime. "Damn," she swore under her breath. Draven seemed not to have heard her, so single-minded was his determination to lead her to his chambers. She felt a peculiar, unwelcome pang in her lower belly.

With a soft, nearly inaudible snick the stunner hidden in her sleeve protracted. It hummed with the rush of crackling energy at its tip. "I am sorry about this, Draven."

He paused. He half turned back to her. "What?"

Chapter Seven

She pressed the tip of the wand against the base of his spine. He dropped to the floor in mid-spin. She crouched down beside his prone form. She gently turned him onto his back. She brushed his long, black hair from his face. "I truly am sorry. I had hoped to enjoy you before. There just wasn't time, I'm afraid."

The clock chimed again, ominously. She flew to her feet. She hurried to Silas' desk. She rifled swiftly through the papers. Her eyes darted frequently towards the prone soldier several feet away, lest he require another jolt to pacify him. King Silas' papers were in far better order than had been the Duke's. It took her only the briefest moment to discover her object.

My esteemed Brother

I, too, agree that Queen Jila's methods are heavy-handed and counter to our brokered peace treaties. Your concerns are of great consequence to me, and I shall endeavour to assist you in any way I am able, per our agreement. Our country has always enjoyed a unique partnership with yours, and I have no wish to see that partnership fail now, in your darkest hour. Please call upon me in the event that I can be of service to you in your struggle against the Queen...

Kai's gaze snapped unconsciously towards Draven. She sighed deeply. Her heart thumped heavily in her chest. She tucked the missive swiftly into her corset. Jila would be beside herself when she received the news. There was little time to spare in delivering it. The clock chimed again. She stepped over Draven's body. She avoided gazing down upon him, as if seeing him would somehow shake her resolve. Her resolve had never once been shaken before, she reminded herself sternly. Now was hardly the time to change that.

The guard did not spare her a glance as she hurried from the room, as if an unaccompanied woman emerging, dishevelled, from the King's chambers was unworthy of his notice. She did not spare a moment to consider the grim implications of this. When she was out of the guard's line of sight, she broke into a run. She avoided the ballroom and the main entrance. She hoped this time to remain out of sight of the crowd. One narrow escape from an unfamiliar palace was enough for a lifetime.

Several moments of searching and running into dead stops at the ends of corridors, however, offered no convenient egress from her eminent capture. Still, if she merely wound her way through the ballroom, avoiding the gazes of Colonel and Mrs Grimes, perhaps she could use the crowd to obscure her escape.

She was brought up short in the entrance hall at the sight of an enormous, perfectly motionless sentinel in the livery of a Tyran guard. He blocked the path outside. Damn. She wove into a crowd of handsomely adorned ladies. She turned her head to avoid his gaze. She knew instantly upon passing him that he had recognised his query, for he snapped to attention at once. His brilliant eyes glittered with sudden, terrible life.

His eyes did not leave her. They grew distant, as if he were looking far away. She was certain he was communicating in that strange, silent way with the other guards. They were likely stationed all around the palace. How had she not anticipated the guards' presence? Julian was, after all, a tenacious man. Her transgression had been most egregious. She should not have allowed herself to become unvigilant, particularly in the superficial security of Draven Lockley's arms.

She did not pause to concern herself with how many more of them were waiting outside and around the palace for her. She broke through the crowd. She raced out of the entrance hall into the cool, night air. Behind her, there were cries of surprise. She ignored them. Her heart thumped excitedly in her chest.

Her fortune must have been dreadful. There were two Tyran guards outside, patrolling the courtyard grounds. They did not speak. They had already been alerted to her. They converged upon her instantly. She spun in mid-step and raced in the opposite direction. She drew up short at a wall of tall, green bushes. She had reached the King's widely revered courtyard labyrinth spread out across the acres of forestland behind the palace. Tossing a glance over her shoulder, she raced along the labyrinth wall. She groped for the opening. When she found it, she dashed inside.

The night was glittering with stars. The labyrinth was dark. A scant few glowing blue Abyssal torches lit the pathways. She melted into the shadows. She slid along the walls with her back against the foliage. She felt her dress tear. For a brief, amused moment, she pictured Jila's horror at the tattered state of yet another lovely borrowed gown. She heard the pounding of the guard's feet as they plodding through the maze after her. They quickly lost themselves in dead ends and false turns.

She prayed she would emerge outside near the footpath upon which she could find her way to the circus grounds outside the palace walls. Her Abyssal senses were heightened. They were still no match for the Abyssal guards. Their superior hearing picked up her breath and the rustle of her skirts against the brush. Why had she not spent more time studying them and determining how to deactivate them? Her stunner was little use against them. How had she not anticipated her own danger?

It was highly out of character, failing to foresee jeopardy, to protect, above all things, herself. She cursed. She burst through an opening in the labyrinth and came out in the centre. It was a wide, open space, paved with smooth, shining bronze. A large fountain spurted streams of water into a shallow pool. Her eyes darted quickly around her. There were three gaps in the wall around the fountain identical to the one from which she had emerged. She wasn't sure which one had been hers.

The openings filled suddenly with three Tyran guards. They materialized out of the night and the trees in the same moment, as if the move had been carefully choreographed. It probably had. They were of one mind. That mind was turned towards her capture. She glanced wildly over her shoulder. She could return the way she came. They would follow. She could not conceal herself in shadow and silence. They would catch her up. There was nothing for it but to fight.

She brandished her stunner, poised for an attack. When they converged upon her, she launched into motion, stunning them in quick succession. It was little use against them. As quickly as she had stunned the third, the first had regained himself. She had no sufficient weapons to use against creatures such as these. She had only her fists and her legs, with which she struck out at them, and a length of copper wire twined round her ankle. It probably wouldn't be enough.

She crouched low. She swiftly unwound the wire as she danced out of the way of their grasping hands. She snapped the wire out at them like a whip. Though it would have brought a normal man to his knees, it barely startled the indomitable guards. She might keep this up all night. She would tire sooner than they. It was a matter only of time before she fell to them.

She whipped the wire through the air. It lanced a guard's exposed cheek and drew blood. He merely grunted and moved towards her again. Her eyes darted wildly about for an escape. In her desperation to evade them, she had placed them between her and the labyrinth's openings. Perhaps she could confuse them, duck under their enormous, flailing arms to reach the exit...

A figure in black emerged from the shadows behind the guards. Her eyes widened in shock. The guards had not noticed him, despite their superior senses. They were focussed on she alone. She dropped to her knees to cover her head. The figure drew a large gun from a holster on his belt. His movement and his bearing were eerily familiar. She did not waste time to distinguish his face behind the barrel of his gun.

Beams of blue light arced through the air. The guards fell heavily around her before they were able to register the absence of their brothers' consciousnesses beside them. Then all was silent around her. The air crackled with energy and the metallic scent of blood. She lifted her arms from her face. She looked up with shock into the cold, black eyes of Commander Draven Lockley.

He strode towards her. He holstered his gun in the same movement. She looked around at the guards. "They're dead," she said dumbly. "You killed them."

"Yes, of course," he replied shortly. He dropped into a crouch beside her. He caught her shoulders. His brow was furrowed in concern. "What happened, Kaia? Did they hurt you?"

She shrugged off his hands. She pushed herself to her feet. He did not leave off. He rose to his feet in a swift movement and gripped her arms. "What's going on?" he demanded. "Did they attack me to capture you? How did you get down here?" Kai took a step back. She attempted to break free of him. His hands clenched around her elbows. He yanked her back towards him. "All I remember was walking towards the door in the King's office."

"Let me go, Draven."

"I'm sorry." His words startled her. She stilled and peered up into his eyes. He smoothed her dishevelled hair back from her face. "I did not know they were here. I did not know they would present a danger to you."

"Let me go!"

His expression changed. He seemed to look at her for the first time. Her eyes were wild and angry as she struggled against his grip. He loosened his hold. He looked bemused and sheepish. "Are you all right?" he asked again in a low, anxious voice. "Did they hurt you?"

"Don't touch me--" But he was examining her closely, checking her arms, her clothes and her body for signs of damage. "Stop it--"

"What is this?" His face was stony as he held the missive up between two fingers.

"It's mine. Give it to me."

But his eyes were scanning it rapidly. When he looked up at her again, his eyebrows were knitted together in an expression of surprise. "This is the King's handwriting. He wrote this. Why do you have it? Where did you get it?"

She lifted her chin, ignoring the gnawing, guilty feeling in her belly. It was not the time for guilt. It was not the time to respond to the wounded look in his deep, dark eyes. He had, after all, led her right to it. "Let go of me, Draven," she ordered through gritted teeth.

"Not until you tell me what the bloody hell is going on!" He spun her around abruptly. He trapped her against his chest. He ignored her struggles and her outraged sputtering. He slid his hands over her, over her arms, her legs, around her waist and under her corset. She was mystified for a moment. She wondered how his thoughts could shift so rapidly. But, no, there was no sensuality in his embrace or his touch. He was frisking her for weapons. And he'd found them.

He held out her arm to examine the stunner strapped to her wrist. He had seen it before. He knew exactly what it was. "What is going on, Kaia? Why did you bring this here? Who are you really?"

She said nothing. Her breath came out in angry, ragged huffs.

"You're the one who stunned me." Her silence was all the confirmation he required. He hugged her tightly against his chest with one arm. He groped in his back pocket with the other. "Stop struggling, Kaia."

When the shackles snapped onto her wrists, she reacted as if he'd shot her. She dropped out of his arms to the ground. He was faster than she, tired as she was from her scuffle with the Tyran guards. He pinned her to the ground. He leaned over her with burning, furious eyes. "What are you doing?" she hissed.

"Stop struggling! I'm sorry; you'll have to come with me. If you won't walk, I will shackle your ankles and drag you."

She hissed at him like an angry cat. He lifted her to her feet. He guided her silently through the labyrinth as if the path were engrained in his memory. She could feel the anger radiating off of him in waves of heat. His fingers bit into her upper arms. She considered attempting to escape him. She could, after all, likely outrun him, given the chance to regain her energy. She did not.

He led her out of the labyrinth, around the back of the palace, which had seen less attention than the obverse and the courtyards. A rusted metal door shrieked when Draven pulled it open. Darkness swallowed them. There were stairs beneath her feet. She stumbled. Draven tightened his grip. He caught her around the waist to carry her bodily down the remaining stairs.

He had led her to the dungeon. It was scantly lit with glowing orange torches, which feebly combated the dank, chilly air around them. The cells around them were empty. Kai wondered what was done with the prisoners here. A faint, sickly sweet scent hung in the air. Were they left for dead, carried out and burned? Was that Draven's intention for her, now that her treachery had been exposed?

He spun her to face him. He did not meet her gaze as he removed the shackles from her wrists. Curious, she did not speak or move. She waited, watching the tight line of his mouth as he leaned towards her. He reached behind her. He pushed open the cell door. With a gentle shove, he locked her inside.

The walls of her cell were stone. The bars were cold, hard steel, which she gripped in her hands as she leaned against them. He did not move. He merely stood in silence for a long moment. He peered at her through the metal grate that separated them. Finally he ordered, "Tell me who you are. Tell me why you have this. Why did you stun me?"

She tilted her head slightly. She stared back at his closed, expressionless face in interest. Instead of replying, she asked, "How did you manage to wake up from that so quickly?"

He scowled. "I am a soldier. I'm trained to withstand many weapons of this sort. It only caught me out for a moment. That is not the point! Who are you, Kaia?" He sighed deeply then. He lowered his head for a brief moment. He looked back up at her. "Is that even your name?"

Kai stared at him blankly.

"Damnit!" He pushed his hands through his hair in agitation. He spun to pace restlessly for a moment before returning to face her. "What are you doing here? Why do you have this letter?"

"Let me out of here."

"No! Not until you tell me what's going on!" For a moment, they stared at each other. Draven's chest rose and fell rapidly. Kai's expression was perfectly calm. "You were just using me to get to the King's chambers to steal this letter?"

She considered this question a moment. "Yes."

His eyes flashed. Then his expression grew glacial. It was so much worse than the heat of his anger. "And I led you right into them. I never even suspected. I should have known you weren't real." She studied him. She did not offer a response. "Is anything about you real?" He sighed. He looked away from her. He did not wait for a reply. "Of course it isn't."

"Some of it." Her voice was peculiarly gentle. It was almost kind. His head snapped back up.

"What part?"

"Let me out, and maybe I will tell you."

He scowled. "I'm not letting you out! You're not going anywhere until I figure out what the hell you're doing here! Why would you want this letter, anyway? What does this have to do with you?"

She lifted her chin. Her expression was blank.

"Are you a terrorist?"

She considered. "Sometimes. But not right now."

"What does that mean?"

"It means I am whatever I need to be when I need to be it."

He frowned. Then comprehension dawned on his face. His eyes narrowed. "Who do you work for?"

There was nothing in her eyes, not a hint of warmth or guilt or fear.

"If you don't tell me something, Kaia, I will have to turn you over to the King." When she merely looked at him with that empty expression, he stepped up to her. He seized her wrists through the bars. His voice was fierce. "He will probably have you executed for espionage!"

She met him halfway. She pressed closer so only the thick, metal bars separated them. "Will you be the one to hang me, Draven?"

He reeled back as if she had struck out at him. "No! I would never..." He trailed off. He spun his back on her.

She held out her hands to him. "Go ahead, Draven. You have already disarmed me. Take me to your King."

He glanced over his shoulder at her incredulously. For a long moment, he seemed to have nothing to say. "No." His voice was barely audible.

"No? You must. Is there any other choice?"

He looked at her without comprehension. "I will not."

She raised her eyebrows. "Why not?"

They stared at each other for an endless, silent moment. Suddenly Kai understood. She felt a terrible, unfamiliar swooping sensation in her belly. She stepped back from the bars, away from him. Pity. Draven had cared for her--for the woman she had pretended to be, anyway. She was sorry that that woman didn't exist. She regretted that he would suffer over her loss.

"Tell me what was true." His voice was low and morose. She turned her face from him. She could not meet his gaze. "Did you feel anything when I touched you?"

She sighed. She turned her back on him. "I work for Queen Jila."

He paused. "Jila?" She turned back to face him. She inclined her head. "She sent you to steal from Silas?"

"No. She sent me to discover evidence that your king intends to betray her and align with the Duke in war against Varuna."

Draven looked utterly flummoxed. "War? What? Why would the Queen suspect Silas is intending to go to war against her? They have no quarrel."

She hesitated, eyeing him narrowly. She wondered briefly how much was prudent to divulge to him, the Commander of Silas' guard. She was completely certain that Draven Lockley would not harm her. He would not let her come to harm. She answered him honestly. "There have been attempts on my Queen's life. We are endeavouring to discover who is behind them."

She watched the struggle in his eyes. The desire to forgive her, to believe her, warred with his sense of duty. Pity coursed through her again. Comprehension dawned on his face. Did he think her noble? He was loyal to his monarch, to his King. He valued loyalty. She did not share his values. She did not share much of any of his tender and noble sentiments. She wished he would not look at her as though he was persuaded that she did. "You are protecting your Queen?"

"In a manner of speaking."

"Leza has no interest in war against Varuna."

She was caught out by his conviction. "Then what is that missive?"

"The Duke has appealed to the King for a loan to pay his debts to Varuna."

"How can you know for sure he is not in league with Julian against my Queen?"

"I am his second! I know what he is planning. If war is to be declared, I would be the first to know." She was not convinced. He stepped forward. His was voice resolute. "You misunderstood. You intended to bring this to your Queen as evidence of the King's treachery."

"As evidence he may intend treachery in the future or be persuaded by the Duke."

"It is not so."

She lifted her chin. She exhaled heavily in relief. "My Queen will be most pleased to learn of this."

"If you had simply asked, I would have told you what you wanted to know."

She was not persuaded by this assertion. "I did not believe I had a choice in resorting to subterfuge."

"You didn't have to lie to me! You could have told me! I would have understood." He sighed. "You could have trusted me."

"How could I have done, Draven? I don't know you at all."

His expression was openly wounded. "You know me rather better now." She looked away. "Is that what you do? How you get close to people?"

She considered shouting at him. She considered insisting that it was not. She was not sure why she had allowed herself to become so entangled with him. She had lost herself completely in the intensity of his regard. She did not tell him any of those things. Her reply was flat. "Sometimes."

He exhaled heavily. He pushed his hands through his hair. He turned his back to her.

"What will you do with me? Will you take me to your King to await my execution?"

He glanced askance at her. His eyes were inexplicably sympathetic. "You used me."

"Yes. I did."

He sighed again. He turned and strode forward to unlock the door to her cell. He threw it open. He stepped aside. "Were I in your position, I might have done the same."

This time, the pity shown on her face. "No, Draven. You wouldn't have done."

He frowned. "You're right. I wouldn't have used you. I wouldn't have hurt you." She lifted her chin defiantly. "Just go. You can report to your Queen that Leza has no intent to go to war."

Kai did not move. She stared at him. "You killed three of the Duke's men, Draven. If you let me go, how will you explain it? You may face retribution. The Duke has likely placed a handsome price on my head; he will not take to this continuing encumbrance lightly."

He narrowed his eyes at her. "What do you care?"

She hesitated. "I would not wish for you to suffer unnecessarily."

He laughed bitterly. "Would you not?" When she did not reply, he squared his shoulders. "The Duke's guards were attempting to harm the King's guest at his own palace. They were acting on our land without the permission of the King or his guard. If Duke Julian attempts to seek retribution against the guard who interfered with their unlawful acts, it would be grounds for war. It would be a grave diplomatic error. On balance, Julian will not be so foolish."

He gave her an austere look. She did not consider lying to him again. "Why is the Duke really after your head, Kaia? You aren't who you say you are....was your story true then, or had your lies already begun?"

She looked away again. She did not answer him.

"What crime did you commit?"

"You would not wish to have that knowledge, Draven. It is safer for you not to know."

He strode forwards abruptly into the cell. He caught her shoulders. "If I am to cover this up for you, I will know why!"

"I did not ask for you to cover anything up! I can take care of myself."

They glared at each other. He gave her shoulders a gentle shake. "You can trust me, Kaia. I will not see you come to harm."

She sighed. "I came into possession of some of the Duke's private papers. Papers that would suggest he is contemplating treachery."

Draven lifted an eyebrow. "As you did the King's?"

She smirked. "Very like."

He did not seem to want to contemplate this very closely. He released her and tucked the King's letter into his jacket. "I never saw this. You'd better go before the Duke realises what's happened and sends more men to seek you. The quicker you are in your own land, under the protection of your Queen, the better. I cannot ensure that I can keep you safe for long."

She nodded curtly. She strode past him towards the dark stairs that offered freedom.

Behind her, Draven spoke. "I won't clean up for you again."

She paused on the bottom of the stairs. She did not turn back to him. "I did not ask you to the first time."

She looked over her shoulder then. She saw a flash of hurt in his eyes. She sighed. "Fine," he said gruffly. "Just go."

"Good bye."

CHAPTER EIGHT

Queen Jila sipped her tea daintily. She peered at her companion over the top of the delicate china cup. Kai sat across from her. She had not touched her own tea, which was cooling, forgotten, on the table before her. Kai's expression was utterly grave. She had not spoken since Abraham had shown her into the sitting room. Jila raised her eyebrows. She had never seen her friend this way. She wondered what had happened to her on the King's land to have drawn from her this sombre, almost melancholy mien.

Despite her interest in her friend's uncharacteristically emotive mood, Jila required her report of the King's position. "Kai, is something wrong?"

Kai's head snapped up. "What?"

"You seem different this afternoon. What happened last night? Did something go wrong?"

"Yes. Very, very wrong."

Jila raised her eyebrows. "What do you mean?"

Jila's voice was sharp. Kai shook herself. Her Queen was nothing if not observant, and she was certainly not without impatience. "Sorry, My Queen," she said brusquely. "I was lost in thought a moment. It will not happen again."

Jila's expression was wry. "Come on, Kai. I'm your friend, not only your queen. You may talk freely to me."

Kai shook her head vigorously. "I have nothing to talk about. All is well."

Jila looked unconvinced. She did not press the issue. "All right. What did you learn, then?"

"Silas is not intending to engage you in war, Your Highness. In fact, he seems quite unaware of what Julian is planning."

"How can you be sure of this?"

Kai looked away. "My information is reliable. It is from a source I believe to be wholly steadfast."

"I see."

Kai did not meet the Queen's gaze as she studied her. There was no sense of satisfaction for a job well done—or even a bad job done well. Kai had achieved her objective. She had escaped without harm or overt peril. Could she not meet her Queen's eyes with honour? How had she come by this uncomfortable, discontent feeling in the pit of her stomach?

Jila's voice jolted her out of her pensiveness. "And who might this source be, Kai?" She leaned forwards when Kai did not reply or meet her eyes. "Kai. I'm your friend," she reminded her gently.

Kai looked at her. Her mouth twisted into a small smile. "The commander of his guard," she admitted.

"Really?" Jila sat back in her chair with an expression of surprise. "Draven Lockley? Again?"

Kai sighed. "He has proved most useful in our efforts so far."

Jila smirked. "He has, indeed. How fortunate you came upon him again, so unexpectedly. I might be convinced he has taken a certain shine to you." When Kai scowled, she continued more seriously, "He has a reputation for being an adept and competent leader. He is highly prized by his King and well-respected in all our three nations. He is very steadfast indeed. His information can usually be relied upon to be accurate and most up to date." She raised her eyebrows archly. "But I suspect you know him rather differently?"

"No. I do not know him at all."

"I might remind you, Kai, that impertinence in my chambers can be grounds for execution."

Kai laughed. "You would not execute me. Who else would run around on mad missions doing your bidding without asking questions?"

Jila grinned. "There is truth to that, I'll allow. And I quite like having you around, on balance. But tell me, Kai, how did you come upon this information? What occurred between you and Commander Lockley?"

Kai stiffened. "Nothing occurred. We merely conversed."

Jila looked sceptical. "I am quite shocked, my friend. You are usually such a gifted deceiver. I wonder, then, how it is that you now seem so stumbling and inelegant in your subterfuge." Kai looked away sullenly. Jila smirked. "No matter. I am satisfied you obtained this information discreetly. Should I expect retaliation from the King or any of his subjects?"

"No, my Queen."

Jila nodded. "Well done, then, though not without certain strife and obstacle, I shouldn't wonder. Still, I have learned over the years it is best not to ask you too many questions." She rose to her feet. She paced restlessly as she spoke, as if to herself. "I will speak to Silas immediately regarding his part in the potential skirmish. I mean to secure his detachment as soon as possible so that I may take the matter of the Duke into my own hands without his interference. It will not be long before Julian moves against me, I am sure, especially if he suspects I am aware of his plans and intend to move against him first."

A metallic chirp signalled an incoming communication. Jila strode towards her console. Her fingers danced across the large, brass keys of the keyboard. A small slip of paper printed out on the console beside it. She glanced at Kai. "It is the King of Leza."

Kai shot to her feet. "Silas?"

Their expressions were mirrored in grim surprise. "Should I answer it?" Jila asked wearily. "Have you done something to incite his ire? Should I prepare myself for a declaration of war?"

Kai looked doubtful. "It's a very polite declaration of war, should it be one. Usually war is declared by a simple, unannounced invasion."

Jila laughed. "Of course." She pressed the large, glowing red dome in the centre of the console. The glass screen swirled. "King Silas."

The screen cleared and filled with the image of an unremarkable middle-aged man with short, steel-grey hair dressed in a sensible, straightforward suit. There was nothing flashy, ostentatious or particularly handsome about him, though his slightly lined features were patrician, even and pleasing. Jila curtsied to him. "Your Majesty," he replied in a deep, even voice.

Neither his voice nor his expression gave anything of his intentions away. Kai braced herself for his words. She saw movement behind him. Her eyes snapped to the silent guard at his back. Draven stood very straight. His expression was utterly blank. Despite the tight control in his bearing, he appeared curiously relaxed as he stood behind his King. The position suited him.

Kai moved to stand behind Jila. She presented an unlikely contrast to Draven's crisp uniform in her soft, worn leather pants and scuffed jacket. His eyes met hers. They flashed incomprehensibly. She took a deep breath. Her heart thumped. What had he told his King?

Jila must have sensed the tension in the air. "What can I do for you, My Lord?"

"My Commander has apprised me of what happened in my labyrinth last evening."

Jila glanced slightly over her shoulder. Her face did not reveal her surprise. Her voice was amiable and politely interested. "My Lord?"

"Is this the young lady?" Kai lifted her chin. She bowed slightly at the waist. She met Jila's eyes. Her Queen was inscrutable. "My Queen, I understand that we find ourselves in a quandary regarding the Duke."

Now Jila's eyebrows rose. "A quandary, My Lord?"

"He presents a grave danger to the continuing peace among the nations of the Abyssium zone."

Kai stepped forwards to stand beside her Queen. She shot a look at Draven. His face showed nothing. It revealed no expression or emotion at all. He could have been one of the Duke's inactive Abyssal guards. "Yes, Your Highness," Jila said. She glanced sidelong at Kai. "I believe he just might."

"It has always been my preference to remain impartial in these matters, as you well know," Silas continued earnestly. "However, I am compelled to remonstrate in the event of assassination attempts and his Abyssal guards attempting to apprehend foreign nationals on my own soil without my knowledge or permission."

Kai exhaled heavily. Her entire body relaxed. Draven had remained true to his word. Jila seemed to have sensed the release of her tension. She glanced at her again with a keenly elevated eyebrow. She would have some explaining to do once the Queen had conducted her business with the King, she shouldn't wonder.

Silas' next statement was delivered in such a moderate tone, its gravity was nearly lost. "Jila, I am prepared to stand behind you in the event this tension intensifies into all out war."

His words hung in the ensuing silence a moment. Draven lifted his chin. His expression was austere and resolute. The declaration did not come as a surprise to him. Jila looked completely caught out. "My King. Silas, are you certain of this position? There has been peace among us for so many years, and Leza has always remained impartial."

"It was Julian who chose to breach that peace and disrupt my position," Silas replied firmly. "Leza will not declare war on Tyr unless it is absolutely dire, but I am prepared to show my support on the side of Varuna."

"My Lord?"

"Jila, I offer you the protection of a guard of my very best men to stand beside you in the event of another assassination attempt."

Kai scowled and opened her mouth to dispute this, to inform the King that the Queen had all the protection she required. Jila must have sensed her intention, for she quelled her with a sharp, warning glare. Jila turned back to the King and inclined her head. "That is very generous, Silas. I recognise your cooperation and deeply appreciate your support."

"My men will stand as warning to Julian not to overstep his boundaries lest he face disapproval and opposition."

Jila nodded. "Let us hope this trouble does not spiral down into war, Silas. Our people have enjoyed peace and prosperity far too long to see it fall apart now."

"Just so. We will endeavour to achieve accord in the event of a conflict, but I will not see our efforts of the past many years lost in a single, rash and foolish act of an excessive and greedy ruler."

"I am in accord, Silas. Thank you for your support."

Silas inclined his head. "My men will arrive tomorrow morning. I will leave you but remain in touch." He sighed deeply. "I am obliged to inform Julian of the disposal of three of his guards. It is my sincere hope your day goes slightly more smoothly."

Jila smiled. "Thank you. Good day, Your Majesty."

"Good day, Jila."

Kai met Draven's eyes in the brief instant before the screen swirled again. She was still considering him when Jila turned to her sharply. "Well, that was unexpected," Kai said mildly.

Jila's expression was shrewd. "The disposal of three of the Duke's guards?"

"Not by me, I assure you. That was the Commander's doing."

"Is it to you whom I might attribute this most fortunate turn of events?"

Kai looked back at the screen where Draven had been. There was nothing to see. "I assure you, Your Majesty, I had nothing to do with it."

Jila did not appear convinced. "You will behave yourself in the presence of the King's guard, won't you?"

"Naturally. I cannot imagine how you would expect I would be anything less than perfectly poised."

Jila's smile was wry, but she nodded. "Right." She turned her attention to Kai's clothes. She shook her head in disapproval. "You will require a uniform."

Kai was startled by the abrupt change in topic. "Your Majesty?"

"I cannot have you meeting the King's guard in such an ensemble."

"I beg your pardon? I thought I looked rather smart."

"Abraham will have you fitted in full livery."

"But, My Queen, I am a mercenary, not a soldier!"

"You are whatever I say you are," Jila replied sternly. "And right now, I require you to be one of my guards in order to keep an eye on the King's men. This is a most unexpected gesture on Silas' part. We cannot be absolutely certain this is not merely an elaborate ruse to spy on our guard and our resources for the Duke."

Kai was startled. "Do you think that is a possibility?"

Jila sighed. "I know not, but I will take nothing for granted, not in this perilous and uncertain time." She pointed towards the door. "Go."

Kai sighed petulantly. "Yes, Your Majesty."

* * *

The day was unseasonably bright and warm under the brilliant rays of the sun. Kai shifted uncomfortably in her uniform. It was stiff and restrictive compared to her customarily soft leather gear. The double-breasted jacket buttoned smartly up to her chin and the pants were tucked into shiny, polished boots with flat, uninteresting heels. It was dark blue, the exact shade of her eyes. It felt as if she were simmering slowly in the heat.

The holsters on her hips were heavy. She prodded the long, tight, pale blonde braid that fell down her back. "Stop fidgeting," Abraham ordered sternly out of the corner of his mouth. "They are nearly here."

The Queen's white airship gleamed in the bright morning light. It looked sleek and beautiful against the clear blue sky. In the distance, Silas' vessel neared. It grew rapidly larger as it began its descent. Like his chambers, the airship was unadorned, without unnecessary fancy. It was larger than the Queen's. It was designed to carry a great number of men long distances. It was not likely to be used for pleasure jaunts or outings to impress foreign dignitaries.

Kai straightened her shoulders. She laced her fingers together behind her back. Jila was tense beside her. She silently awaited the King's men between her friend and her major-domo. She glanced at Kai briefly. Her expression was grave. Though Kai had argued over the necessity of it, a tall, wiry guard stood behind them, prepared to move in the event of sedition from the King's company.

There appeared to be none, at least not in the offing. The ship landed gracefully. It was silent despite its considerable size. Its door opened upwards. Five men disembarked, dressed in the livery of the Lezan guard. Kai was familiar now with the uniform. She was even more familiar with the man at the head of the company. He strode determinedly towards them.

She lifted her chin, but her throat caught at the sight of Commander Lockley, dressed in his finest black uniform. His decoration glittered in the sun. For a brief, terrible moment, Kai stared at him, lost in the memory of their last parting. Jila glanced sharply, shrewdly at her. Kai stiffened. She regained possession of herself. Her face was blank when the guards reached them.

Draven did not glance at Kai when he approached them. He paused before Jila and bowed low at the waist. "Your Majesty," he greeted in a low, even voice.

Jila raised her eyebrows. She smiled. "Commander Lockley. I did not expect to see you among my assigned sentry."

He straightened. Though Kai was unable to look anywhere else, he did not return her gaze. "Your Highness, the King has sent me to ensure your continuing security. He is dedicated to your cause and your safety, and he has sent his very best men, including myself."

Now he flicked his eyes to Kai. She could not read his expression. Jila looked between them in interest. "I welcome you, Commander."

He returned his attention to the Queen. He spoke in crisp, confident and formal tones. "We will remain steadfast by your side, Your Majesty. We will be with you constantly and oversee your day to day activity, provide security and assist in the investigation and discovery of any treachery known and hitherto undiscovered. I am hopeful that you will accept our protection."

Jila inclined her head graciously. "I am grateful, Commander. You may commence your charge at once by accompanying me and my guard to the throne room. I have audiences with my subjects today. I am most confident there is no treachery awaiting me there, but I must accept that, even in my own home, my safety is not ensured in the current political climate."

Draven bowed. "Certainly, Your Majesty. We are at your service."

Jila's smile was ominously radiant. When she spun on her heel, Kai spun with her. She could feel Draven's eyes on her back as the Lezans trailed behind them. She felt them as surely as she felt a sense of deep foreboding when she met the twinkling eyes of her Queen. Kai's cheeks heated. She was anxious to be inside, out of the sun and out from under the shrewd, clever eyes of her meddling Queen.

"Well," Jila said slyly. She glanced sidelong at her. "This should be fun."

Kai groaned. "Yes. For you, I'm sure it will be."

* * *

The Queen's subjects were already lined up outside the grand, scarlet draped throne room to await their moment with the beloved monarch. Abraham stood dutifully beside the ornate golden throne, close enough to bend down and murmur in her ear. On either side of them stood a large, menacing guard. At the Queen's feet, a page waited to announce each visitor.

Draven's men were stationed at the entrance hall. They held Abyssal sensors aloft, poised to detect Abyssium powered augmentations or weaponry. Jila entered the throne room. She paused a moment to allow her subjects to bow reverently before seating herself comfortably upon the plush scarlet cushion. A young, dark-haired guard strode towards her from the entrance hall. He bowed as he spoke. "Permission to search the subjects, Your Majesty?"

Jila scowled imperiously. "No! The sensor is invasive enough. I will not subject my people to such indignity. It is bad enough they will witness my increased security measures. I would not wish them to think I suspect them of sedition. It is not my subjects about whom I am worried."

The guard opened his mouth to protest. Draven appeared at his side. He laid a firm hand upon his shoulder. "Yes, Your Majesty," the guard replied.

"We would not wish for you or your subjects to be inconvenienced," Draven told the Queen mildly. He nodded to the dark-haired guard, who inclined his head to him.

Kai's eyes followed Draven from where she stood silently behind the throne in a position to view the entirety of the room. She could not hear his voice as he directed his guards. She saw them snap to attention when he addressed them. They took their positions around the throne room. He watched them for a brief moment, apparently satisfied with their formation. He turned towards the head of the room.

He strode without hesitation towards Kai. He stationed himself beside her. He did not look or speak to her. She lifted her chin. They watched silently as the Queen conducted the drudgery of her weekly business with her subjects, a series of businessmen, tax collectors, farmers, nobles, Abyssium traders and desperate peasants. Kai wasn't interested in their information or pleas. Her attention was wholly occupied by the tall, stony and perfectly motionless man beside her.

He barely seemed to breath, he was so still. Kai was bored out of her mind. She wondered how he managed to remain so at ease. She was sure she could not bear another moment of remaining there, motionless and inactive and superfluous. Indeed, she had not missed her calling when she had neglected to enter the palace guards. She marvelled at Draven's ability to remain so perfectly erect and immobile without shifting or even twitching a muscle. She resisted the urge to turn to him and ask how he was managing it. She stared straight ahead. If he could do it, she could do it better.

When he spoke, she nearly jumped. "So, you are a soldier?"

She glanced sidelong at him. His voice and face were perfectly even. She could not determine his mood. "I am today."

He frowned. "What does that mean? You never told me who you really are."

"Yes, I did. I'm Kaia." She met his eyes. "It is my real name."

"Kaia what?"

She hesitated. She had not spoken aloud her true name for so many years. She had realised long ago that, in her line of work, it was best to simply forget it. It felt foreign on her tongue. "Kaia Valela."

"Kaia Valela." It sounded equally odd from his lips. "Are you a spy?"

"Sometimes."

He scowled in dissatisfaction. "You're a mercenary."

"Yes." She studied him. She was amused by the irritation that crossed his features. She smirked. "Does that offend your delicate militaristic sensibilities?"

He hesitated. "I have not met many mercenaries who act within the structure of law and order."

She laughed. "If we did, Draven, we would be soldiers, like you."

His voice was harsh. "You know nothing about me."

She shrugged. "Perhaps you are right about that. But I know you are a man of law and order and integrity."

He glanced at her. "And you are not?"

"I suppose that is a matter of opinion. I follow the orders of my Queen."

He studied her a long, silent moment. "I have never met a mercenary like you." He considered. "You should be forced to wear symbols or something so the rest of us can identify you."

She raised an eyebrow wryly. "The rest of you?"

"Decent, law-abiding people who act within the confines and with respect to the law."

"While I understand your ire, Draven, I believe that would defeat the very purpose of hiring something of my profession and abilities in the first place."

He scowled. "I don't know why someone would need to hire someone of your profession at all."

She raised an eyebrow at him. "Don't you? Surely you are not so limited in your reasoning. There are some things that require the bending and occasional breaking of the structures of the law you so highly esteem." She smirked. "And I am effective, am I not?"

He scowled, looking away. "Kai!" His head snapped back up as Jila called to her.

Kai stiffened immediately and strode towards her Queen. Jila beckoned her. She bent down. "Your Majesty?"

Jila's smile was mischievous. Kai was instantly wary. "What do you and Commander Lockley have so much to speak about?"

Kai's expression was bland. "Nothing, Your Majesty. Merely discussing the practicalities and strategy of the guard. He seems rather averse to people of my profession."

"Is that so? I did not receive the impression that he has a particular aversion to you."

Kai glared at her warningly. "Don't start developing fancies, Jila."

Jila laughed. "And why not? I am the Queen. I do what I wish." Kai scowled. Jila smirked at her. "I am confident my safety is ensured within the palace with the protection of my guard and Silas' company. I believe your services may be better utilised in the city." Kai narrowed her eyes. Jila's tone brooked no argument. "Take Lockley with you. Attempt to uncover any leads on anyone who might be discontent and likely to take up with Julian."

Kai raised her eyebrows. "Draven and me?"

"I did not realise you and the Commander were already on first name terms."

Kai's mouth tightened. "Do you not have spies and investigators to accomplish this sort of task?"

"Yes, I do. However, they are not yet conscious of the situation, and I do not wish to make them aware any sooner than necessary. I believe you and Lockley will be a finer team, besides." Kai sighed petulantly. Jila ignored her. "You have contacts my people do not. Speak to some of them. Perhaps they are aware of someone hiring an assassin. If it wasn't the Duke who commissioned the attempt on my life, we could be making a grave political mistake that could unnecessarily lead to war."

Kai sighed again. She nodded in resignation. "Yes, Your Majesty."

"I am confident you will not fail me, Kai."

CHAPTER NINE

The Fool's Errand was a dilapidated, unsavoury establishment. Stooped and hooded figures milled about outside, waiting in the shadows on the darker side of the street for an unwary passer-by. It was difficult to suss if the twisted creatures were men or women. They all carried with them the distinct scent of decay and poverty, a static crackling around them, and the repellent aura of utter madness. They did not attempt to molest Kai and Draven as they strode past them towards the tavern. Perhaps they sensed, despite the madness, that they were no unwary travellers.

Draven glanced at Kai sceptically outside the rusty, dented metal doors of the Fool's Errand. "What are we doing here, Kaia?"

She smirked. She was enjoying his discomfort. He appeared as out of place in the soft, movable brown leather civilian clothes as she had in a soldier's livery. He shifted restlessly beside her. She wondered if the uniform was imbued with some mysterious confidence the calfskin pants and long coat did not possess. She did hope this was not actually the case. He needed all the confidence he possessed to navigate the potential perils within The Fool's Errand.

"Are you feeling slightly out of place, Commander?" she asked in a low, amused voice.

He tilted his head to peer at her from underneath the wide brim of the scuffed, brown leather hat atop his head. For a moment, he looked completely roguish, like a highwayman or brigand. His sour look belied the impression. "I am perfectly at ease, I assure you."

She smirked. "Are you?"

He narrowed his eyes at her. "Would you prefer to hear I am off balance in your company or that I feel uncomfortable beside you?"

She shrugged. "I have no preference."

He looked slightly offended for a moment before he lifted his chin. The floppy brim of his hat concealed his expression. "I am fully prepared for any circumstance in which you intend to place me."

She inclined her head gravely. "Right, then. I need to speak to someone. He is found, most times, in here. It is where he conducts his business."

83

Draven angled his head to look at her. He raised his eyebrows. "It seems an unlikely venue for business meetings."

"Yes, it is, which is why it is so popular with people of his persuasion." At his curious look, she said, "He will assist us in our investigation."

"In what way may he be of help?" She smiled, looking up to encompass the crumbling stone building with her gaze. He looked suddenly wary. "What is this place, Kaia?"

"It is the headquarters of the Assassins' Guild. If anyone has hired a Varunian assassin, they will know."

Draven swept the building with a scrutinising glance. "Will they talk to us?

"They will talk to me. You keep quiet. Do not reveal your name or who you are. If you want to live past the hour, say nothing, if possible." She looked up at him. Her matter-of-fact expression belied the gravity of her words. "And do not offer information. Speak only if you are addressed, and if you are asked, you are my associate."

For a moment, he looked irritated, as if her instructions were offensive. Then his expression cleared. He seemed to decide she was better versed in the etiquette of these sorts of meetings. He did, in fact, want to live past the hour. "As you say. I am thus at your service."

Their eyes took a moment to adjust to the dim, shadowy interior of the dusty, shambling tavern. The tables were nearly empty at this time of brilliant, sunny day. Only a few stragglers and malcontents bent silently over their drinks or at the bar, looking vacant. Many of the patrons' faces were hidden or covered behind hoods, veils and, in some instances, tarnished bronze masks that obscured half or more of their faces. The masks likely hid the horrifying effects of Abyssium exposure.

The customers did not bother to look up at them or eye them cagily. They were wholly disinterested in the new arrivals. They assumed they were, as they, merely two more lost souls wandering in for the comfort of oblivion. Kai glanced at Draven. His face was rigidly set in a closed expression. He nodded shortly. He followed her as she approached the publican. He was a tall, ebony-skinned man with brilliant blue eyes. They were not the glowing, toxic blue of Abyss but the clear, sky-blue of a fortunate inheritance.

He was strangely sexless and indefinably beautiful. He nodded to Kai when he saw her. There was no sign of recognition in his peculiar eyes, but nor did he seem surprised to see her. "Two pints of your darkest," Kai requested, holding the publican's gaze. He nodded. He poured the beers from a tap without looking at it. His gaze held Kai's steadily as if she were a dangerous, volatile animal. "I am here to see Ptolemy."

The bartender pushed the beers across the worn wooden bar towards her with a vacuous expression. His eyes flicked to Draven then back to Kai.

"He is with me," Kai assured him in a low, dangerous voice.

The dark-skinned man nodded. He raised his hand, pointing towards the back of the room. Kai did not turn to look where he had pointed. Just as Draven began to think the man could not speak, he told them, "You may have to wait." His voice was low and smooth. It resonated deep in his chest. It sounded like pure music. "He is hosting a client."

Kai nodded curtly. "Thank you." She passed a stack of banknotes to him across the bar. He returned her nod without a smile or polite parting. Kai caught the crook of Draven's arm and steered him towards the back of the tavern. A man with long, white dread-locked hair sat in a dark corner, facing out into the pub. His black clothes and dark skin nearly blended in with the shadows. His eyes were coal black and oddly slanted. Draven could make out only flashes of white as they moved around the bar with remarkable watchfulness.

His eyes snapped to Kai when she and Draven approached the nook. He nodded almost imperceptibly at her. He turned his attention immediately back to the client in front of him, whose back faced Kai and Draven. Kai tilted her head at Draven. They slid into a table nearby their unusual contact, just out of earshot. Curiously, Kai sat with her back to her contact. Draven took the seat across from her where he could eye the white-haired man.

Kai did not speak to him as they were seated. She sipped her pint almost reverently. Draven took a sip of the beer. His face screwed up in distaste. It was as thick as molasses, pungent and so strong, he felt it must surely go instantly to his head. Kai smirked, as if she knew exactly what he had been thinking. He lifted his chin, bracing himself. He took another swig. It went down easier after the initial shock of its consistency and strength. He allowed it to roll over his tongue a moment before swallowing it.

They sat for a long moment, sipping their drinks and peering at each other as if in a silent match. Finally, Kai broke the silence. "When Ptolemy is free, we will approach him. You will not speak to him."

Draven's jaw set resentfully. He nodded curtly. "Clearly you have more experience with assassin protocol than I, being one yourself, I suppose "

Her face and eyes did not reveal any emotion at this. "I am not an assassin."

"You're a mercenary. It is the same thing, is it not?"

Now she frowned. "No, it is not. My work is more delicate than simple, inelegant murder."

He raised an eyebrow. "Well, what sort of work, exactly, do you do?"

"Whatever I am asked." She hesitated, then added, "Within reason."

"What do you consider 'within reason,' then? Do you often seduce foreign soldiers in order to steal their King's secrets?" His voice was venomous. She scowled.

"I might remind you, Commander, that it was you who attempted to seduce me."

His mouth jaw stiffened. His mouth thinned to a tight line. He did not respond to this. He narrowed his eyes. "How does one get into your line of work?"

She shrugged. "It is different for all of us."

"Are there many more like you?"

"Oh, yes, surely, but we do not work together well and stay out of each other's way."

"Really."

"If we worked well with others, Draven, we would not do the work we do."

This caused him to chuckle. "All right. How did you get into this line of work?" She considered a moment. He raised an eyebrow at her reticence. "It may be a while before your man is ready for us. He seems to be disputing something with his client." When Kai sighed, he added, "You are not, I assume, an aerialist, as you would have had me believe. Though, I must admit, you do have a certain talent for it. I was thoroughly convinced."

She smirked. "I was an Abyssium miner."

This information startled him, and he tilted his head back to meet her gaze from beneath his hat. "You were a miner. So you are Abyssal, after all."

She hesitated. "Yes. A bit."

"I could not tell. I see no signs."

"Well, you wouldn't. My augmentations are very subtle."

"What are they?"

She looked away. "I am equipped with the typical augmentations of the Abyssium mine workers: enhanced lungs, agility, strength, dexterity and sight." Her mouth tightened slightly, as if she meant not to continue. When she spoke, her voice was almost cheerful. "I was injured while working in the mines."

"Injured how?"

"I was gored by a sea creature. I nearly lost my life. Many of my organs had to be replaced."

He blinked. "You bear no scars. Unless they are in areas I've yet to see."

Her lips twisted wryly. "And should not expect to," she added promptly. His mouth pursed slightly in irritation. "But no. No scars. The Abyssal engineer was very talented, very thorough."

Draven considered this. "How did you come to work for the Queen?"

This time, Kai hesitated a long moment. She took another swig of her beer before she replied, "She is my cousin."

"Is she?" He was astonished.

"Our mothers share a mother, who was a minor noblewoman. It was Jila's father who was royal. Her mother was the eldest, and my mother married beneath her. My father was an Abyss trader and a commoner. She was disinherited and disowned by her father, but she was happy; she married for love. Jila and I have been life-long friends, despite my mother's disinheritance, and long since before her parents were killed, leaving her the throne."

"I had no idea she had family."

"Only me. It was she who financed my Abyssal engineering."

"Was it she who also recommended your profession?"

"No, it was my choice. I complete errands and missions of which she has need and cannot send anyone else."

"You work exclusively for the Queen?"

"No. Sometimes I work for others. Eventually, people in my line of work make contacts, and people who are in need of us find us easily enough."

Draven silently contemplated the unexpected information. He was still deep in thought when Ptolemy's client walked away. Kai's eyes followed the man. When he reached the door, pulling it open and casting a prism of sunlight across the floor, she stood. She turned to Ptolemy. She met his dark gaze. With a small, barely perceptible gesture, he motioned them to join him.

Ptolemy eyed Draven suspiciously. "Hello, Kai." His voice was smooth as velvet, as deep and melodic as the publican's.

"Ptolemy."

"Sit." They obeyed him, sliding into the seats across from him with their backs to the door. Draven felt a brief sense of foreboding. It was ill-advised to leave their backs vulnerable in a place such as this. Kai was relaxed. She did not seem to share his reservation. "Have you come seeking one of my people?" Ptolemy asked brusquely.

"Not today."

His eyes were icy steel. "Then why have you come to disrupt my business?"

She smiled. "I will make it worth your while, as always." She slid a stack of banknotes across the table.

Ptolemy looked at them distastefully for a moment. Then he lifted a large, thick hand. The money disappeared beneath it. "All right." His voice was slightly more amicable. His coal black eyes were curious. "What can I do?"

"I require information." When he inclined his head, she continued. "I am interested to learn if any foreigners have commissioned any of your people recently." As Ptolemy considered this, she added, "Or if you have heard of anyone outside the guild working in the city."

He raised an elegant eyebrow. Then his eyes narrowed suspiciously. "Now why would you be needing to know such a thing? You aren't one of us, Kai." She eyed him. There was cold steel in her gaze. He sighed. "I have not taken any foreigners as clients, and, as far as I know, no one has been working who isn't one of the guild."

His dark, almond-shaped eyes darted about the tavern, as if attempting to discover listening persons or flies on the wall. Kai's expression was austere. "Ptolemy, I am looking for the one who attempted to do the Queen."

Ptolemy scowled and looked away. "I do not know anything about that."

"I think you do. As you said, there have been no foreigners in the area, and no one outside your guild is working."

Ptolemy looked around again. His voice was low when he spoke. "I didn't know about it. It was not commissioned through me." When Kai raised an eyebrow, he continued, "I suspect the job was taken behind my back, as I would have sent the client off straight away. I heard about the attack at the Carnivale. It was around the same time one of my guild brothers disappeared." Ptolemy scowled. "If he was taking work behind my back, he likely fled the city, fearing retribution."

"Who was it?"

Ptolemy sighed. "Argus Wick."

"No ideas who might have hired him? Someone he knew, or someone who knew who he was and approached him?"

"There is no way to know. It could have been anyone."

"Have you looked for Wick?"

"Yes, of course. I have sent my best people to find him, but they have failed to recover him."

Kai nodded. "Where does he live?"

Ptolemy considered that for a long moment. He stared at her with narrow, inscrutable eyes. Then he scribbled upon a slip of parchment with a pen he seemed to have produced from thin air. He slid the parchment across the table at her. She tucked it into her jacket pocket without looking at it.

"Thank you, Ptolemy."

"I expect this information will remain between us."

"Naturally. Our intent is not to disrupt the guild, as you know." She rose quickly. She dipped at the waist in a swift bow.

Draven followed her lead. He inclined his head to Ptolemy, who eyed him a moment before tilting his own head in response. Draven did not speak to Kai as they left the pub. They blinked in the sudden, startling brilliance of the afternoon sun outside. When they were at last alone, he asked, "What do you intend to do next, Kaia?"

She glanced at him. "I believe Wick is the likely perpetrator of the attempt on my Queen."

"Do you expect to find him at home?"

She snorted. "Of course not. When Ptolemy says he sent someone to find him...well, he is likely buried in an Abyss mine by now, if he was caught up."

Draven nodded gravely. "Then perhaps some evidence can be uncovered at his home to explain what happened to him, who hired him, or where he might be now."

"Just so. It is our most promising lead at the moment. And I'm afraid it is not all that promising."

He smiled wryly. "No, not especially. But, at the very least, it will give us something useful to do."

She glanced at him. Her eyes twinkled slightly. "Step lively, then."

* * *

The dilapidated tenement building in which Argus Wick had lately resided was in a grim, dangerous and dodgy part of town. As they stood side by side, looking up at the rotting metal staircases and crumbling stone walls, the residents of the street passed by them, averting their eyes as if to avoid notice. From a dark, filthy alley, a thief eyed them cagily for a moment. Kai's sharp, menacing glance sent him reeling back into the darkness between the buildings.

She looked up at Draven. Her mouth set in a grim line. "Shall we?"

"Yes, I suppose so." His expression was twisted in distaste. "It's a bit dodgy, isn't it?"

She chuckled. "Where would you expect an assassin to live?"

He shrugged. "At least in a nicer place. I mean, if one's going to have such a risky profession, it seems it should at least pay well."

She lifted a shoulder. "Usually it does. Maybe he isn't a very good assassin."

"Well, clearly not, considering he failed to kill his target and is now rogue from his guild."

"Yes, I suppose that's true enough."

They stepped forwards simultaneously. Draven paused. He allowed her to precede him upon the creaking, rusted staircase to the third floor. Draven gripped the railing anxiously. His eyes followed Kai carefully, lest she step wrongly and upset the stair, sending them plunging down into the street below. It did not give beneath them. They paused at Wick's doorway. Kai tried the door. The handle did not spin; locked.

She looked at Draven. She gestured an invitation. He smirked. He raised his foot to kick the decaying wooden door. It yielded almost too easily, as if the wood were rotting off the hinges. Kai looked at him sternly. "I'm not paying for that."

He shrugged. "I suspect the management will be hard pressed to determine the difference between the use of force and the door crumbling of its own accord."

She chuckled and turned her attention to the interior of the flat. The furniture was overturned. Effects were strewn everywhere, as if it had been recently, inelegantly ransacked. She exchanged a glance with Draven, frowning. She snorted with laughter when he stepped forwards, burying his boot in a soft pile of putrid food.

He groaned in disgust. He bent to wipe his shoe clean with a handkerchief from his breast pocket. He tossed the kerchief aside with a revolted expression. "This place hasn't been ransacked at all; it's simply filthy. How does someone live like this?"

Kai shook her head. She rolled her eyes. "Let's just get on with it. I'd prefer to find something and get out of here without any further mishaps."

"I am beginning to rethink this."

"This is hardly the time to lose your mettle, Commander."

He sighed. "Come on, then."

The flat was so tiny, it required only moments to determine there was no one inside. Judging by the smell, there had not been anyone there for a very long time. No personal effects identified the erstwhile occupant of the flat. They would not have expected such, owing to the nature of the tenant's particular line of work. There were no pictures, no keepsakes. The flat seemed furnished in equal parts of old newspapers, rubbish and scattered paperback books.

"I don't see anything," Draven muttered. "Nothing personal at all. He might not have been anyone."

"That's likely the point. If he's caught or someone like us decides to kick in the door looking for him, he'd not like to be identified." She looked around the flat with her hands on her hips. "It's probably the first rule of the guild: remain anonymous."

But he wasn't, not entirely. Kai's augmented eyes narrowed upon a handwritten note on the floor a few feet away. She swept a stack of newspapers aside and stooped to pick it up. She shook a brilliant red fruit rind from its corner. The words were smudged, as if the person writing them had been weeping. Of course, it might simply have fallen victim to the filth of the room. The spidery, elegant scrawl was neat and legible. She held it up to Draven.

Dearest Argus, it has been so long since you were beside me. I fear something terrible has happened to you. Are you well? Ptolemy has refused to give me any information regarding your whereabouts and I fear he is hiding something terrible. Please, my love, give me word. Come home and prove that you are not hurt or worse. I await you and long for the moment when we are together again, side by side as we are meant always to be. Please, do not leave me long in this purgatory, in this fear and worry for you. My love always, Kang

"Kang?" Draven asked, his brow furrowed.

Kai shook her head. "I don't know who Kang is."

"I do."

"What?" She stepped towards him, surprised.

"It's here. Finnis Kang."

"Where? Where do you see it?"

"On the envelope."

"You have an envelope?"

He held it up between his fingers. "It was just here."

"Is there a return address?" She stepped forward to snatch it from his fingers.

"No. Just this one and his name."

She sighed, turning over the crumpled envelope as if it might yield more answers. It did not. "It is good enough."

"Do you think Wick went to Kang?"

"Maybe. Probably. If Wick attempted to assassinate the Queen and was unsuccessful, he was probably in a lot of trouble. He might have sought comfort."

Draven frowned. He stared at her a moment in silent disapproval. Finally he said disparagingly, "Or he would have stayed away, in case he got his lover into trouble with him. Do you understand love at all?"

She looked at him. She ignored his tone. "It is worth finding out which. It may be our only chance to discover where Wick is, what happened to him and who hired him to kill Jila."

"Will we be able to find him?"

"Yes, I think so. Abraham maintains a record of all the Queen's subjects."

Draven raised his eyebrows. "How does he manage it? There must be hundreds of thousands."

Kai smirked. "He has his ways. I have often been surprised by the information he possesses."

Draven shrugged. He watched as she pulled out a small, tarnished brass communicator from her jacket and punched a button. He leaned over her shoulder as Abraham's face appeared on the tiny screen. "Kai?" he asked, his face expressionless.

"Abraham, we might have a lead on the assassin. We need an address for Finnis Kang."

CHAPTER TEN

*K*ang's cottage could not have been more different than his lover's flat. It was elegant, small but carefully maintained, nestled in a verdant forest on the edge of the city. It was the last house before the long, winding dirt road led out of Zooni, into the sparse countryside of Varuna between city and sea. Draven stepped off the deck of Kai's small flyer onto the tall, lush green grass around the house.

"Again, this is not what I would have expected for an assassin's country home."

Kai shrugged. "People do not always fall into your perfect little profiles, Draven."

He looked at her. She was surprised he did not appear offended. "I am beginning to see that. You continue to prove it to me."

She turned away. She wasn't sure how she should receive the remark. She chose not to receive it at all. She strode purposefully to the door. She knocked loudly. They waited, glancing at each other. When no sound issued from inside, she pounded on the door again. "Mr Kang!"

Draven shrugged. He stepped towards the door. He lifted his leg to kick it in.

Kai raised her hand. He paused. "My turn this time, yeah?"

He smirked. He watched as she struck out at the door. His smirk faded as the door flew smoothly off its hinges, landing several feet away in the antechamber. She winked at him and preceded him inside. Inside the quaint, neatly arranged cottage, they found the sitting room empty. Dust danced in the rays of sun peeking through the half-drawn drapes. Kai tilted her head at Draven, indicating the back of the house. He nodded. He drew his pistol from beneath his jacket.

The house was empty and as silent as a grave. A grave it was, in a manner of speaking. They found Kang in the bedroom. He was a large, ruddy, well-muscled man. He looked diminished in death. His curling black hair fanned out over the pillow. His tanned, slightly lined skin was stretched tight across his bones. It looked unnaturally ashen and parchment thin. Kai strode towards the bed and leaned over him.

"Kaia, stay away from the body," Draven ordered sharply.

94

She shot him a withering look. "I need to determine how he died."

"Why?"

"To discover if it was Wick."

"How will you know?"

"Each assassin has a signature. They all have their preferred modes of operation. If it was Wick, we will be able to identify his particular style."

"Which is?"

"I don't know. But Ptolemy will." She turned back to the corpse. She leaned over him. A long, thin, puckered line spanned across his throat, barely visible against his dark skin. She scowled.

"What do you see?"

She shook his head. "That's peculiar. His throat is slit, but there is no blood."

"So he was killed somewhere else?"

"Yes, and I reckon posed here. He was a very large man. I wonder how the killer was able to get over on him." She stepped away from Kang. She gestured as if to allow Draven to inspect the body himself. "The wound is very clean. Precise. There was no struggle. It was over in a heartbeat. He might not have even heard his assassin before he came up on him."

"Or Kang was incapacitated somehow." Draven did not approach the remains. He seemed satisfied to trust her conclusions.

"Maybe." She stepped towards Kang again, fluttering her fingers across his eyes. Draven opened his mouth to protest. She peeled back the corpse's eyelids, ignoring him. Kang's glazed, sightless eyes were smooth, honeyed amber. They were not saturated blue. Nothing indicated he'd been touched by the glowing, toxic Abyss. He'd been strong, but he could not have worsted an Abyssal man. She shook her head. "It doesn't matter, not really. He's dead. Whomever killed him got over on him somehow."

Draven raised his eyebrows. "You think it could have been Wick?"

"It's impossible to know. It might as well have been one of the guild assassins sending Wick a warning."

"A warning."

"Wick might have gotten it, too. He may have found him like this and fled."

Draven sighed. "Or he's dead, too, and his body's been taken off somewhere."

"Right. Well, there's not much we can do here."

"We aren't finished. I want to look for traces of blood and try to figure out where he was actually killed."

"I suppose it might give us some clues, but I doubt it." She frowned. She followed him outside into a small quad. A meticulously maintained garden of brilliant, colourful blooms lined the perimeter of the house. Beyond, on the expanse of thick, green grass, was a small lean-to.

They glanced at each other and stepped towards it simultaneously. It yielded nothing more than a carefully organised collection of gardening tools and bags of seed and soil. "Clearly Kang was the nattier of the two, eh?" Draven remarked. His tone was morose.

Kai frowned thoughtfully. "There are no signs of blood anywhere. Do you think Kang was killed somewhere else?"

"The assassin may have cleared up after himself. Or he was killed outside and the blood washed away in the last rain."

Kai sighed. She nodded. "Yes. Well, we will have Abraham send the clear up men to get him out of here." She looked up at him. Her eyes were suddenly alight. "There may be a way to find out what happened here."

He raised his eyebrows. "Indeed?"

"Yes." She smiled mysteriously. "We will consult a fly on the wall."

* * *

The unmarked steel door in the bowels of Queen Jila's palace opened into a large, circular room. The walls were covered from floor to ceiling in prismatic screens, faceted like the eyes of thousands of tiny flies. In the centre of the strange, disorienting room, a young, pale man was seated on a revolving chair. He spun continuously in a circle as if to view all the screens at once. When Kai and Draven entered, he paused. He looked up at them. He nodded at Kai. "Madam Kai. Abraham said you would be coming to review some images."

"Yes."

Draven wasn't paying attention. He was staring, his jaw slightly slackened, at the thousands of images on the walls. "What is this place?" he demanded.

"This is the Hive," the young man replied. "I'm Emile Ainsley. I am the Keeper."

"The Hive?" Draven repeated dumbly.

"It is where all the information from the clockwork sentinels positioned around the cities are recorded, stored, and reviewed."

"The Queen is spying on her own people?" Draven was aghast. Kai shot him a sceptical look.

"And Silas is not?"

He considered, peering around him at the screens. "Not like this. He has people in the cities listening for him, but it is nothing so elaborate as this."

Kai lifted her shoulder negligently. "Well, the Queen possesses rather more sophisticated equipment, as you can see."

"What is it you are looking for?" Emile asked keenly.

Kai glanced down at him. "We can take things from here, Ainsley."

He did not pause to argue. He nodded. He rose from his chair. He scurried from the room as if he were relieved to be away from them. Draven glanced at Kai with a smirk. "You seem to have a way with people."

She shrugged. "I have a reputation. It isn't my fault it's been blown completely out of proportion."

He snorted. "Has it?" She ignored him, dropping into the spinning chair. Draven stood behind her. He crossed his arms over his chest. "Do you know how to work the displays?"

"I am sure I can manage to suss it out."

Attached to the arm of the chair was a small console with tiny symbols carved into the keys. In the centre was a large, brass ball, which was shiny and smooth, as if it were polished relentlessly by the touch of Emile's nimble, constant fingers. She spun the ball and watched the images upon the screens slow and begin to move rapidly the opposite way.

There were innumerable images, places and people. She spun the ball swiftly backwards, searching eagerly for their query. They watched the changing scenes for what felt like hours, marvelling at the happenings in the cities and homes of Varuna's people. After several long, unrewarding moments of silence, Draven groaned, rubbing the back of his neck. "How will we know when we have the right fly?"

She shook her head. "There are so many. It probably moved once there was no life left in the house." She sighed. "We'll have to back it up until we see the house again."

The pictures reversed so quickly, they could barely make out the faces and locations. There were thousands of images: people fighting, making love, working, people merely sitting alone, in the dark. People drank and slept, talked and laughed in pubs and taverns and in the ostensible privacy of their homes. "Is there sound?" Draven asked.

"Yes, but it probably remains turned off until the right fly is selected. Otherwise, it would just be a noisy jumble."

"Wait. Go back."

"Where?"

"There. That one." He raised his arm, pointing towards a screen on the ceiling. "That's Kang's house."

Kai lifted her hand off the control. She squinted at it. "Are you sure?"

"Pretty sure. Look." She moved her hand over the brass ball again. She examined the console beside her. She pressed a likely-looking button carved with a plain, square symbol. The screen he had indicated moved forwards, as if suspended in midair. "That's it. Kang's there. His body."

She frowned. "So we have the right image, at least."

"Back it up. See what happens."

They watched the fly's strange, faceted view in reverse for a time. Then there was movement: a figure, moving slowly, walking backwards. He was a tall, reedy man in a tattered black suit. His velvet cape was incongruously luxurious. It billowed slightly in the breeze. The man sat down on the bed beside Kang's body, bent over him. As they watched, he cradled Kang's head in his lap. Tears dripped onto the dead man's closed lashes. The thin man kissed his forehead. He pressed his face to his neck for a long moment.

"So it wasn't Wick who killed him," Draven muttered.

"Unless we haven't gone back enough."

"Back it up some more, then."

She did. Eventually a different man appeared on the scene. He moved slowly, eerily backwards. They did not recognize his face. In fact, he seemed not to have a face at all. His features were scrambled and blurry. They shifted and transformed so rapidly, they were gone before Kai and Draven could make them out. The rest of his body, wrapped in a faded brown duster, was perfectly normal.

The Kai and Draven looked at each other. "What's wrong with his face?" she said.

"I can't tell."

"Is it some sort of mask?"

"Maybe. Or some sort of Abyssal instrument."

"It keeps changing. I can't get a clear image of it." She sighed. "But it certainly isn't the Duke, anyway. Even with a mask, there's no way this man can be him. He isn't near large enough."

"Did you expect the Duke?" He sounded surprised.

"No, indeed not. But it would have made things much more straightforward than a man with no face."

He chuckled wryly. He cut off as they turned their attention back to the moving picture. The faceless man was carrying Kang as if he weighed nothing, despite the dead man's extreme bulk. He laid him carefully on the bed. He brushed his curly black hair from his face almost tenderly. "Further."

The fly had followed the movement. Its tiny sentience was perhaps somehow cognisant of the significance. It might simply have been drawn by the only life in the house. The faceless man carried Kang. He was moving backwards, from the house to the quad. He had come upon Kang in the garden, while the burly man had been pulling up weeds. The anguished lover had not heard his stalker's approach. His blood, deep crimson, spurted over the flowers. It turned them all to garish ruby-red. He'd been weeping. Tears trickled from his eyes as they closed. He pitched forward over the flowers.

Kai moved the ball again. She spun it so they could view Kang in the moments before his death. She froze the image upon the man. He sobbed over his gardening. "He was worried over Wick," Draven said in a low voice. She glanced at him. It was terribly tragic and senseless. For a moment, an awful despondency passed over Draven's face. "Turn it off."

He sighed. He dropped his head. Kai rubbed her eyes tiredly. As Draven checked his pocket watch, he said, "Perhaps we should take a break. We can think it all over in the morning. Maybe we can learn something about a man with no face. Or an Abyssal mask that can constantly change his features like that."

She reached her arms over her head, stretching languidly. "Sounds like the best idea I've heard all day. As long as Jila is safe, it can wait until morning." He waited as she rose. They walked together towards the door. "I'm starving," she remarked.

He looked at her. "Will you be going home for dinner?"

She smirked. "Trying to come home with me?"

He stiffened indignantly. "No! I was simply curious if you have a home. Or if you live here."

She shook her head. "I have a home. Actually, I have two homes. One in Zooni for when I am working, and one in the countryside for when I want some peace and quiet."

He raised his eyebrows, looking at her. "You must do very well in your profession."

"Yes. Well, I'm very good. But I will be staying at the palace until this is all sorted out. Jila has insisted." She glanced at him. "Come with me. We can eat in the kitchen with the servants."

He smiled slightly and nodded. After the constantly moving, three dimensional images in the Hive, the flat, empty corridor was disorienting. They walked in silence. They were lost in their own troubling thoughts. When they reached the entrance hall, Abraham materialized. He blocked their path towards the kitchen. He dipped a quick, ironic bow.

Kai narrowed her eyes at him. His face did not reveal any emotion. "Commander. Miss Vale," he said in a very formal voice that dripped with sarcasm. "The Queen requests your attendance in the dining hall for dinner in five minutes."

Kai sighed loudly. Draven inclined his head politely. "Thank you, Mr. Abraham," he said graciously. "We will be delighted to join the Queen. We will be there directly."

Abraham nodded. He spun on his heel. His footsteps echoed through the hall as he strode smartly away. Kai groaned.

"You do not wish to dine with your cousin?" Draven asked.

Kai looked at him sharply. "You don't know my cousin."

* * *

Jila sat at the head of the ebony table in a large, ornate and plush-cushioned chair. The table was long enough to accommodate a party of dozens. It seemed terribly garish without the addition of guests. It was typically set for one and so silent, the Queen might have been in mourning. Kai knew Jila rarely used the table or the dining room with the exception of special occasions or to impress visitors and diplomats. She dined most days alone in her chambers, reading or listening to a small music box in her sitting room.

Jila had dressed for dinner, as if for a party, in a rich, emerald green gown. Her hair was twisted into a carefully braided crown. Kai suspected the flourish had everything to do with Commander Lockley. Why the Queen would seek to impress the foreign soldier, Kai knew not. Perhaps it was simply that Jila, locked away in her grand, empty palace, was lonely.

Kai sighed. Jila smiled luminously when they entered. They bowed to her. She gestured at the seats on either side of her. They were already set with her finest polished silver. Bowls of rich, red soup steamed in delicate china bowls on either setting. Kai and Draven sat. They met each other's eyes for a brief instant before they turned back to Jila. She was watching them in interest. "Good evening," she greeted warmly. "Thank you for joining me. I rarely have occasion to dine with others. This is a special treat."

"We are honoured you have invited us to join you, Your Majesty," Draven replied graciously. His posture, expression and bearing were so perfectly, unaffectedly appropriate that Kai felt like a misbehaved child beside him. She rolled her eyes.

Jila waved her hand with a smile. "You are very gallant, Commander." She picked up her spoon. She dipped it into the soup and took a very small, dainty sip. Once she had done, she motioned them to do the same. The soup was as rich as it appeared, salty and thick with tiny shellfish. They were silent for several long moments. Kai and Draven looked at each other bemusedly across the table as they enjoyed the luscious first course.

Finally, Jila cleared her throat. She placed her spoon delicately on her saucer. Kai sighed.

Jila smiled brilliantly at her. "So," the Queen began in a deceptively cheerful voice. "Have you two learned anything interesting today?"

Kai glanced at Draven. He nodded to her politely. This was her show. She frowned. "We have discovered information regarding who may have been hired to assassinate you."

Jila raised her eyebrows. "One of my people?"

"One of the Assassins' Guild. He was not hired through the guild leader, however. It was an unauthorised assignment. The guild seems rather in your favour, actually."

"That's somewhat reassuring, I suppose. Have you, then, discovered the rogue assassin's whereabouts?"

"No, not as yet, but we are hopeful that one of the flies may have followed him."

Draven studied the Queen. He seemed highly interested in her reaction to the mention of her spies. She inclined her head. There was no expression of abashment upon her face. It was her country. She did as she liked.

"I will have Emile review the records. You need only direct him to whom he is to look for. He is quite gifted. I am sure I am unable to review the necessary information in even half the speed, and have grown quite good at it."

Jila looked at Draven as she spoke. She peered directly into his dark, inscrutable eyes. She might have been measuring his reaction. He was as unreadable as she.

"He has a knack for locating exactly which fly has tracked the subject of our particular interest." Jila smiled in the answering silence. She laid her hands primly on the table in front of her. "But, that is not a matter for dinner conversation, is it?" she asked cheerfully. "Death, murder and treason are hardly topics about which I prefer to speak over lamb chops." She gestured over her shoulder. A servant appeared immediately, as if he had been awaiting her command through the conversation.

The servant laid plates before them. He bowed before he disappeared again. Wherever it was he waited to serve his Queen, they could not see him. Kai had the uncomfortable suspicion he could see them quite perfectly.

Jila motioned to her guests. She seemed perfectly content to eat her main course in perfect silence. Her eyes darted between the two of them inquisitively. Kai glanced across the table into Draven's eyes. They shared a guarded look. The Queen's insistence they dine with her was peculiar. It was even more so that she had no apparent intention to glean what they had learned earlier in the day.

Nevertheless, the meal was pleasant. When they had cleared their plates, the servant appeared to sweep them away. He replaced them with steaming mugs of fragrant coffee. It was strong, rich and black as deepest night. Jila sipped hers first. She peered at them demurely over the rim of her porcelain mug. She closed her eyes in reverence. "Ah, this is my favourite part of the meal." She smirked. "And, Kai, too, enjoys it, do you not, cousin?"

Kai smiled stiffly. She inclined her head. "It is very pleasing."

"And there is no better place to enjoy it than the palace." She leaned towards

102

Draven conspiratorially. "She orders it all hours of the day when she is staying with me."

"Don't go giving him the idea I'm petty and indulgent," Kai objected.

Jila laughed. "Ah, no one could possibly think such a thing of you, my cousin. You tolerate the least nonsense of anyone I know." She turned to Draven. "And you, Draven? What is your vice? What do you have brought to you in the middle of the night when you cannot sleep and wish for refreshment?"

He smiled. If he was unused to being addressed so informally, it did not show upon his face. "I cannot say I have any particular vices. I have been a military man practically my entire life. I have become accustomed to restraint and deprivation."

Jila laughed delightedly. "I have not known many commanders to abstain from all manner of vices, Draven. Is there not a single cordial or tea you prefer?"

He inclined his head. "I do enjoy a fine red wine now and again. I find that, when I am off-duty, imbibing reasonably can be very gratifying."

Kai rolled her eyes. Jila smirked at her. "Do I sense you believe Commander Lockley not to be in earnest, Kai?"

Draven glanced at her. He raised his eyebrows. Kai lifted her shoulder. "No, I believe he is in earnest. Perfectly in earnest."

Draven looked at her expectantly. She did not offer any further comment. Jila smirked over the lip of her mug. "Commander, you are an honoured guest in my home. You should feel at liberty to order anything you please at any hour of the day."

Draven inclined his head with measured, gracious reserve. "I am most grateful, Your Majesty."

Jila's face transformed. There was suddenly a very wily, very mischievous glint in her dark eyes. Kai narrowed her own eyes warily and glanced at Draven. If he noticed the capriciousness of the Queen, his expression remained impassive. "So tell me, Commander, have you left a wife and children at home in Leza?"

Kai sighed. She knew what her cousin was about. Draven appeared to receive the question without guile. "No, Your Majesty. I am unmarried."

"Are you indeed? How is that so?"

"I don't understand the question, Your Majesty."

She smiled widely. "You are quite fine-looking, to be sure, and a very powerful figure in His Majesty's court. Do you not have your pick of desirable women?"

Draven paused. He looked momentarily caught out. He answered carefully. "I regret to say, Your Majesty, that I have met many desirable women, and yet my position makes it difficult to court them in the manner they deserve."

Jila raised her eyebrows. "Surely you have your free moments."

"Yes, Your Majesty, I do have free moments."

"Perhaps you simply have not met a woman worthy of filling them."

Draven smiled. He inclined his head dutifully. "I am not fool enough to contradict a Queen or a woman, Your Highness, in matters of the heart. You are clearly my superior. I confess I know little about them."

Jila laughed. "And yet your management of whimsical women is quite masterful, Commander."

He chuckled. "I am gratified by your praise, Highness, undeserving as it may be."

Jila's eyes sparkled. She seemed to be enjoying the Commander. She winked cheekily at Kai. Kai shook her head wryly and looked away pointedly. "Well," Jila said smoothly. "I will leave you two to your evening, whatever it may hold for you. I confess I am not used to such excitement as the two of you may be." She rose. She smiled radiantly at them. "I will be off to bed now." They rose quickly to bow to her as she swept from the room with a coy wave. Her eyes twinkled in merriment. "Good night to you both."

When she was gone, Kai sighed and dropped back into her seat. She screwed up her face in a petulant expression. Draven did not return to his seat. He raised his eyebrows at her. He looked amused. "The little busy-body," Kai muttered, surprising him.

"I am quite certain it is ill-advised to speak like that about your Queen."

"It may be to speak about your Queen, but I will speak about my meddling cousin however I want to."

Draven chuckled. He moved around the head of the table to offer her his arm. "May I escort you to your chambers, Kaia?"

She hesitated. She wasn't sure she wanted his company. She finally inclined her head and took his arm. They walked slowly towards her chambers. His abrupt question surprised her. "Do you enjoy the castle?" When she looked at him in bemusement, he added, "I mean, do you prefer it to your own home?"

She sighed and shook her head. "No. Not really." Her tone was slightly resentful. This surprised Draven. She held out her arms, as if to encompass the entire palace. "Though it is very luxurious, very grand, I prefer my freedom. I feel, often, that every move I make in this place is watched."

Draven chuckled. "By the look of the Hive, it probably doesn't matter where you are."

She shrugged. "Yes, perhaps. But it is not necessarily about having privacy; it is mostly feeling as if I do that appeals to me. There is always noise and bustle and light here. When I am alone, in my flat or my cottage, I hear nothing. I can sit in full darkness and silence and simply be alone."

"Do you prefer to be alone?"

She considered. "Sometimes."

"Other times?"

"Other times, I prefer to be with someone else." He looked down at her. She had stopped moving. "These are my rooms."

He smiled. He inclined his head politely. "I will leave you here, then."

Her returning smile was reserved. It was almost genuine. He raised his eyebrows. "Thank you, Commander, for seeing me here."

He peered down at her for a long moment without stepping back. She dropped her head back to return his gaze. In the long moment that passed between them, she knew he was remembering their interlude in the King's sitting room. She was remembered the heat and the spark that had ignited within her when he had touched her. She took a deep breath. A strange, tingling sensation slithered down her spine. He leaned forwards. His eyes dropped languidly to her mouth.

She frowned and leaned away from him. He drew back sharply. He nodded curtly to her. "Good night, Kaia."

She backed up, away from him. She smoothed her features into a blank, unreadable expression. "Good night, Draven."

He spun on his heel. He strode swiftly. She listened to his heels click smartly on the polished marble floors.

He did not look back. Kai slipped alone inside her dark chambers alone.

CHAPTER ELEVEN

*D*raven was waiting outside her door when she left her chambers the following morning. She was still slightly groggy from the night's light, fitful sleep. He smiled at her and raised a mug of steaming coffee towards her. The strong, pungent smell filled her senses. She sighed reverently. She took a sip before smiling gratefully at him. He stared at her with a look of blank disbelief. He seemed as startled by her smile as her appearance. "I have never seen your hair down," he said. "It's lovely."

"I couldn't bear another day in that wretched uniform. I prefer my own clothing."

"It would be quite appropriate for a brigand, I expect."

She laughed. Her good cheer seemed to unsettle him further. He watched her warily, as though she might turn on him and strike at any moment. She was more relaxed in the loose, silky blue pants, white chemise and soft, black leather corset than she had been in the Queen's stiff, woollen livery. She almost felt herself. Her step was uncharacteristically buoyant. She tossed her hair. She fluttered her eyelashes at him. She smirked at his unease. It had indeed been worth eschewing the Queen's orders to see the disconcerted expression on his sculpted features.

He cleared his throat. "Good morning," he said belatedly.

"Good morning. Thank you for the coffee."

He inclined his head. "Shall we go?"

She smiled. She fell into step beside him. They strode slowly towards the Hive. She did not speak for a long moment. Finally, the rich, dark coffee worked its particular magic. She felt enlivened. "I am not accustomed to such early mornings."

He glanced down at her. "Are you not? I am usually up with the sun."

"Of course you are. I am in a line of work in which many of my duties are traditionally performed in the evening or the wee hours."

He considered this. "I suppose that makes some sense, though I do not like to think too closely about what you might be getting up to in the wee hours."

She looked at him. She smirked. Challenge glinted in her eyes. "Do you not?"

He tilted his chin. His jaw set in a rigid line. He did not respond. When they reached the Hive, Emile was watching the screens with wide, unblinking eyes. He spun relentlessly in his chair to view the lot at once. He barely glanced at them when they joined him. He gestured absently over his shoulder at the two new seats placed beside his.

Kai and Draven glanced at each other. They sat and attempted to follow the rapid speed of the changing images. After a few minutes, Draven pinched the bridge of his nose. Kai sighed. Emile did not seem to notice. He did not speak for a long time. His nimble fingers manipulated the brass ball with a practised, expert ease. Kai did not wish to see the murder again. Emile apparently did not, either. It was over in the blink of an eye.

The young man lifted his hand. It hovered over the ball. Kang's killer froze upon the screen. Emile pressed a button on the console. Another screen moved to the fore beside the first. The image was familiar. Wick frozen in departing the home of his dead lover. Emile turned to them. His expression was expectant as he awaited further instructions.

"I want to follow those two people," Draven told him. He leaned forward. "Can we do that?"

Emile nodded. "I have already done it. It is interesting."

"Why?"

"Because shortly thereafter, they meet."

"What happens?" Kai demanded keenly.

"Here you are."

His hand spun over the ball. A new image swirled on the screens before them. Argus Wick hunched over at a table in a filthy, crowded tavern. Wick was not alone. They could not make out the face of his companion. His features shifted and blurred. "Is that the same person?" Draven demanded. "It doesn't look like the same person."

Emile nodded emphatically. "It is the same person. I followed them both. This is where they both went."

"He doesn't look the same. Did you lose track of him and pick up someone else?"

"I did not lose track of him."

"Did you see him change?"

"No. He just did."

"But that doesn't make sense. If you watched him the whole time, how did you not see when his face changed?"

Emile shook his head. "It difficult to make out. It is like he can scramble the fly's vision somehow, but nothing else changes."

Kai and Draven exchanged a deep scowl. They leaned forwards to view the meeting upon the screen. "Is there sound?" Draven asked.

"Yes. If you like."

Emile's fingers fluttered over another button on the console. Voices flooded the room. It was as if a sound barrier had been lifted. The din of the tavern carried with a curious clarity. Argus Wick's voice was shaky when he spoke.

"It's all wrong. It's all gone wrong. My friend is dead." He slammed his mug on the table. Beer sloshed over the brim. "He's dead! Ptolemy sent someone for me, and Finn is dead." Tears leaked from his eyes. He closed them tightly. "It is the way of the guild. There is no way to leave, not alive. They do not accept desertion. I had no choice but to run. If I had known they would kill Finn, I would have turned myself in..."

The featureless man was listening silently. If he was reacting to the rambling monologue, it did not show on his face. Nothing showed on his face.

Wick went on as though he had forgotten the man with him. "If anyone finds out what we've done, we'll both be hanged for treason or worse. I have heard stories about what the Queen does with people who act or speak against her."

His companion nodded. He finally spoke. His voice resonated strangely. It sounded as if it came from deep inside him rather than out of his mouth. It was low and grating. His mouth continued to shift and change. If it moved to form the words, it was impossible to tell. "No one will find out."

"How do you know?" Argus demanded. His voice cracked with desperation. "I heard she has spies everywhere!"

"No one will find out. I won't tell anyone. The only other person who knows what we've done...is you."

The fly's focus shifted abruptly. It zoomed across the room towards another table. It seemed to have lost interest in the conversation. The other voices in the tavern drowned out the assassins' dialogue. Draven grunted in frustration. "Can we hear more?"

Emile waved his hand. "It isn't important. You have all the information that you require. What's important occurs next."

They turned back to the screen in interest. They watched Wick and the changing man walk outside, into the dark, filthy alley beside the tavern. Wick shifted from foot to foot. His expression was both desperate and tremulously sad. His companion was perfectly calm. He stared at Wick in still, perfect silence.

"What will we do?" Wick spoke in a jerky, pleading voice.

"Keep your head down. Keep your wits about you. It will all sort itself out. No one will know what happened." His voice was oddly soothing. Even the spectators were lulled. "Get out of the country as soon as possible. Hide in Tyr. You'll be safest there."

Wick nodded feverishly. He looked relieved. "Yes. Yes. All right. Good." He paused. "Will I see you again?"

"No."

Wick bent in a strange, erratic bow. He turned away from his companion. He did not make it to the street. The changing man reached into his long, black jacket. He removed a straight, thin-barrelled pistol. He aimed it at Wick. He did not hesitate before he fired. The weapon made no sound at all. Blue light arced from it, crackling through the air. Wick shuddered as it struck him. His entire body glowed an eerie, lethal blue. Then he simply disappeared, as if he had never been there.

Kai looked at Draven. His puzzled frown was a mirror image of her own. "So, Wick is dead," Kai said with a sigh.

"Then we have to find the man with no face," Draven added grimly.

"Emile, can you follow him?"

Emile shook his head. "The flies are sentient, but they have no real intelligence. They don't understand when something criminal or unusual happens. They sort of go where the most activity is. It went back into the tavern when the killer walked away."

Kai frowned. She pressed her mouth into a tight line. She stood. Draven rose beside her with a curious expression. "Emile, keep monitoring the flies. You know what we're looking for."

"Yes."

"Report to us if you discover anything out of the ordinary or if you catch up this man again."

"It could be a woman," Emile said thoughtfully.

She blinked. "Could it?" Draven asked doubtfully.

"Well, it's hard to tell, really. I think it's a man, but...I've never seen anything like it."

Kai exhaled in a stern sigh. It did not really matter whether it was a man or a woman. It only mattered that they located them. "Well, let us know what you find."

She tilted her head at Draven. Outside the Hive, they peered at each other thoughtfully for a long moment. Draven murmured, "Who could it be?" His question was in vain.

She shook her head. "No idea. One of the Duke's people maybe?"

"Or one of Jila's." His voice was low.

She nodded. "The only thing we can do now is continue to monitor the Hive and listen around the city. It could take a long time to discover something, if there's anything at all to discover."

He frowned. He paused in the corridor. His dark eyes slid away thoughtfully. Then he nodded resolutely, as though to himself. He turned back to her. "We could go to the tavern where Wick was killed. Perhaps we can find out something there. Perhaps someone knows something about who Wick has been meeting."

Kai shrugged. "It's worth a try. Anyway, a life of leisure doesn't particularly suit me."

* * *

The Tattered Wing made the sinister-looking Fool's Errand appear agreeable by comparison. It was precisely the sort of place a ruthless killer might meet and murder his accomplice. This time, Draven did not pause outside the battered wooden door. He strode resolutely inside, trusting Kai would remain by his side. She did. They turned together towards the proprietor. He eyed them warily from behind the bar when they approached.

Draven looked askance at Kai, as if he expected the proprietor to recognise her. It appeared the man did not. This was not the sort of place Kai often had reason to patronise. They approached the bar with grim purpose. They must have looked ominous. The publican watched them with narrow, suspicious eyes. "What do you want?"

"Beer," Kai replied smoothly.

He looked sceptical. He poured them each a draught. His eyes followed them cagily as he passed the drinks across the bar to them. "You've got a look in your eyes," he said tetchily. "What do you want?"

Kai passed a stack of banknotes across the table at him. He eyed it interestedly, quickly calculating the substantial tip. When he glanced back up at her, his expression remained guarded. "We're looking for Argus Wick. Do you know him?"

The publican hesitated. "I might have seen him around," he admitted. "He in some kind of trouble?"

Draven shrugged. "Maybe. He was with someone the other day. Someone with a strange face."

The bartender's lip curled up thoughtfully. His eyes widened almost imperceptibly. His face transformed into a blank, obtuse mask. "I don't know what you're talking about. I don't know anything like that." His voice was completely flat. "I haven't seen Wick in here for an age." When they returned his gaze with identical forbidding expressions, he scowled. "This isn't the place people remember names. We barely remember faces."

"You remember Wick," Draven reminded him levelly.

The publican frowned. "Now that I think about it, maybe I don't know who you're talking about, after all. It's better that way. Safer, if you get me. You know what sort of place this is?"

Kai raised an unimpressed eyebrow. "We have an idea. We're beginning to get a better one."

"Are you? You'd best be careful asking questions like that." She exchanged a glance with Draven exchanged. The barkeep added, "Watch your back. You could find more trouble."

"We're perfectly well equipped to handle trouble."

"You might think you are."

Kai frowned. She leaned across the bar to speak to him in a low voice. "You'll let us know if you see anyone familiar, won't you?"

"I won't."

She tilted her head at Draven. They spun away from the publican in a synchronized movement. They peered out into the throng. "This is getting us nowhere," she muttered irritably to Draven. "Someone wants Jila dead. Someone hired Wick to do it, either for the Duke or for someone else. And even though we've seen him, we can't figure out who he is." She cursed under her breath. "If only we could get a fly into the Duke's palace. If the assassin is reporting to him, we might at least hear something useful."

Draven shook his head. "He is watching for that sort of thing. His guards are extremely alert. They barely sleep, and they can hear a fly buzzing in the next room."

Kai considered. She cocked her head to one side. "I could try to get in there again."

He spun to her abruptly. He caught her by the shoulders. "No. Don't be preposterous. The Duke knows you now. He has a price on your head." His brow furrowed as he peered down at her with a petulant gaze. "Speaking of that, are you ever going to tell me what happened in Tyr the night we met?"

She shrugged off his hands. "Jila sent me to find proof he was plotting against her. I did. He caught me, and I ran. I told you."

He scowled. "You used me to escape."

"Yes. And you were very accommodating," she replied in a sing-song voice. His face darkened in anger.

He spun away from her. He stormed past her towards the door. She did not hurry to catch up with him. She glanced once more at the publican, who avoided her gaze, before joining the Commander outside. He was standing beside the glass-domed flyer. He glared at its wide, gold and white wings without seeing them.

"What now?" Kai asked.

He took a deep, steady breath before turning to her. When he spoke, it was as if their row in the bar had never occurred. "I don't know. We could hang around the tavern a few nights, see if we can see anyone who resembles our killer. Not that we could tell, probably."

"How hard can it be to see someone with no face?"

Draven shook his head. "I don't know. I suspect slightly more difficult than we anticipate."

* * *

Draven's posture was rigid as he sat beside her in a dark corner of the

Tattered Wing. Kai was amused. She did not rebuke him as he slid closer to her. His hooded eyes glared around the room at the men eyeing Kai cagily. They likely took her for a scarlet lady or worse and were plotting how best to take her from Draven by force. Kai did not trouble over them. Whether or not Draven was capable of defending her, and likely he was, she was not the sort of woman who was easily taken.

They did not speak to each other as they sipped their pints slowly. Their eyes swept continuously over the room. They watched the door. There was no sign of the man with no face. Nevertheless, the bar was raucous. Two men argued loudly nearby. Their words were slurred by spirit. Draven's gaze snapped to them. Kai felt him tense as the first fist was thrown.

She laid a restraining hand on his arm as he rose to break up the altercation. "Don't, Draven," she said in a low, warning voice. "You don't want to call attention to yourself."

He tossed a scowl at her over his shoulder. "I can't let them just go on beating on each other."

"It's not your fight. It's not your country. Stay out of it." Her voice was sharp. "We have something more important to do."

He looked at her coldly. "Is that what you do? Stay out of it?"

She lifted her chin. "If it doesn't concern me."

"Unless you're being paid, I shouldn't wonder."

"Yes. Unless I'm being paid." She raised her eyebrows. "You think me heartless? You think me without conscience?"

He blinked. His expression cleared slightly. "I don't know what I think of you, Kai. I just don't know." She shrugged. She looked away. "Don't you care?"

"About what?" she asked crossly.

"What I think of you."

She frowned. "Why would I care?"

He sighed. "I don't know. I don't know anything about you."

"Well, I don't care," she said forcefully.

"Good."

"Right, then."

They sipped their drinks in sullen silence. They forgot their quarrel several lengthy moments later when their vigil was remunerated. The door swung open slowly. A man strode inside. There was nothing distinguished about him. He wore a faded, brown leather duster. His hair was short and toneless brown. His face bore no discernible features or shape. It was as though the arrangement was constantly shifting. Kai squinted her eyes. His face remained bizarrely blurred, as if he were moving at astonishing speed. He wasn't. He walked with a slow, relaxed gate.

Draven stiffened. He moved closer to her, as if he intended to intervene in the event the changing man darted for them. She rolled her eyes. "It's him," Draven said. "It can only be."

Kai laid a hand on his arm to stop him rising to confront the assassin. "Wait."

"But he has committed crimes for which he should be detained."

"Not yet. This isn't Leza, Draven. We are here to learn now, not act. Wait. There's more to see; he isn't here for nothing."

Draven sighed in frustration. He settled down beside her. His hooded gaze tracked the assassin towards the corner of the room. The changing man sat alone at a table. He faced out into the tavern. No one paid him any attention. It was impossible to make out the direction of his gaze. "He's waiting for someone," Draven muttered.

"Yes. And we need to see who."

They didn't have long to wait. A heartbeat later, another man strode into the bar. He wore an outlandish, powder blue suit and bowler hat. He looked out of place in the rabble. His face was a mottled shade of green against the blue of his clothes. He looked anxious and frightened. When he spotted the changing man in the corner, he hesitated. He looked reluctant to join him. After a moment, he did. He sat down without awaiting a gesture or word of invitation from the assassin. He leaned forward to speak urgently to him.

They could not hear the man's words. They watched in narrow interest. "He's not Varunian," Kai said. There was a definite edge of triumph in her voice.

"No. He dresses too outrageously," Draven agreed.

She looked at him in excitement. Her fingers clenched around his arm. He looked down at her fingers, startled, and peeled them off. He held up his arm with an incredulous expression. Four small bruises were already beginning to darken on his skin. "Sorry," she said absently. "Do you think he's Tyran?"

Draven exhaled heavily through his nose. "It's more likely than Lezan."

"Can we get closer?"

"We can try."

They stood together. He wrapped an arm around her waist to keep her close in the throng. It was not difficult to avoid the eyes of the changing man in the thick, rowdy crowd. They did not blend well among the malcontents, but no one was paying them any mind. Another brawl had broken out amongst angry shouts and jeers. Draven spun her around. He turned his back to the flying fists and bottles to shield her from the scuffle.

She did not protest. She opened her palm as they struggled through the crowd. A small, humming brass fly flitted amongst the squabbling patrons and zoomed obediently towards the changing man and his companion's table. The assassin's face did not change expression. Rather, it merely continued to change without reason or emotion. He turned his head slightly around. He seemed to be watching the fly buzzing around his head.

The brawling crowd concealed them. The changing man turned his head about as though searching the tavern for whomever had released the tiny clockwork spy. He held up a hand to his companion to silence him. He half-rose from his seat. His hand struck out abruptly. He snatched the fly from mid-air. He peered at it a moment then looked around again. Kai and Draven were otherwise engaged in avoiding the skirmish around them. They clung to each other as they disentangled themselves from the crowd.

The changing man crushed the clockwork between his fingers as if it were no heftier than a grape. His companion shot to his feet. He reared suddenly backwards. The appearance of the Queen's spy had apparently spooked him. Whomever he was, he did not want to be seen with the changing man. Without another word to the assassin, he fled towards the door.

"Damn," Kai muttered. She ducked to peer between the flying arms of the brawlers around them. "He's going. We have to follow him or we'll never know who he is."

"What about the man with no face?"

"Split up?"

"Absolutely not."

"Fine. We'll come back for him, but right now we need to follow the Duke's man, if that's who he is. Whomever he is, he may be the only one able to tell us what we need to know."

Draven nodded, He gripped her hand tightly. He steering them expertly through the crowd. He deflected the fists that flew inadvertently in their direction as though he was accustomed to situations such as these. In moments, they had broken free of the horde. "Not too quickly. He's watching for us."

Kai nodded. She slackened against him without warning. He caught her. He wrapped an arm around her waist and bore her awkwardly towards the door. She clung to him, as though she was too weak to support herself. The air of the cobblestone street outside the angry, stuffy tavern was crisp and clear. Kai straightened and brushed herself off.

Draven looked at her incredulously. "What was that?"

She waved her hand. She scanned the street for the Tyran. He was walking quickly away from them. His tall, pointed black heeled boots clicked rapidly on the stone beneath his feet. Kai scoffed. She gestured for Draven to follow her. It was a dangerous part of town, home to ne'er-do-wells, brigands and worse. The Tyran in his blue velvet suit and bowler hat was a likely target for crime. Many a tourist had wandered lost into the wrong side of Zooni and had never been seen again.

He was not accosted, despite the glittering baubles on his neck and fingers. It was a wonder, for he seemed to be entirely unaware of his dogged shadows. He led them directly to his accommodations. They were a seedy, shambling inn on the darker side of a torch-less street. Kai and Draven paused outside the dilapidated inn. They exchanged a dubious glance. Kai shrugged. Draven yanked open the door without ceremony. He motioned her to precede him inside.

The Duke's man did not pause for a meal or a drink in the quiet, vacant dining room. Without a word to the publican, he marched towards the winding stairs leading up to the rooms on the second floor. He step was slow, heavy and weary, as if he had run many miles and found nothing at his destination. Draven did not wait for Kai's input. He strode to the bar and slapped a stack of banknotes in front of the publican.

"We want a room," he said in a low, authoritative voice.

The publican eyed the stack of money with interest. "That's more than the cost of a room," he said. There was a slight note of reluctance in his voice. An honest man in this part of Zooni was rare, indeed.

Draven inclined his head then tilted his chin towards the stairs. "We want the room beside his."

The publican raised his eyebrows. His gaze followed the man trudging dejectedly up the stairs. He considered for a long moment. He eyed them shrewdly. Finally, he nodded. He reached under the bar for a long, rusted skeleton key. "Room 6 is occupied, but Room 7 is available, sir."

Draven nodded in understanding. "Thank you."

The second floor was as dingy as the dining room. The yellowing paint was peeling off the walls. The wood floors were scratched and dusty. Draven paused at the battered door to Room 6. He listened outside a moment for signs the Tyran was moving around. He shrugged and continued down the hall to the Room 7. He inserted the rusty key into the lock. It took several tries to open it.

His lip curled in distaste as they walked inside. The room was old and encrusted in a layer of grime. The bed was made. The linens had been freshly laundered, but they were threadbare and flea-bitten. Draven avoided it, as though he feared moving too near might taint him. Kai rolled her eyes in amusement. She held her fingers to her lips when he groaned in disgust. He'd trodden upon a pair of stained, soiled knickers half tucked under the edge of the bed.

"That is twice," he complained. Kai shushed him.

As he wiped gingerly at the sole of his boot, Kai strode to the wall between Rooms 6 and 7. She pressed her ear against it. She frowned slightly as she strained to listen. She glanced back at Draven. She shook her head. It was silent as a tomb in the room next door. He sighed. He looked around him as if he were unsure where to stand or sit to avoid soiling himself. Kai smirked. She lowered herself unceremoniously to the floor and sat with her back against the wall.

Draven stared at her for a moment, appalled, before bracing himself and joining her. They did not speak to each other. They sat side by side and listened for any sign of life on the other side of the wall. It felt like hours. Kai's eyes started to droop. Her head dropped forwards. There was a noise from next door.

Kai's eyes flew open. She nudged Draven. He was already alert. He'd risen to his knees and pressed his ear to the wall. The door to Room 6 opened and closed with a barely audible creak. There was a low murmur. A shaky, frightened voice asked, "You?"

They glanced at each other in alarm. When they heard a soft, suspicious thump, they shot simultaneously to their feet. They raced for the door. Kai reached into her jacket as they burst into the hall. Draven slammed his shoulder into the Tyran's door. Kai released the anxious, purring fly. It zoomed down the corridor, as if seeking a more interesting venue.

"Kai." Draven's voice was urgent. She saw no more than a glimpse of the dead Tyran on the floor. He lay in a pool of thick, glutinous blood. The blood still trickled relentlessly from his exposed throat. Draven spun on his heel in a swift move. He caught her hand and dragged her with him out into the corridor after the Tyran's killer.

The changing man's footsteps echoed on the cobblestone outside the inn. They caught a glimpse of his brown coattails as he rounded a corner. "After him!" Kai growled. She did not wait to ensure Draven had followed. She pelted through the streets after the killer. She was barely aware of Draven's swift footfalls beside her.

If he knew they were behind him, the killer made no indication. He did not look back. He did not slow down to confront them. Nor did he seem to speed up to evade them. Though he moved with a relaxed, carefree gate, they were unable to catch him up. He remained ahead of them, as if he were gliding smoothly and effortlessly though the streets. He led them through the dark, stinking alleys of the poverty-stricken district of Zooni towards the Sulis River. They kept pace with him.

"He's heading for the bridge," Kai told Draven breathlessly.

When they emerged onto the river walk, the changing man was illuminated under a feeble, flickering blue street torch. He walked unhurriedly, as though he were taking a pleasurable stroll along the waterfront. The water sparkled like glass under the stars. The riverboats along the pier bobbed serenely on the surface. Glittering coloured lights garishly adorned their masts. They flickered in and out of view as they moved up and down on the waves.

The bridge was a wide, stone path barely large enough to accommodate a carriage. Though it was illuminated with small, glowing torches along the way, it was empty of travellers so late in the night. The killer turned towards the bridge. Kai and Draven broke into a sprint.

They did not catch him up, despite his casual pace. He paused in the centre of the bridge. They leapt onto the footpath in pursuit. He turned to confront them. His features shifted in the pale moonlight. The scant, soft glow from the torches cast flickering shadows across the moving planes of his face. Nevertheless, Kai was grimly certain that he smiled.

"No!" she shouted. She raced towards him with a desperate burst of speed.

It was too late. The changing man hoisted himself over the side of the bridge in one fluid leap. She and Draven rushed forwards. They bent over the railing to peer down at the glittering water below. He was gone. Draven cursed vehemently. Kai growled in frustration.

A loud, echoing whir of wings from under the bridge beneath their feet silenced them instantly. A frosted glass-domed flyer lifted into the air. Its rapidly beating wings stirred the air around them, forcing them to take a step back from the railing. They watched the airship as it soared away. It disappeared swiftly over the water. In seconds it was out of Zooni, headed towards the Scyllan Sea.

"Damnit!" Draven shouted across the rippling water. He spun away from the railing and shoved his hair back from his face in aggravation.

Kai shook her head. She panted slightly. They shared an angry, frustrated glare. Draven sighed. His entire body relaxed as he leaned against the rail. "Well," he said in a deceptively calm voice. "At least now we can tell Queen Jila the man who hired the assassin was probably one of the Duke's."

"Unfortunately, he's dead and unable to confirm the allegation."

Draven's chuckle was bitter and humourless. "Why the hell did the assassin kill the Tyran?"

Kai shook her head. She stared out over the silent water. "No idea. Maybe the Duke's man hired him to kill Jila, and he contracted it out to Wick, who obviously failed. Maybe it all went wrong and he's just trying to clear up after himself."

Draven scowled doubtfully. "That doesn't make a lot of sense."

"I don't understand it, either."

He dropped his head back. He grunted petulantly. "How the hell are we supposed to catch him now?"

Kai smirked. "Calm down, Commander. All hope is not lost. One of Jila's little spies found its way into his jacket."

"You released a fly?"

"Just. At the inn."

He considered. "Think he'll find it?"

"Maybe. Probably. But until then, maybe we can learn something about who he is and where he came from."

Draven's lips twisted in a small smile. "I like the way you think."

She nudged him. "Oh, now you do."

He snorted. "Come on. Let's get back to the castle. I suspect we have some explaining to do."

CHAPTER TWELVE

*Q*ueen Jila looked small and deflated and powerless curled up on the corner of the settee in her thin, green dressing gown. Her expression was grave. Her eyes were weary and infinitely aged, as though she had lived several lifetimes in the span of mere days. "So, it is certainly the Duke who commissioned my attempted assassination," she said in a low, sombre voice.

"All circumstances suggest so, Your Majesty. Him, or one of his people," Draven replied in an equally solemn voice. "Unless someone has taken extreme measures to mislead us."

She raised her eyebrows. "Is that possible?"

"It is not impossible," Kai replied reluctantly. She glanced askance at Draven. "We have yet to discover the identity of the dead man. We only assume he is Tyran; we are not yet certain. Abraham is looking into it."

Jila nodded. "Yes, very good. We must be sure."

"We can likely assume that the Duke is aware of the order," Kai said.

"We can assume nothing at this point! The only thing I might assume is that someone very clearly wants me dead."

Draven sighed. He laid a hand gently on Kai's wrist as she opened her mouth to retort. "I am sorry, Your Majesty. We had hoped to know more at this juncture," he said gently.

Jila shook her head. "You two have done well, under the circumstances. I did not mean to snap. I will have Emile continue to monitor the Hive for further leads."

Draven rose. "I will report these new developments to Silas right away. He will want to know our progress on the matter and the likelihood of coming conflict."

Jila nodded. She waved a hand to dismiss him. He did not leave. The Queen turned to Kai. "Who is this man with no face? Is he one of my people?"

Kai sighed. She slouched in her chair beside the Queen. "We cannot know, Your Majesty. We were unable to glean the information from his conversations. We suspect he was hired by the Duke's man and contracted the job to Wick."

"We do not know why he would have done this when he has proven to be perfectly capable and probably more effective," Draven put in.

"Then I am glad he did not do the job himself," Jila murmured. "I rather value my life. If it is Wick's incompetence I have to thank, I do so willingly. Well." She lifted her chin imperiously. "I will not allow this dreariness to ruin my life. I will not hide away under the covers and wait for another assassin to claim me. If the Duke wants something from me, he can take it himself. Or die trying. Most likely die."

Kai smirked. "We sent the man with no face off with a fly. He is very clever, but maybe our sentinel will be cleverer still."

Jila smiled bravely. "Good. I anticipate we will soon identify him. Now." She rose in one fluid motion to her feet. She brushed her long, black braid over her shoulder. She straightened. Her tone when next she spoke was brisk. "Right now, however, we need to coordinate security for the Bicentenary Ball. I will not allow this unfortunate situation to keep me from it. It is one of my particular pleasures. Julian will be here, with his Abyssal guard."

Draven frowned. "Your Majesty," he began carefully, "Are you certain it's wise, in the present climate, to continue with the Ball and accept the Duke into the palace?"

Jila's glance was glacial. "I am the Queen," she said in a sharp voice. "And I will not show weakness now. I will have a challenging time of it playing nice with Julian, but I expect you all to do the same."

Draven sighed. He exchanged a glance with Kai. They nodded to the Queen in resignation. "Yes, Your Majesty. As you wish."

* * *

As the evening of the Bicentenary Ball loomed ever closer, the castle deteriorated into an unbearable state of tension and excitement. Draven was especially edgy. He still strongly disapproved of Jila's decision to hold the ball in the dangerous political climate. He did not voice his concerns, but he was in a constant strop. If Kai shared his dissent, she did not let on. She was even graver than usual. She spent her time hovering silently around the Queen. She watched her constantly with wary, vigilant eyes. Queen Jila was an intolerable companion. She snapped and snarled each time an order was not fulfilled to her satisfaction, which was, apparently, never.

When the night finally arrived, however, the palace was turned out in its most lavish finery. The walls, ceilings and floors twinkled with subtle hints of sparkling gold and jewels. Delicate scarlet silk draped the windows, tables, and chairs and hung in streamers from the ceilings. The palace was brazenly feminine. It suited the lovely, audacious young queen. The pandemonium with which she had conducted each minute detail of the arrangements had resulted in a stunning display. If she was to die that evening, she would do it elegantly and in style.

Despite her haughty bluster, as Jila finished dressing in a beautiful brocade gown of pale pink and copper, her strain was palpable. Her ubiquitous guards stood on either side of her vanity mirror. They did not tonight resemble the tacit, capable sentinels to which she had grown accustomed. Kai shifted uncomfortably from one foot to the other. She scrunched up her face in silent protest of the tall, impractical high heels and thin, flowing blue silk gown. She glittered from head to toe. Her long, moonlight pale hair was braided with a silver ribbon down her back. Her throat, ears and wrists sparkled with the Queen's palest blue jewels.

"Stop fidgeting, Kai," Jila ordered irritably. She slammed a dazzling jewelled comb on the vanity table.

"I look ridiculous. How am I to protect you if I'm dressed like a silly courtier?" Kai grumbled. She fingered the end of her braid as if she meant to unravel it.

Draven reached over the top of Jila's head. He stilled Kai's fingers sternly. "Don't."

Kai turned her glare on him. There was an intense, unreadable gleam in his dark eyes that silenced any retort she might have hissed at him. A tremor crept up her spine. She ignored it resolutely. They had more important things to think about at the moment than the last ball they had attended together. The changing man was still at large. Duke Julian would be arriving with his entourage in a matter of hours. There wasn't any time to waste on trivial diversions and fleeting attractions.

The absence of mischief from the Duke's kingdom was unsettling. There had been no signal from Kai's surreptitious fly. It might be entangled in the changing man's jacket. More likely, it had met the same fate as the first and been crushed between his powerful fingers as though it were nothing more than a troublesome insect. They could not predict what treachery might ensue at the Queen's approaching celebration.

Jila rose abruptly. She spun to face them. She took a deep breath. She inclined her head and held her hand out to Draven. He folded it into the crook of his elbow. "It is time," she announced imperiously. Her brave expression faltered for an ephemeral instant. "Please do not allow anyone to kill me tonight."

Draven's expression was grave. Kai smirked at her cousin. "You know I won't. How will I support myself without you?"

Jila laughed. "You know perfectly well you can support yourself without me."

Kai's expression was suddenly serious. "Well, despite my cheek, I prefer having you around."

Jila tugged her hand out from Draven's elbow. She strode forward to embrace her cousin. Kai seemed as surprised as he at the sentimental outburst from the usually reserved Queen. She patted Jila's shoulder awkwardly, but a smile danced across her lips. "Come now, cousin," Kai chided gently. "You aren't dying yet. Cease your emoting."

Jila laughed. This time she tucked her hand into her cousin's elbow. "Right, then. Let's get on with it. Step lively, Commander."

A company of Varunian and Lezan guards waited outside the Queen's chambers to escort them to the ballroom. They bowed to the Queen and saluted their Commander. Then they turned and preceded them brusquely through the corridors. Draven trailed behind the two women as they strode side by side towards the entrance hall with their heads held high.

The Queen's courtiers and guests were already inside the ballroom when the escort arrived outside the entrance. The guests were laughing and mingling gaily. They were thoroughly unaware of the tensions rising in the kingdoms. Jila stepped away from her cousin to be announced to the party. Her subjects and guests sunk to their knees in tribute to her arrival. Kai and Draven remained behind her. They regarded the assembly assiduously. Jila spoke to them through the teeth of her stiff smile. "I don't think Julian is here yet."

Draven's brow furrowed as he scanned the crowd for signs of the Tyran Duke or his guard. "Do you think he will rescind his promise to attend?"

Jila shook her head grimly. "No. It would dreadfully impolite and politically foolhardy. He will arrive. Eventually." She smiled and lifted her chin. "I must greet my guests."

"We will be watching you," Kai assured her quietly.

Jila nodded. She stepped boldly forwards to receive the attention of the court. They converged upon her instantly. Her guard remained nearby. Kai and Draven slipped past them to precede her into the elegant ballroom. The Varunian nobility were turned out in their finest gowns and suits, resplendent and exhilarated by the lavish party. It was always the court's most highly anticipated event of the year. Haunting, melodic music filled the room. There was no band.

The sound issued from an undetectable source. Couples were already dancing, tossing their partners around in a free-spirited dance.

Draven paused a moment to watch them in interest. Kai paused beside him. "Ridiculous, isn't it?"

He chuckled. He watched the men spin their woman in enthusiastic but ungraceful circles. "It looks rather entertaining." She eyed him sceptically. She snatched a flute of clear, sparkling wine from a server's tray as he passed. Draven frowned at her. "We need to be focussed tonight, Kaia. You should not be drinking."

She rolled her eyes. "I assure you, I am perfectly focussed." She wasn't, though. She could not place the source of her disquiet. "One drink will scarcely impair me."

His features did not soften. However, he spun to catch the server before he had disappeared with the drinks. Draven raised his glass to her. Kai smirked. Draven took only one sip before he placed the glass onto another passing waiter's tray. "One drink," he said. He inclined his head to her gallantly.

Her sour expression smoothed into one of complete impassivity when a short, thin man appeared in their path. He smiled ingratiatingly as he approached them. Possessing black, oiled and slicked hair, a long, curved nose and narrow features, he resembled nothing more than a small, sycophantic rodent. His coal black eyes darted between them in keen, gleeful interest. Kai stiffened. She felt Draven step closer to her side, as if to intervene in the event the man attempted to accost her.

"Ah, Miss Valela."

Kai blinked. She did not recognise the smarmy little man. He bent over her hand to kiss it. Her skin crawled. Silver satin gloves covered her arm to the elbow. They shielded her from his thin, moist lips. It wasn't enough. She resisted the urge to wipe her hand on the folds of her skirt, as if to wipe the memory of his kiss from her flesh. He was higher born, a nobleman, she knew, for he wore a Varunian family coat of arms on his breast pocket. She did not know his name. Jila would not forgive insolence towards her nobles, especially on an evening of such sombre importance to the realm.

Draven's eyes narrowed. Kai curtsied politely. "I don't believe we've had the pleasure," the rat-faced man said. His smile seemed fixed upon his face. "I am Baron Omari Gregori."

The name was not entirely unfamiliar, though Kai knew she had never met him face-to-face before. How had he known her name? She inclined her head, despite the rising disquiet. "Baron."

Gregori turned his coal black eyes on Draven. They swept over his black livery and glittered with the barest hint of disdain. "And you must be Commander Lockley. I heard you were attending the Queen."

Draven glanced at Kai. His eyes were blank. His tone was rigid with the effort of maintaining his customary civility. "I am."

"Is she in particular need of protection?"

Draven's response was lightning quick. "King Silas has sent his company along in his stead as a courtesy. He is unable to attend the ball due to pressing matters at home."

Gregori's thin lips twitched. "Is that so? Matters so pressing they require the King to remain without his guard?"

Draven's smile was razor sharp. "The King is well-attended."

"Ah, but I have heard he is unable to go a single day without his trusted Commander by his side. I see these rumours are merely fancy."

Draven inclined his head politely. "I would never presume to judge the nature of a rumour, my lord. However, I am fully confident the King is well-protected in my absence."

"And the Queen is well-protected in your presence?"

"If she is so in need, indeed she will be."

Gregori seemed to find this remark amusing. His black eyes glittered. His gaze returned to Kai. "And you, Miss Valela? To what do we owe the pleasure of your return to Varuna?"

Kai hesitated a split second. He had caught her out. She felt Draven shift beside her. He wrapped an arm around her waist. He drew her up to his side. She relaxed and smiled slightly. "Nothing less than the promise of a thrilling evening, my lord."

Gregori smirked. His canny eyes suggested he did not entirely believe this. "Well, then. I will allow you two young people to get on with your thrilling evening."

He bowed again. This time he did not linger over Kai's hand. He inclined his head to Draven. In the instant before he spun away from them, they saw his lips twist in a smirk. When he was out of sight, Kai shuddered dramatically in Draven's arms. "That man is utterly creepy."

Draven stepped away from her. His brow furrowed. "Do you know him?"

She shook her head. "No. I have heard of him." She frowned up at him. "I do not know how he knows my name. I have not worked for him before."

He considered. "Should that be cause for alarm?"

She shook her head. She still felt extremely disquieted. "I have worked for many nobles. He may merely have heard my name from one of them." He seemed no more convinced than she. She sighed. "The Queen has plenty of protection here. I want to look in on the Hive and inquire as to whether Emile has located our missing fly. I want to know the moment the Duke arrives."

Draven remained troubled. "I do not suspect we will require the services of the Hive to spot him; he is wholly singular, after all." He offered her his hand. She took it. She was grateful to leave behind the music, laughter and dancing in the ballroom.

When they reached the Hive, Emile spun in his chair to greet them. Behind him, a hundred screens monitored the ball. They saw everything: the guests, the dancing, the private interludes in the darker corners of the ballroom. Emile looked as if he had been expecting them. Kai narrowed her eyes. She looked around for a fly. "How is the party?" Emile asked. There was a wistful expression on his face.

"Dreadfully dull," Kai told him bracingly. He did not look as if he believed her.

"Have you found our assassin yet?" Draven asked. His voice was sharper than usual.

Emile shook his head. He appeared completely untroubled by the commander's tone. "I'm sorry. Nothing new. I have been watching the flies all day and night."

"Don't you sleep?"

Emile shook his head. "I am Abyssal. I do not need sleep."

Draven blinked. This seemed to startle him. "I did not realise."

Emile's expression was impassive. "I am connected to the flies. I see what they see. I am awake as long as they are awake."

Draven frowned. "Forever?"

"Until I die." Now his smile was slightly sad. "I see everything, but I will never live it." Kai and Draven exchanged an uncomfortable glance. Emile perked up

127

immediately, as if he had not spoken the brooding observation. "I will notify you, should I discover the whereabouts of your assassin. I assure you, nothing will escape my scrutiny."

"Thank you, Emile."

Emile smiled. They left him alone in the Hive, surrounded by thousands of tiny eyes. Draven was scowling. "What's the matter?" Kai demanded.

"I did not realise Emile lived in such a way."

"Yet something else of which you disapprove, Commander? Emile chose this life. If he had not been augmented and joined to the flies, he would have died."

Draven blinked. "How so?"

"He was very sick as a boy. His family could not afford the Abyss to heal him. They came to Jila for help. She offered to extend his life through the Abyss, but he would forever live through others. He can only ever watch now. Nevertheless, he chose it over death."

Draven was silent a long moment. "I am not sure which is the lesser of two terrible alternatives."

"It doesn't matter which you think is lesser. Emile thinks this is."

He sighed. "All right. That's fair."

He lingered in troubled silence as they strode back towards the ballroom. She did not speak to him. She did not consider Emile's situation a matter about which he had any business forming conclusions or judgments. The terrible din from the ballroom echoed through the entrance hall when they arrived. She instantly forgot her consternation.

They did not pause to exchange a glance. They rushed into the ballroom. Kai stumbled slightly in her heels. Draven caught her arm to steady her without even glancing her way. He dragged her the rest of the way into the Queen's state room.

The cause of the din, to their exasperation, was merely Duke Julian's arrival. He was turned out in his finest royal blue velvet suit and flanked by several of his guards. The Tyrans towered above the Varunians, who were exclaiming delightedly over the appearance of the foreign sovereign. They sank to their knees in reverence. He greeted them in a booming, jovial voice, as though he desired nothing more in the world than to see them all there admiring him.

Kai swiftly scanned the ballroom for her cousin. Jila was in perfect condition.

Her cheeks were flushed. Her eyes sparkled. At Julian's arrival, she glided towards the centre of the room to receive her foreign guests. Kai suspected only she had recognised the wary glint in her cousin's eyes. She started forwards to flank her Queen.

Draven caught her arm. He dragged her back towards him. "No, Kaia," he hissed. "Not yet. We don't want him to see you before he must. He will surely recognise you."

Kai scowled. "I need to be close to her."

"She's perfectly all right. She is surrounded by hers and my people. Julian will not be foolhardy enough to make an attempt on her life under these circumstances, in front of all these people."

She sighed, but she allowed him to draw her away from the converging crowd in the centre of the room. Apparently, the spectacle of Queen and Duke together had trumped the dancing. All eyes were on the sovereigns. A fleeting, wild suspicion that they were all aware of the simmering tensions passed through her mind before she dismissed it outright. Nonsense. The nobles were merely gossip-mongers and cheap thrill-seekers.

Julian approached Jila. He paused to wave and smile luridly at the crowd around him. He seemed to love nothing more than the attention. He might have been a cheap carnival act or a magnificent show pony. He greeted Jila heartily. The Queen curtsied gracefully. "Good evening, Duke Julian," Jila greeted with a gracious smile. "I am so pleased you were able to attend my humble do."

He bowed low over her hand. His smile was radiant and brilliantly white. "Not at all, Your Majesty. I would not have missed it for the world."

There was no sign of tension between them. Julian's garish blue eyes darted almost imperceptibly towards the Lezan guards in their distinguished livery. Though he did not remark upon them, his bearing was taut when he straightened once again. "I most sincerely hope you enjoy yourself, Your Grace," Jila told him sweetly.

"I am certain, Your Highness, that I will. With your leave, I will avail myself of refreshments and enjoy a dance with a willing partner." Jila inclined her head. He bowed over her hand once more. His voice, though huskier than before, carried clearly across the crowded floor. "I should most earnestly desire a dance with you later, My Queen, if it is not too much trouble."

She smiled. "Of course, Your Grace. I am most gratified."

He turned from her. He continued to smile hugely around him. The smile did

129

not reach his electric blue eyes. His gaze swept narrowly over the crowd, as if he were searching for someone in particular. Draven seized Kai's hand abruptly. He spun her into his arms. "Come. Dance with me," he ordered curtly.

She was completely caught out. "What?"

His expression brooked no argument. "If we are dancing, there is slightly less chance one of the guards will recognise you, activate the others and cause a politically devastating commotion."

She snorted, but she accepted his hand. The melody was slow and sensual. Draven drew her close against him. He led her into a gentle sway. She looked up into his eyes. For the briefest moment, she exulted in his arms. She melted into the strength and warmth of his body against her and the brilliance of his pure, dark eyes. The moment passed quickly. She turned her head sharply to search out her Queen amongst the crowd.

Draven's long, slender fingers gripped her chin. He tilted her gaze back to his. He did not speak for a moment. She sighed deeply. "What will we do when this is all over?" he asked finally.

His words were as startling as the abruptness of their utterance. "What do you mean? We will return to our lives. You to your country, and me to my work."

He raised his eyebrows. "I think you know what I mean."

She looked away. "I was under the impression you were quite keen to be shot of me."

"Were you?"

She frowned. She averted her eyes from his intent gaze. When the song ended, she stepped sharply away from him. "I need to refresh myself," she muttered.

He sighed, but he did not try to stop her. She hurried towards the entrance hall. She was unsure where she intended to go. She drew up short when Gregori stepped into her path, smiling that slippery, obsequious smile. "Miss Valela," he purred. "You look slightly flushed. Is there anything I can do for you?"

She opened her mouth to rebuke him. She remembered her manners. She swiftly closed her mouth again and lowered her gaze demurely. "No. Thank you, my lord."

He stepped closer to her and lifted his hand. His fingers brushed across her cheek, as soft, subtle and unsettling as a spider's leg. She stiffened. "Are you quite sure? There are many things I can do. I would be delighted to show you what some of those things are."

Her skin crawled. Nausea welled in her belly. Nevertheless, she remained firm. "I am grateful for your gracious offer, my lord, but I am quite well. If you'll excuse me, I'm off to the ladies."

He bent low over her hand. He tilted his head up to smirk at her. She pulled away from him as swiftly as courtesy allowed. She shuddered as she peered over her shoulder at him. When she turned back, her revulsion for Baron Gregori was instantly forgotten. She reared back from the massive form in her path. She looked up into Duke Julian's glittering blue eyes. Her stomach sank into her knees.

He stared down at her in utter incredulity. "You," he hissed. For a moment, he appeared completely at a loss, as if he were unsure what to do with her now that she was so near.

Then he lifted his hands. He reached forward as if to seize her. She angled away from him, stepping swiftly to the side. Draven was beside her in an instant. He wrapped an arm firmly around her waist to draw her up to his side. He bowed smartly to the Duke. His jaw was rigid. He still looked perfectly at ease. "Your Grace."

Julian's face was peculiarly blank. His cheek twitched. He glanced between them with a slightly hunted expression in his eyes. "Commander Lockley," he greeted in a booming voice, despite the tension in the air. "I didn't expect to see you here tonight. Have you come in King Silas' stead?" His eyes darted towards Kai again.

Draven smiled. "I see you have met my intended, Lady Kaia."

Kai glanced sharply at him. She felt his hands clench around her waist. She closed her mouth with a snap. Julian blinked. "Yes, it seems we have met. How do you do, Lady Kaia?"

She curtsied demurely. "Very well, thank you, Your Grace."

"Well..." Julian's smile was deceitful. It chilled her. "It has been a pleasure to make your acquaintance. If you'll excuse me."

"Certainly, Your Grace." Draven bowed. He watched the Duke drifted back into the crowd with narrowed eyes.

Kai dug her elbow into his ribs. They could see the Duke's head over the top of the crowd. He greeted the guests and nobles with all of the gusto of before. Now his smile was tense. "Why did you tell him that?" she hissed.

Draven caught her hand. He dragged her towards a corner of the ballroom out of earshot of the other guests. "If he believes you belong to me, he will not attack you again. Moving against my woman is as decisive as moving against King Silas. He is not such a fool. He requires Silas' camaraderie and alliance to further his goals." Draven frowned at her, as if she should understand this. "You are safe now from him."

She considered with a frown. Then she shrugged. "Well, that was quite cunning and unexpectedly auspicious."

Draven chuckled. "Is that a thank you?"

"The closest you'll get."

He smiled. "That will have to suffice. Remain by my side, Kaia, and you will be most impressed by just how cunning I can be when the need arises."

* * *

Kai and Draven stood side by side. They watched the guests trickle slowly out into the entrance hall. The ball had been a smashing success, despite Jila's tension and the presence of Julian and his menacing guards. Kai's gaze was not on the Duke as he bid brash, deafening goodbyes to Jila and her remaining guests. Her eyes followed Baron Omari Gregori, who still lingered in the ballroom, as if waiting for the last of the guests to exit before taking his leave. Perhaps it was merely that he was waiting for someone in particular. Kai did not wish to deliberate too extensively about whom that might be.

Draven noticed her wary attention to the Baron. He did not remark upon it. He focussed his attention upon the Duke. Julian bowed over Jila's hand one last time before finally leaving the ballroom with his guard. Julian did not glance around for Kai as he left. Nevertheless, Draven slid an arm around her waist. Kai rolled her eyes. She sighed in relief when Julian's massive back had disappeared into the darkness of the palace grounds.

As the last of her guests bid her farewell, Jila returned to the Commander and her cousin. The Queen looked visibly strained, as if her face were tired from the effort of maintaining her smile. Her cheeks were flushed. It appeared she had enjoyed herself immensely, notwithstanding the perfidious atmosphere.

She smiled at them. "Well, I cannot be the last to leave my own party; it wouldn't be demure," she announced. "I am taking my leave of the evening."

Draven chuckled. Kai smirked. "You, demure?"

Jila held up a warning finger to her cousin. "Do not sass your Queen, Kai."

She smiled and bowed her head to them. "Good night."

"Good night, Your Majesty."

Her guards flanked her to guide her back to her chambers. Draven stepped aside to murmur to his men. He returned to the Queen. He bowed. "My men will watch over your chambers, Your Majesty."

"Thank you, Commander."

"I will join them," Kai announced.

"No," Draven replied. There was a sharp edge in his voice. "There is no need." When she scowled, he added, "My men are perfectly capable. You should get some rest. You need to be prepared to continue our investigation afresh in the morning."

She considered arguing. It had been a long, tense night. She would welcome the solitude of her chambers. The Queen would be in very good hands. "And you?"

He smiled. "I will watch over your cousin for you. She will not come to harm."

Her lips turned up slightly. "Thank you."

"Shall I have someone escort you to your chambers?"

She scowled. "No. I am perfectly capable of seeing myself to bed, thank you." She spun away from him. She bowed to Jila. "Good night, My Queen. I will see you in the morning."

Jila smiled at her. "Good night, Kai."

Alone in her chambers, Kai sighed luxuriantly. As she soaked in the steaming, porcelain tub, her mind replayed the day's and week's events. They were troubling and wearisome. She rose from the flower-scented water. She wrapped herself in a thick, white dressing gown, and she sighed deeply. The hour was late, nearly morning. It was not the time to keep herself awake, forming and discarding strategies for the coming day.

She loosened the long braid. She tossed the silver ribbons aside as if they had mortally offended her. She combed out her long, pale blonde hair. Her thoughts turned unbidden to Draven. They often did when she was alone and unguarded. She slammed the comb on the vanity counter. She shook her head violently as though it might dislodge him from her mind. She wasn't a woman of fancy and sentiment. She hardly needed a man like Draven Lockley disrupting her perfectly ordered and satisfying existence.

She dressed in a soft, silky nightgown borrowed from the Queen. She climbed into the large, four-poster bed. She determinedly ignored any troubling thoughts of faceless assassins, treacherous dukes and disquieting soldiers. She was asleep the moment her head touched the soft, goose-feather pillows.

* * *

Kai bolted upright in bed. Her eyes darted warily around her chamber. She did not see anyone lurking in the shadows. She was certain she had heard a soft noise. She sensed a subtle shift in the air. She couldn't see them or hear them breathing, but she felt someone in the room with her. She breathed in slowly, silently. She squinted into the darkness. She considered reaching for her stunner on the nightstand. She hesitated to alert the intruder to her awareness of him.

The air shifted again. Before she could reach belatedly for her weapon, the intruder was upon her. She had time only to gather a deep breath before the intruder pinned her beneath him. She could not see him well in the dark, despite her specially trained eyes. She could make out his movements. She didn't expect the first blow when it came, striking her face with perfect aim. She did not cry out. She tasted blood in her mouth as her teeth jarred and bit down on her lower lip.

She attempted to deflect the blows as they fell. Her attacker was faster than she and much stronger. His hand groped at her throat. He squeezed. She struggled against him. She could not peel his clenched fingers from her neck. For a moment, he leaned over her to peer into her face. Her vision was blurred by the blood in her eyes. She thought she could still make out a familiar face. It was a face she had seen only hours ago.

She forgot its name the moment it crossed her mind, for two hands were squeezing now at her throat. She felt the delicate bones snap beneath the relentless assault. She could not catch her breath to gasp or scream. She did not intend to waste it on such things if it were to be her last. She was strong. She had always been able to best any opponent in the past, but he was stronger than she. Her struggles merely stole the last of her energy.

She struck out at him feebly. The blow barely glanced off his head. He tilted his head only slightly to evade her strike. His hands tightened around her neck. Her body was constructed almost purely of Abyss. Her attacker was more impossibly powerful than she.

Stars exploded on the edges of her vision. She heard a strange, distant and echoing shout. The door to her chambers crashed across the floor as it tore from its hinges. Whomever had shouted, whomever had finally come, was too late.

She stopped struggling. She allowed the cold, empty blackness to swallow her completely.

CHAPTER THIRTEEN

shock racked her entire body. Kai jerked convulsively. She gasped and tried to sit upright. There was a weight pinning down her chest. Her eyes flew open. She struck out, but she paused as her eyes focussed upon Draven's dark, flashing gaze. He caught her flailing hand. He pressed it to his chest as it rose and fell with his shallow, heavy breathing. In his other hand, he held a long, thin gold wand resembling her own stunner. Its tip glowed blue. It still buzzed with energy.

"Kaia?"

He climbed off of her. He moved to assist her into a sitting position. She waved him away. She lifted herself from the waist. A spasm seized her entire body. He tried to catch her shoulders to still her convulsion. He paused to watch with wide, shocked eyes as the cuts and bruises on her face and throat closed and healed in a terrible, unnatural instant. He stared at the smooth, unblemished skin. She was still as pale as alabaster.

"Did he get away?"

Draven blinked. He stared at her throat where once there had been the dark, livid bruises left by the assassin's hands. "What?"

"Draven! Did he get away?

Draven sighed. He lowered his head. "Yes. I tried to catch him, but I was losing you."

She shook her head. Her eyes flashed angrily. "You should have gone after him. I'm Abyssal. I heal quickly."

He looked down at the wand in his hand. He tossed it away from him as if it had burned him. "What is this thing?"

"It stimulates the Abyss to speed the healing process." She glared at him. "I would have lived!"

"I wasn't going to take that chance."

She sighed. "Where did you get it?"

"Jila."

"Always clever, my cousin. How did you know about the assassin?"

"Emile. He was watching the flies."

She frowned. "Was he able to follow him?"

"He tried. I don't know if he was successful. I was concerned with your safety; I did not check back with him."

"I'm fine."

He moved so quickly, she reared backwards. He sat on the edge of the bed beside her. He examined her throat with deft, gentle fingers. "Were you hurt anywhere else?" His voice was low and husky. His eyes were oddly hooded. They smouldered. She shook her head and batted his fingers away. "Are you sure?"

"Do you want to check me?"

His nostrils flared. He drew back, scowling. "Did you see who it was?" he demanded. Her eyes slid away. She struggled to remember the blurred vision of the face looming over her. After a long moment, she nodded. He sat straight up. "Who?"

"Baron Gregori."

He was caught out. "What? Are you certain?"

Kai pushed herself up as if to rise from the bed. "We have to go after him."

"No." Draven's voice was sharp. He pushed her back against the pillows. "Absolutely not. You were just violently assaulted. We'll have someone else get him."

Kai's temper flared. "I can take care of this myself." She tilted her chin defiantly.

His expression turned stony. "No. You need to rest."

"I perfectly rested. I want to go after him!"

"You're shaken."

"No, I am not."

"I am!" He shot to his feet. He pushed his hands through his long, black hair.

Kai blinked. She stared at his rigid back. His shoulders hitched with his harsh, laboured breath. "Draven?"

He half turned his head. A muscle twitched in his cheek. She stood on slightly shaky legs. She paused a moment to regain her bearing. She was not as fit after

137

her near-death as she would have liked to believe. She could still move easily enough. She laid a hand on his arm. He whirled abruptly, catching her out. His dark eyes flickered strangely. She opened her mouth to speak. No words came. She blinked up at him. The intensity of his glared startled her.

He took a step towards her. She remained where she stood. She lifted her chin insolently. And then he reached for her. He wrapped an arm around her waist to drag her up against him. His other hand fisted into the hair at the nape of her neck. Giving herself up, she tilted her face up to receive his kiss. She clutched the back of his neck with both hands to hold him closer to her.

There was no slow seduction in the way his tongue stroked against hers. He kissed her voraciously. He stole her breath and her senses. Heat coursing through her from head to toe. He lifted her effortlessly. The firmness of his body pressed against every inch of her. She moved against him urgently. She met his kiss without shame or reserve. He moved forwards. When she encountered the edge of the bed, she dropped down upon it. She broke the kiss to scrabble at the buttons of his jacket.

Her fingers were quick and nimble. They were not fast enough for him. He batted them away impatiently. His urgency had not stolen his efficiency. Kai had only begun to yank at the belt around his waist when he shrugged the jacket off his shoulders to drop to the floor. He paused a moment to allow her to yank the thin, black underpinning over his head, and then he was upon her again. He pushed the thin nightgown up her legs with more deliberation than he'd shown with his own accoutrements.

His fingers brushed over her thighs with a moth's wing lightness. She moved restlessly against him. She yanked him back down to meet her parted lips. She moaned as his fingers stroked against her upper thighs, towards the throbbing heat of her centre. She opened her legs. She leaned back. Sensation rippled through her entire body.

He trailed hot kisses across her throat. His hands slid up abruptly to yank the thin, silky night gown over her head. She did not move to cover herself or preserve her modesty. She allowed him to look at her a long moment. His eyes darkened eloquently until they were nearly black. The moment was too long. She pulled him back down to her. His hands slid over her skin. He did not return to kiss her mouth. Tingles spread across every inch of flesh he touched. She moaned as his fingers flicked across the sensitive tips of her breasts.

His lips followed his hands. He reached slowly down between them as his mouth closed over her nipple. His mouth was hot. It seared the tingling, energised flesh. She hissed his name. In response, he slid his hand under the waistband of her knickers, down to her throbbing centre. He exhaled in a low, savage growl. His fingers grew slick with her arousal. He lifted his head and returned to her mouth with renewed vigour.

She fumbled at his waist. Her fingers were clumsy with desperation. She unbuttoned his trousers. She shoved at them with a soft, impatient noise. Draven smirked against her mouth and lifted himself above her. He peered down at her as he kicked the offending trousers aside. He cupped the side of her face in his hand. With the other, he reached down between them. He cast aside her knickers effortlessly.

She arched up into him. He groaned. In one swift, fluid movement, he pushed inside her. She threw her head back. She gasped for breath. He cradled her face in his hands. He stared down into her eyes as he moved. His eyes glittered. Her body rocked with the force of his thrusts. She clung to him. She lifted her hips to draw him closer. He leaned down to kiss her. His breath was harsh and ragged against her mouth.

Brilliant sensation rippled through her entire body. It built up at her centre with each stroke of him inside her. She clung to him and squeezed her eyes shut. She threw her head back as waves of pleasure suddenly crashed over her until she was senseless and weak. She clutched at him, crying out as he moved faster and faster.

With a feral, agonised growl, his body hitched and trembled. He arched as his climax seized him. He lowered his head. He panted into her neck for a long moment. Then he collapsed to his side to stare up at the ceiling. His breath was still erratic when he turned his head to look at her. His lips curved into a smile. She looked at him archly.

"Still shaken?" she asked.

"Yes. Still shaken. You?"

"Yes, I'm a bit shaken."

* * *

Light filtered in through the thin, sheer blue drapes in Kai's chambers. It cast prisms across the floor. A tinkling noise issued from somewhere on the floor near the bed. Draven awoke groggily. He groped for his trousers over the side of the bed. Beside him, Kai stirred. She opened her eyes blearily to look at him. He smiled at her and flipped open the communicator.

"Who is it?" she murmured petulantly.

139

He smirked. He brushed her dishevelled hair from her shoulder. "It's Lieutenant Rhames."

"Our people have captured Gregori," Rhames informed his commander. Draven angled the compact carefully away from her. Kai could not see Rhames' face. She didn't need to. The tone of his voice was excited.

"So quickly?" she murmured. She frowned thoughtfully.

Draven listened a moment longer. He closed the communicator and looked at her. "What's wrong?"

She shook her head. She was troubled. It seemed unlikely her Abyssal assassin had proven so easily captured. He had been quick, powerful, and she had been no match for him. Did Draven's men possess abilities she could not imagine? "How did they catch him?"

He did not seem to understand her reservation. "One of Jila's flies pursued him. Our people caught him up at his estate."

"Is he here now?"

"They are bringing him now."

She sat up straight. "I want to see him."

Draven nodded. "Of course. When he arrives." She turned from him to slip out of bed. He caught her shoulder. He rolled her onto her back. She smiled as he leaned over her and pressed his mouth to hers. "Are you so eager to be away from me?"

She caught the back of his neck. She held him against her for a long moment. He moved atop her and nudged her legs apart to accommodate him. She pressed her hands to his chest. She pushed him away from her. She sat up. "We should apprise Jila of the situation. She will want to be informed."

He raised a cheeky eyebrow. "And which situation, exactly, is that?"

She rolled her eyes. "I had not intended to describe in detail the complete events of the night, if that's what you're getting to."

He smirked and leaned towards her again. "Abraham will have told her everything by now."

"Draven," she scolded. This time he allowed her to slip away. He watched her with intent eyes as she moved towards her washroom.

He rose from the bed. She glanced over her shoulder at him to watch him yank on his trousers. When he noticed her attention, he paused. He strode towards her to catch her up into his arms. He kissed her languidly. "I will meet you in the Queen's chambers."

The feeling in her stomach as she washed and dressed was one with which she was not acquainted. She had felt an intense sensation of satisfaction before. She had felt relaxed and serene. She had never felt light and giddy. Giddy was a sensation that other people felt--foolish people. The state of affairs was sombre indeed. It hardly seemed an appropriate time to be feeling so jocular. She pushed aside the wistful memories of her night with Commander Lockley and turned her mind to the more crucial and disquieting matters of the realm.

The assassin this time had been one of the Queen's own. He was one of her treasured aristocrats. Though he had attacked Kai and not the Queen, the enormity of it seemed to have affected Jila even more deeply than it had her cousin. She greeted Kai and Draven grimly when they entered her chambers. She looked weary and sober. She had dressed in her most austere black dress. Her corset was laced so tightly, her waist was positively waspish. Her hair was drawn tautly back from her face in a severe bun. She appeared as though she were in bereavement. Her expression was terrible.

"I have heard of what happened last evening," she told them. Her jaw set rigidly. She looked at them closely for the first time. She paused. Her eyebrows travelled almost imperceptibly towards her hairline. For the briefest moment, the stern expression softened. She strode forwards to fold Kai into an embrace. "Are you well, cousin?"

Kai smiled self-consciously. She stepped out of the Queen's embrace. "Yes. Quite." She smirked. "I do wonder by what premonition you thought to give the Commander the wand."

Jila smiled. "I am well-acquainted with your unruliness, cousin. I thought it might come in useful, and I trusted the Commander to know what to do with it and when." She turned her smile on Draven. "And I am relieved I could rely upon him. I would not have wished to lose you."

The corners of Draven's mouth twitched. He glanced at Kai. "Nor would I have."

"No, I don't suppose that you would have." Jila's expression turned downcast once again .The tender moment passed. "You are certain the assailant was my subject, Baron Gregori?"

Kai hesitated a moment. She frowned. She nodded reluctantly. "Yes, Your

Majesty. I was caught out myself, but I am quite sure. I saw his face clearly, if only for a moment."

Jila sighed. She turned away to pace towards the window. "Do you think he is in league with Julian?"

"It is impossible to know. We shall know more when we are able to interrogate him."

Jila spun. "My subject, Baron Gregori, is in the dungeon?"

"Not yet, Your Majesty," Draven replied. "He is en route. My people caught him up at his house."

Jila looked at her cousin. "His house?"

"Yes, Your Majesty."

Jila's expression was a mirror of Kai's own doubt. "I see. Inform me directly how the interrogation proceeds."

Draven bowed. "Yes, Your Majesty."

She flicked her fingers over her shoulder, dismissing them. They bowed and strode from the room. Draven removed his communicator from his jacket pocket. He flipped it open. "Anything?" Kai asked tensely

Draven shook his head. "Nothing new yet. They mustn't have arrived with the prisoner." He turned to her. His lips curved into a sly smile. "We have a little time yet."

"Time?" She understood when he caught her around the waist. He drew her against him. She turned her head up to meet his mouth and returned the slow, languorous kiss. He lifted his hand to thread his fingers into the hair at the nape of her neck. He tilted her head back to deepen the kiss. She pressed herself closer to him. Surely she'd had enough of him the night before. The heat of his arousal against her belly surged through her. Apparently, she hadn't.

For a long moment, she wrapped her arms around his neck and held on as his tongue stroked drowsily against hers. Her more practical thoughts intruded like a bucket of cold water. This was hardly the time nor the place for such things. He seemed to be thinking the very same thing. He seemed to be thinking it wasn't the place, anyway. He tore away from her. He seized her hand to drag her hastily towards her chambers. Her fingers set to the buttons on his jacket the moment the door closed behind them. He attacked her corset with equal ferocity. He yanked her chemise over her head and tossed it to the floor on top of his jacket. He lifted her smoothly and dropped her onto the large, four-poster bed.

She sat up to watch him work at the buckle of his belt with a hooded gaze. When he came to her, she tugged him down beside her on the bed. He kicked his trousers aside. Kai rose to her knees and tugged at the waistband of his trunks. He looked at her in surprise. She smiled at him. She pressed him onto his back. She climbed lightly atop him. Her long, pale hair brushed across his chest. It surrounded them like a veil as she leaned down to press her mouth softly against his.

She moved down the length of him. She reached between them. He gripped the back of her head to draw her down to his mouth. Slowly, she slid down upon his arousal. She tossed her head back. He groaned low and deep in his throat. She moved languidly. He endured it for several moments. Then he caught her around the waist and rose abruptly to his knees. He flipped her onto her back in one fluid motion. He smirked at her and pressed deeply inside her. She lifted her hips to meet him.

They moved, frenzied, towards release. It erupted around them in a wave of intensity and left them gasping and slick with a sheen of sweat. Draven collapsed beside her. She smiled at him. He pulled her up to his side. She curled contentedly against him.

The communicator in his jacket, discarded several feet away on the floor, squawked insistently. Draven let out a frustrated growl. Kai leapt up to retrieve it without bothering to cover herself. Before she could flip it open eagerly, Draven prised it from her hands. He angled it away from her so his lieutenant did not see the shocking state of her. She smirked at him.

Her expression sobered when she heard the message.

"He's arrived."

Kai was already on her feet, quickly tossing on her clothes. He did not move for a moment. He simply watched her. She gave him an impatient look. "Step lively. Get dressed. I want to see him," she ordered.

Draven sighed. He did not argue. When they were dressed, she started for the door. He caught her arm, drawing her back. "We could let him sweat a while," he said. He smiled. "We don't have to go right this moment."

She lifted her face to receive his kiss for an instant. She pressed her hands to his chest. "I want to see him. Now."

Draven sighed. "All right. Who am I to stand between a woman and her revenge?"

She seized his arm and dragged him towards the door. "You are a smarter man than I would have thought."

He chuckled. Their elation did not last. The dungeon was located in the deepest bowels of the palace. It was dank and chilly. Baron Omari Gregori was alone in a small, dingy cell. He sat calmly on the packed dirt floor. He looked exactly as he had the night before: oily, smarmy and smiling sycophantically through luminous white teeth. He did not look like a man who had spent the night attempting to murder a young woman or escaping the Lezan palace guard.

He looked up at them through the veil of his greasy black hair as they approached. He rose to his feet. He bowed low at the waist. "Ah, Miss Valela. I admit, I regret to see you looking so well. So...flushed."

She ignored the suggestive tone of his voice. "I am sure you do, considering your attempt to murder me last night," she replied in an even voice. She paused to face him through the bars.

Gregori inclined his head. He pursed his lips in strange self-deprecating disappointment. "It seems I underestimated you, Miss Valela. You must have more Abyss inside you than I realised. You do not look it. How is it that I did not kill you?"

"You did kill me," Kai replied smoothly. "I just did not die." Draven, standing beside her, glanced sharply at her. She ignored him. "Why did you do it? Are you working for Duke Julian? Did he order it?"

Gregori considered. His coal black eyes practically crackled with the intensity of his internal deliberation. "No. My desire to kill you was all my own. I have developed a taste for it, you see. And you were so...desirable. It is a dire shame I was unable to complete the ritual."

Draven scowled. He stepped forwards, but Kai placed a hand on his arm to calm him. It did not seem to make sense. If the man acted independently, if he was merely a blood-thirsty noble...how had he been so strong, so powerful? Was there no more to this? "Do you know Argus Wick?"

Gregori raised his eyebrows. "An interesting question. I knew him. I hired him to kill the Queen Jila."

There was a long, stunned silence. "What?" Draven demanded. He looked completely caught out.

"Yes. I hired him, and I murdered his lover to punish him when he failed to complete his task." He smiled. "Then I murdered him so he would not expose me."

Kai pinched the bridge of her nose. She squeezed her eyes shut. Draven frowned. The confession had been so matter-of-fact, so calmly delivered, that it rang hollow in their ears. Surely, this was not their man. They had seen the murders with their own eyes. They had seen the changing man who had killed Kang and Wick without difficulty or passing consideration. Had he been so easy to capture, after all? Could this truly be the man with no face?

"You did this on behalf of Duke Julian?" Kai repeated.

Gregori tilted his head to the side. "Why do you keep asking about the Duke? He has no part in this. It was I who hired Wick. It was I who intended Jila dead."

"Then why did you murder the man in the hotel? Why did you speak to him in the tavern and follow him to his hotel? Who was he?"

Gregori smirked. "He was no one. It's nothing to do with this. He owned money to me, and, as I said before, I have developed rather a taste for the... perverse arts."

Draven frowned sceptically. "For what did the man owe you money?"

"I lent him in order to acquire Abyss." Gregori lifted an eyebrow. "You know how people are when they're addicted."

"Why did you really kill him?" Kai repeated.

"He told me he could not pay. He would not pay."

Kai shook her head. "You are lying."

"I assure you, Miss Valela, I am in earnest. Why confess my treason if I intended to alter the facts?"

Her mouth tightened into a thin line. "What reason do you have to wish the Queen dead?" Draven asked.

Gregori turned his head away from them. "Revenge," he hissed. "Of course."

"Revenge for what?"

His coal black eyes flared. For the first time, there was genuine anger in them. The glibness of his tone was gone. "She took everything from me! She ruined my life."

"What are you talking about?" Kai growled. She stepped forwards.

"In the night, her guards took my wife. I never saw her again."

"Why would she have done that?"

"You are not foolish, Miss Valela. You know what happens in Varuna at night. You know what happens when people speak out against the Queen. Sometimes they disappear, and they are never heard from again. It happened to my wife. I have never forgiven her loss."

Draven glanced at Kai. Her expression was utterly blank. She lifted her chin.

Gregori leaned against the bars. His lips curled in a sneer. "I know who you are, Kai Vale. I know what you do. It may have been you who took her, out of her bed. It may have been you who stole my life from me that night." His eyes narrowed. "If it wasn't you who took my wife, it was you who took someone else's. I was justified in protecting the others from you."

Kai was perfectly still. She did not return Draven's glance. He turned back to Gregori. "So, this is a simple matter of revenge?"

"I assure you, revenge is never so simple."

"Nor can it be all there is to this. Tell me what it has to do with Julian."

Gregori glared. "I have told you! He has nothing to do with any of it." His thin lips turned up in a small, humourless smile. "I have told you all. I am guilty. What will you do with me now? Will I receive a trial? Or will you simply shoot me in the back without fanfare? I am prepared for my punishment." He turned his eyes to Kai. "I would prefer you to be the one to exact it, Miss Valela. I should think it would be quite poetic."

She opened her mouth to retort. Draven caught her arm abruptly. He whirled her away from the prisoner. She did not resist him. He led her up the thick, stone steps out of the dungeon and into the brightness of a torch-lit corridor. "What the hell is going on here?" he demanded.

She stared at him. She shook her head in bemusement. "I don't know."

Draven's brow furrowed. He released her arm and stepped away from her. Anger flashed in his eyes. He turned his back to her. "Could it be the Duke is not plotting against Jila, after all?"

She lifted her chin defiantly. "It seems rather unlikely, considering the damning missive and his guards' subsequent attempts to suppress it. I stand by my conclusion."

He sighed heavily and looked down. "I see your point. There could be two who wish harm to your Queen." His eyes flared a moment in anger. "It should not come as a surprise, knowing what you do about what she does to her own people."

"Why, then, has the Duke remained silent so long? Could it truly be that he has not made his move yet?"

"Perhaps. Or he has and we haven't discovered it yet."

Kai exhaled heavily. "That is more worrisome still." She frowned, peering over her shoulder in the direction of the dungeons. "Can it really be so easy to have caught him?"

Draven shook his head. "I, too, was troubled. The ease with which we elicited his confession is suspicious indeed."

Kai considered. "How does he scramble his face?"

"A mask, surely?"

"Perhaps. But he is Abyssal. He must be."

"What does it mean?"

She looked at him gravely. "He allowed us to capture him. He told us exactly what he wanted us to know."

"It is a ruse?"

"I am unconvinced of the veracity of his confession. There is more to this."

"What do you propose we do?"

She sighed. "I don't know. I know nothing about him."

"Then we will hold him until we can learn more." His eyes were cold. "Perhaps your Queen remembers something about him."

She ignored the judgment in his eyes. "Perhaps there is a link between he and Julian."

"You cannot keep him here indefinitely."

"We cannot give him a trial until we learn all we need to know. He must be kept."

Draven was silent a moment. He looked at her as if he didn't know her at all. "Is it true what he said?"

She looked at him sharply. "What?"

"Do you take people from their beds at night? Do you kill them?"

She stepped forwards. Her eyes glittered with anger. "I never killed anyone."

He blinked. "No?"

"No," she growled. "Not unless they were trying to kill me. I am loyal to Jila, but she does not force me to kill." She glared at him. "She is not that sort of woman."

He looked unconvinced. "Then what does she do with them?"

Kai turned her head. Her expression was guarded. "I don't know. I never asked."

Draven scowled. "I would have wanted to know."

She snapped her head towards him. Her temper flared at the sanctimonious tone of his voice. "Well, I do not."

They stared at each other, as if seeing each other for the first time. A sudden loud, strange noise from below jolted them from their glower. It was not an explosion but a deafening pop! from the direction of the dungeons. They spun together and raced down the stone stairs towards Gregori's cell. They did not find him there.

Rather, there was a small hole in the wall, scarcely large enough for a man. They looked at each other wildly. "He escaped," Kai said, as if to herself, as if she could not believe it.

"How?" Draven growled. He yanked open the bars to examine the hole.

"Where did he go?" Kai followed him. She peered over his shoulder into the dark recess.

"Did he have some sort of Abyssal machine?" Draven peered into the hole. He could not squeeze his shoulders through.

"Let me." Kai slithered into the narrow alcove. To her astonishment, it opened into a dark tunnel. She peered back out at Draven. "It's some sort of tunnel beneath the castle. He must be crawling through the walls right now. Should I go after him?"

"No." She blinked, glancing at his rigid face. "Leave it. He has nowhere to go. We caught him once; we'll catch him again."

"Draven--"

But he was already barking orders into his communicator. "Surround the castle. Let no one leave! The prisoner has escaped."

"I am going after him."

"No!" He reached into the hole and dragged her back through. "I cannot go with you that way. I am not letting you pursue him alone."

"I am quite capable--"

"He already killed you once, as you said. You simply didn't die. I won't be able to get through to you to save you again if you go without me."

She sighed. He spun away from the hole, tugging her along with him. "We'll join the guard on the perimeter. Perhaps we can catch him as he burrows out of the palace."

"Unless he tunnels all the way through the city!" she growled. "Then he'll be gone! Let me go in."

"No. Stay with me. We have no idea what traps he's left in case of pursuit. I'm not risking you crawling in there." When she opened her mouth again to protest, he growled, "Don't argue. Come on. If he's to escape, he may return to his home. We'll catch him before he is able to leave the country."

Kai scowled, but she allowed him to lead her out of the dungeon towards the entrance hall. "I am not as confident as you, Commander. There is something very wrong here, and I do not think it will be so easy to sort out what it is."

CHAPTER FOURTEEN

*B*aron Omari Gregori's estate had once been large and elegant. It was run-down and shambling now in the wake of his losses. Perhaps he had squandered his fortune in the Abyss or let the house fall to disrepair when his wife disappeared. Kai's back was stiff. She was unable to feel more than a slight stab of empathy. He had, after all, strangled the life from her, killed three men and attempted to assassinate her beloved cousin and Queen.

The door swung from its hinges as Draven kicked it in. He hadn't bothered to attempt the knob. When they entered, the dark, sullied house was covered in a layer of filth. Dust swirled in the air around their feet. It appeared as though no one had entered the parlour in ages. No one had cleaned anything since the compulsory departure of the Baroness.

They separated silently to creep through the first floor of the crumbling mansion with pistols at the ready. Kai slipped soundlessly into the library. It was as dark, dim and dirty as the parlour and stuffed with books of every influence. The books were scattered about the room. Their pages were torn and sticking out from every cover. It had not been touched, not for a very long time. Her finger turned black with dust as she trailed it along the scuffed, littered reading table in the centre of the room.

She met Draven in the parlour. It seemed his search had turned up little more than her own. He pointed towards the winding, once gilded stairs. The brass railing was tarnished and rusted. Kai nodded. They moved together towards the second floor. The door to the master's chambers was slightly ajar. They glanced at each other decisively before Draven nudged it open, holding his pistol aloft in case of attack.

There was none. They sighed in unison. They lowered their weapons. Then they saw the withering, decaying body upon the master bed. Draven held up his hand to Kai in a silent command to stay right where she was. She did not move towards the Baron's body. She did not need to. She recognized it instantly from across the room. Her stomach sank.

Draven peered cautiously into every corner of the stinking bedroom. He checked the bath and wardrobe, as though to ensure the Baron's killer was not waiting for them behind the curtains or on the other side of the door. He returned to Kai's side. He shook his head. "There is no one."

"There is the Baron." Her voice was low and toneless. "And it appears he has been here a while."

Draven scowled. "Bloody hell. What is going on?"

Kai stepped forwards to examine the body. Draven raised an arm to hold her back. He approached it himself. He leaned over the Baron's diminutive form. He glanced up at Kai. "His throat."

"Slit?"

"Yes. Like the others." Draven sighed, scowling. "He has been dead a while. Too long for it to have been him at the ball. He isn't the man we captured."

Kai exhaled heavily. "What does it mean?"

Draven stepped towards her. "I think it means the man with no face can take any face he likes."

"It was all deception." She looked up at him with a bemused expression. "He allowed us to capture him to convince us the Duke hadn't anything to do with the plot against Jila?"

"Such elaborate subterfuge makes little sense. Why escape us and allow us to immediately realise the ruse?"

Kai shook her head. "I don't know. I don't understand what is happening." She sighed. "We'd best return to the palace. Jila must know what we have discovered. The marauder is still fugitive. And he could be anyone."

His expression was grim. "That certainly does not make me feel any better."

"No, it wouldn't." She looked up at him sombrely. "It shouldn't."

* * *

Jila paced swiftly across the soft, scarlet carpet in her chambers. Her face was drawn and worried, as though she had wearied of the intrigue, the peril and the plots around her. She had preferred life when it was simple and she lost no sleep over assassins or treacherous persons waiting in the wings to do her in.

She met Kai and Draven with this weary countenance when they entered her chambers. "Come," she ordered in a subdued voice. "Join me for tea."

They glanced at each other. They inclined their heads to her and joined her beside an elaborate tea service. Draven opened his mouth to apprise her of the day's events. She held up her hand to silence him. She leaned back in her chair.

She silently sipped her tea for a moment before she spoke.

"We will discuss grim matters when we have had our tea," she told him firmly.

Draven sighed. He sat back in his chair, but he obeyed her reluctantly. Kai was stiff and anxious. She understood her cousin's custom. She understood her need for normalcy in the pandemonium around them. Jila watched them as they drank their tea, nibbling pensively on a biscuit. She seemed aware of the change in the climate around them. Kai herself was unsure what was between them now, after the ersatz Baron's unpleasant revelations.

Jila laid her teacup upon the saucer and placed them delicately on the tea table before her. "So," she said finally. Her tone was carefully neutral. "You lost Gregori."

"No, not lost as such," Kai replied. "We are fully aware of where Gregori is at the moment."

Jila raised her eyebrows. Draven glanced at Kai. He scowled slightly at her flip tone. "Our prisoner was not Gregori."

"I do not understand," Jila said in a deceptively calm voice.

"Baron Gregori is dead. He has been dead for several days. The man with no face murdered him and assumed his likeness in order to deceive us, Your Majesty."

Jila was silent a long moment. She looked at them with wary eyes. "Who is the man with no face, then?"

Draven shook his head. "We do not know."

"All we know is that he could be anyone?"

"That is the brunt of it, Your Majesty," Kai said grimly.

Jila sighed deeply and leaned back in her chair. "What of Julian? What part does he play in this?"

"The assassin insisted he was not in league with Julian, but we cannot know for sure. We do not know who he is. We suspect his acquisition of Gregori's likeness was an elaborate ruse to turn our attention inward to our own people."

Jila's jaw was set when she nodded. "This is very critical indeed. How are we to protect ourselves if we do not know the people we trust are themselves?"

"I am sorry, Your Majesty," Draven told her in a low voice. "You must not leave the palace under any circumstances, in light of the present danger." Jila nodded, but he continued. "Our assassin is a chameleon. He can escape your dungeon, and he can get into places no one else can. You must be constantly on your guard, and you must never be alone."

She sighed and lowered her head. "We must tell Silas. He will want to know what is happening."

Draven inclined his head. "I will speak to him straight away. Kaia, remain with Jila. We must ensure she is always safe."

Kai nodded. She watched Draven go thoughtfully. Jila was silent a long moment. She looked drawn and haggard. Then the Queen turned to her cousin. Her expression had changed. The sombre, rigid calm she had held in Draven's company had slipped away. Her eyes were bright. "I am frightened, Kai," she admitted quietly.

Kai moved instantly to her side. She wrapped an arm around her shoulders. "I do not blame you, cousin," she said softly. "I, too, am very anxious."

At this, Jila chuckled. Her voice wavered slightly. "You? My brave, fearless Kai?"

"I am not fearless when it comes to the safety of my Queen."

Jila looked at her. "Find him, then. Bring him to justice. Stop him. You have never failed me in the past, Kai, and I am confident you will protect me this time."

Kai smiled. "I will stop at nothing. You know that."

"Yes. I know."

When Draven returned, the Queen smiled wanly. When she looked up at him, her dark eyes glittered fretfully. He bowed. "Silas will come. He is planning a trip to Varuna straight away."

Jila rose abruptly to her feet. She flushed slightly. She nodded, as if this were very agreeable news. "Will he bring Leona?"

"No. The Queen will remain in Leza." Draven hesitated a moment before continuing. "Silas believes she is safer at home, away from Varuna."

Jila smiled ruefully. "That, I must say, is very likely true."

"Silas will offer his wisdom. He will have ideas as to how to proceed in the investigation into the matter of the Duke's involvement or lack of involvement in this."

"Very good. I shall prepare for his arrival at once." She inclined her head to him. "I thank you for your protection and attention, Commander. I trust I can rely upon you and your King, and you may trust I will return the favour and good faith when the time arrives for me to do so."

Draven bowed. "Yes, Your Majesty, of that my King and I are in no doubt."

Jila looked between them with a resolute arch to her eyebrows. "We shall prevail. I have the utmost faith."

They bowed to her. They lifted their heads when she had left the sitting room to prepare for Silas' audience in her chambers. Kai sighed. Draven stepped towards her. "The Queen is safe for the moment."

"We should be out there looking for the assassin."

"Do you have any leads or ideas right now?"

She frowned. "No, not really."

"Emile is reviewing the flies. Abraham is investigating Gregori's past. We can be of little use to either of them." He smiled at her gently. The tension and fear she hadn't even realised she had been harbouring melted away in an instant. "Perhaps we might find a constructive way to spend our time."

"But, the Baron--" She twisted her hands apprehensively.

He did not misunderstand her. "I had imagined far worse of you than that," he admitted in a low voice. He sounded almost ashamed. "Though hearing the truth of your transgressions is somewhat worse than not knowing, at least it is hardly as bad I had feared."

She considered this for a moment. "What does that mean?"

"It means I have no illusions about who you are, not anymore."

"And you are not disturbed?"

"I am disturbed." He smiled slightly. "But I think I can learn to live with it."

She raised her eyebrows. She was suddenly uncertain. "Can you really?"

"I intend to try."

This wasn't entirely satisfying. She also had no illusions about who he was. There were aspects of her work, her past and her being he would never be able to understand. There were things he may never be able to accept. She didn't dwell upon them. It was good enough for the moment, anyway. She could worry about his delicate sensibilities when there wasn't a faceless assassin on the loose. He would probably kill them all before any of it ever became a problem, anyway.

* * *

Draven tugged the blanket up to her chest. He rolled on his side to look down at her. His hair was mussed around his sculpted features. His eyes were serious. Her stomach sank a bit. She knew what he was going to ask. "Did you take people from their beds at night?"

She looked away. "You're asking me that now?"

"I want to know."

"Why?"

"Because I don't really know who you are. I know what you are, but not who. I don't know anything about you."

"You know more than most people."

"That doesn't make it better for me. I want to know the truth."

When she looked away, he tilted her chin back to face him. He brushed a long, stray lock of silver hair from her eyes. She frowned. "I thought you preferred not knowing."

"I changed my mind."

She sighed. "I have told you the truth about me. You are the only one besides Abraham who knows I am Jila's cousin. You know my real name. You know about the Abyss inside me." As she said this, a furrow creased his brow. "Do you think I'm a monster?"

He looked at her in shock. "What?"

"Do you think I'm a sort of freak of nature, barely human?"

"You're human," he said forcefully.

She stared at him relentlessly. "I'm nearly entirely reconstructed from the Abyss."

"You're still you. You are the same, inside your mind. Not that I know who that is. You are not a monster simply because your body is Abyssal."

She rolled onto her side. She propped her head on her hand to meet his gaze. "I may have misjudged you, Commander."

He considered her a long moment. "I think we might have been better off discussing this prior to becoming involved with each other."

155

She blinked in bemusement. "Involved with each other?" The words sounded utterly alien.

He stared at her. "Yes. That is, if you'll have me."

She looked away. "I've had you many times."

"That is not what I meant."

"I'm not sure what that means."

He smirked. "I'm not surprised."

"I did take people from their beds. On Jila's orders."

He sucked in a breath. He was startled by the abruptness of her remark. "I don't know what happened to them after that, not really." She sighed. "But I have seen them since, some of them, anyway. They are not dead, but they are never the same again. They are never right." She paused. Her tone was ardent when she spoke again. "I believe my cousin is good. She would not hurt someone who did not deserve to be hurt."

"But stolen from their beds?" he demanded. His eyes glinted angrily.

She shrugged. "I know only that the kingdom is peaceful, and people do not speak out violently against the Queen. I do not know what one must do in order to be targeted in such a manner."

Draven lay back upon the pillows. He stared at the ceiling. "Where do you take them?"

"To the guards."

"You never asked what happens to them?"

"No. And I would not. It is not my place to question my Queen. Would you, were it your King?"

He sighed. "No. Perhaps I would not. But I might endeavour to find out."

She considered. "Well, perhaps someday I will do."

He looked sceptical. "Does it even matter to you? Where they go, how they become the way they are when you see them again?"

She looked away to hide the hurt expression from him. "Things matter to me. I didn't say they did not." She sighed. "It matters. I wonder. Especially after what...well, he wasn't really Gregori, but after what he said...I wondered."

"I'll help you find out, if you wish."

She shrugged. "Perhaps now is not the time for such investigations. We have other areas of more pressing concern."

"My particular area of concern now is you."

"That's very sweet, but I was referring to the situation with the assassin and the Duke and the quietly simmering political tension which might result in a catastrophic war between our three nations."

"I know to what you were referring. You don't have to be Kai Vale, the mercenary, all the time. You can just be a woman for a little while longer."

She blinked at him. "I'm not entirely sure what that means."

"It means that there is a human woman there inside you somewhere. It is all right to give in to that now and again."

"What do you think I've been doing?"

"I know you think you are."

She frowned. "What does that mean?"

He shook his head. "It doesn't matter." He smiled. "I'm sure it will come in time."

"I don't understand you sometimes."

He laughed. He reached out to wrap her tightly in an embrace. "It's all right. I am a patient man."

* * *

King Silas' airship descended with the evening sun. His austere guide flanked him on either side as he strode purposefully across the airstrip to meet his reception party at the gate. Draven bowed low to his King. Kai and Abraham dipped their heads respectfully. Silas clapped Draven on the shoulder. He nodded brusquely to the others. "Come. Lead me to Jila."

Draven fell into step with his King. Kai trailed silently behind them, allowing them to speak alone in quiet murmurs. In Jila's audience chamber, a great, imposing, domed room panelled in brass, Silas stepped away from his Commander to greet the Queen. She awaited them anxiously. She looked fraught and weary. She flushed in pleasure when Silas entered the room, however. She inclined her head as he bowed low over her hand. "Silas. You came."

He guided her to sit by his side. "My dear Jila, my Commander has apprised me of what has occurred in your country. An assassin with no face and no name."

Jila nodded. "He says he does not come from Julian, but how can we be sure? We know nothing about him."

"It is very serious, undeniably. Is there nothing you know of him?"

"Only that he can change his face. He can become anyone he wishes. He can become you or I or any of our people. He can go places no one else can go. He is like a phantom or a ghost. He could be everywhere."

Silas' lips curved slightly. "He could be me."

Jila raised her eyebrows. "He could be you. How can I know it is you, Silas?"

He smirked. "I know things only you and I could know."

"Such as?"

Silas glanced over his shoulder at Kai and Draven. They exchanged a perplexed look. "My Queen, perhaps now is not the appropriate venue for such confessions."

Jila laughed wryly. "No, indeed, now is not the time. I can only hope that it is really you and not a mysterious phantom who will strike when we least expect."

"So he is Abyssal, this phantom?"

"He can only be. We cannot fight him or find him. It is only Abyss that can turn a man to a chameleon."

Silas sighed. "It is a very dangerous situation, but I will stand by your side, Jila. If Julian is involved, we must expose him and determine how to deal with him appropriately."

"Can you still be convinced it is his work, after all that occurred?"

Silas considered, but it was Draven who spoke. "Your Majesty, the assassin allowed us to capture him, in your subject's guise. We believe he could have escaped us at any time. Why allow us to capture and question him if he did not have something he intended for us to hear?"

"You believe he allowed you to capture him in order to lead us astray?"

"Perhaps. We cannot begin to fathom what his intentions are at this juncture."

"Your Majesty," Silas put in, "the Duke has attempted great harm. It is safe to believe he is related to this in some way, if through his people. His full participation must be determined. Even if he is merely aware and had no hand in the plot, he should be brought to task for failing to forestall it. I know of no man in Leza who can become anyone he wishes. Do you know of such a person in your own country?"

"No, Silas. Of course I don't."

"Do you truly believe you would not be aware of such a person? With your resources?"

She considered. "No. You are right. I would have known. My flies and my people keep me apprised of all that occurs in my cities." She sighed, resting her chin on her hand. "This man cannot belong to Varuna"

"So he can only belong to Tyr."

"Or to the lands outside the Abyssium zone."

Kai exchanged a glance with Draven. "Your Majesties, there may be someone who knows something about this assassin," she said. They all looked at her, startled.

"May there?" Draven demanded.

She shrugged. "He is one of our people, but he knows many things. Perhaps he has heard of this assassin from Tyr or beyond our three countries. If anyone may possess the information we seek, it will be he."

"Ptolemy," Draven said flatly.

Kai inclined her head. Silas nodded sharply. "Go. Speak to your contact. Find out what you can about the man with no face, his means, methods, his purpose and who might have hired him."

"He may not know those things, but he may have at least heard something of him. If there is such a man that may be engaged to kill, my associate will know about him," Kai said confidently.

"I'll go with you," Draven announced. Then he turned to bow to Silas. "If that is acceptable, My Lord?"

Silas nodded. "Yes. Yes, go on. Jila and I will stay here where we will be protected." He turned his attention to Jila once more. He seemed to have forgotten them as completely as if they were no longer in the room.

Kai smirked at Draven. They bowed to their sovereigns in unison and ducked out of the room. "To be a fly on that wall," Kai muttered in the hallway.

Draven shook his head. "I don't think I really want to know that much about my King."

"I, Commander, will endeavour to imagine wildly enough for the both of us."

CHAPTER FIFTEEN

*P*tolemy was sitting alone in his alcove in the Fool's Errand when they arrived. His impassive face did not change as they approached him. His eyes widened slightly, as if he were surprised to see them interrupt him without warning. They did not waste time with formalities or observe his customs. When he caught the gravity of their expressions, he gestured them to sit.

"Has something happened?" he asked in a low, sombre voice. "Have you discovered Wick?"

Kai inclined her head. "Yes, Ptolemy. I'm sorry. He's dead."

Ptolemy was silent a long moment. "It was not one of my people."

"We know," Draven told him.

"You know who did it?"

"A man with no face," Kai said. Ptolemy raised his eyebrows. His eyes slid shiftily away. Kai narrowed her eyes at him.

Draven glanced at Kai then back at Ptolemy. "We need to know what you know about him. The assassin with no face who is made from the Abyss."

Ptolemy's eyes darted wildly around the room. His expression was hunted. He looked frightened for the first time since Kai had met him. The look was strange and alien on his smooth, dark features. "I know nothing about such a man," he said in a low voice.

"Yes, you do, Ptolemy," Kai replied coldly.

He stared at her for a long moment. "I did not think he was real. I did not think such a man really existed. He is only a legend."

"A legend?"

Ptolemy sighed. He tossed back the dark liquid in the crystal tumbler before him. "There are tales of a man who is called when all other assassins have failed, when there is no one left who can take a job. Of course, his history is sordid and tragic."

"What is his name?"

Ptolemy shook his head. "He has no name. He is not called anything. He is not spoken of but in rumour and whispers and night time horror stories other assassins tell their children."

"What do you know about him?" Kai demanded insistently.

"He was once killed and brought back to life with Abyss. He's indestructible. He cannot be killed, and he cannot be stopped. Once he is set upon someone, once he has been dispatched, he will not stop until his target is dead."

"How is he reached?"

Ptolemy shook his head. "I don't know. How would I know?"

"I think you know. You always know."

Ptolemy looked down at his empty glass, as if the answers could be found there. When he glanced back up at them, his eyes were guarded. "I don't know if it's real. It's only what people say. When I took over the guild, my predecessor told me, but I did not believe it was really true. I thought he was merely trying to scare me, to tease me."

"Ptolemy, get to the point."

"My predecessor told me he can only be reached at the boundaries of the world."

"The boundaries of the world?" Draven demanded, frowning.

"It's an island. Out on the ocean, as far as anyone has ever gone. It is outside our three countries' boundaries, owned by no sovereignty. It is uninhabitable, all rock. No one can walk on its shores. They can fly but never land."

"Is that a metaphor?"

Ptolemy looked irritated. "No. It's the way it is. An airship or boat would be dashed to pieces on the shore. If you want the man with no face, you leave a stone carved with the name of the person you want dead."

"A carved stone?" Kai asked sceptically.

"Well, yes, it's a legend, you see. It's romantic."

"Romantic?" Draven repeated. "Murder is romantic?"

Ptolemy smirked. "It depends upon whom you ask, doesn't it? Besides, if you want someone dead acutely enough to hire him, carving a stone is nothing." He looked exasperated at their scepticism. "It's symbolic, don't you see?"

Kai rolled her eyes. "All right. Go on."

"And you leave Abyss."

"How much Abyss?"

"A lot. More than most people can afford. He uses it to sustain himself, you see. If you've given him enough, he will pursue your target relentlessly. To the end."

"So you've never actually seen him?"

"How would I know? He has no face. He can be anyone. He could be me." When they scowled dangerously at him, he held up his hands. "All right, all right. Don't get that look on your faces. It was only a jest."

"Humour doesn't suit you, Ptolemy," Kai told him irritably.

He chuckled wryly. "No, it doesn't. Nor does it suit your predicament, I shouldn't wonder, if you're up against the man with no face."

"How do you know we are?" Draven asked suspiciously.

"You wouldn't have asked about him otherwise. No one asks about him, not unless they truly want someone dead. Dead forever. And you two don't seem that sort."

They glanced at each other. "Where is he from?" Kai asked.

Ptolemy shrugged, as if this were of no particular consequence. "I don't know. Maybe here, maybe some other land we've never heard of. Does it matter?"

"Maybe."

Ptolemy looked sombre. "I do not think it does. He is loyal to no one. He recognises no master. He is a machine. He cares only for sustaining himself. He exists to perpetuate his own existence."

They exhaled heavily and glanced at each other. "How is he stopped? There must be a way to call him back," Draven said.

Ptolemy shook his head. "I told you. There is no way to stop him."

"There must be a way!"

"I'm sorry, Kai. Once he has begun, he will not stop. Not until the end."

* * *

Draven flipped open his communicator in the centre of the dark street outside the Fool's Errand. He impatiently jabbed a series of buttons. His Lieutenant's face appeared on the small, circular screen. "Commander?"

"Are Silas and the Queen safe?"

"Yes, sir."

"Keep them in the drawing room. Do not allow them to hold court or audiences," Draven ordered curtly. "They are to see no one, regardless of whom they ask for, until we have returned. Do you understand?"

"Yes, Commander."

"We are on our way back to the palace."

"Yes, sir."

Draven flipped the brass lid shut and looked at Kai. "We have to find something that neutralises the Abyss. We have to find a way to prove it was the Duke who hired the assassin."

Kai sighed. "Just that?" she asked flippantly. "Neither of those are small feats, you know."

"No, they aren't." He frowned. He glanced around the street then back down at her. "What will stop him? What will shut down the Abyss?"

Kai shook her head. Her mouth twitched uneasily, and her eyes slid away.

"What is it, Kai?"

"Draven, I'm Abyssal. If it defuses him, it may do the same to me, as well. I will be unable to help you." He nodded resolutely. She added, "I will not be able to help you if you are hurt."

He smirked. "I can handle myself."

"I want to be sure!"

He blinked. He was startled by her vehemence. "Kai, he is nothing without the Abyss."

"Nor am I," she whispered.

He smiled. "You are not what is inside you." He stepped towards her. He folded her into an embrace.

She relaxed against him, sighing. "Thank you for the reassurance, but that isn't entirely true. I will be powerless if my Abyss is neutralized. I don't even know if I'll still be alive."

"It won't come to that."

"It might."

164

"Then you won't be there."

Kai shook her head vehemently. "I will be there. We'll take our chances. Jila can bring me back if something happens." She paused and looked up into his face. "I don't know what I will do if something happens to you when I am unable to stop it."

He chuckled. "I appreciate the sentiment, Kaia. I will endeavour to stay alive until you are back on your feet."

"You had better do."

He stepped away from her. "What is it? What can we use against him?"

"I don't know, not exactly, but I know someone who will."

"You do seem to know a lot of useful people."

She smirked. "In my line of work, it is beneficial to know all sorts of people."

* * *

They stepped off the flyer onto a narrow, quiet street in a wealthy neighbourhood. The storefronts were sparkling and pristine in their newness and care. The cobblestones were brilliant white. There was no rubbish or debris polluting the streets. Women strode confidently along the thoroughfare without the necessity of an escort. A gaggle of schoolchildren rode shining bicycles with large, thick wheels. They laughed and called happily to each other as they ran in and out of the sweets shop on the corner.

Draven glanced at Kai. His eyebrows arched in surprise. "This is not where I would have expected to find an illicit Abyssal engineer," he admitted.

"No, well, it wouldn't be very clever to work out of a sinister, abandoned warehouse, would it? For one thing, who would trust an engineer who couldn't secure appropriate premises?" Draven hesitated. She looked at him sternly. "Are you under the impression all my contacts are criminal?"

He chuckled. "Well, I suppose I was."

"You're wrong. Dr Creed is licensed. He is one of the very best."

She led him away from the busy thoroughfare, into a dark, narrow and slightly shabby alley. There were no tramps or brigands lurking in the debris. Kai paused in front of a large, bolted steel door which looked as if no man or machine could breach it. "So why isn't his name on the storefront?" Draven asked archly.

Kai glanced at him with a smirk. "It doesn't need to be. If you need Dr Creed,

165

you know where to find him." She pushed a small, nearly invisible button on the stone wall beside the door.

For a long moment, nothing happened. Draven looked at her dubiously. Abruptly, a voice barked over a concealed speaker above their heads. "Identify yourself."

"It's Vale," Kai announced, looking up towards the speaker.

There was another long pause. "Come in, Kai."

A soft, metallic click signalled the door's release. Kai pulled it open without any visible effort. They stepped into a large, open space that glittered with its intense sterility. The walls were polished steel. The entire room glowed an eerie, electric blue. In the centre of the room was a large, strange apparatus: a globular brass ball with a long, wide barrel. Beneath the barrel was a sort of stretcher with tubes, gauges and appendages sticking out from every angle. In the corner of the laboratory, a large, cylindrical brass tank pumped liquefied Abyss through the long, glowing blue tube that fed the apparatus.

A tall, thin man in a white lab coat with hair like steel wool and lustrous, manic blue eyes greeted them with a nod. It was difficult to determine his age, for his face was pale and unlined, strangely stretched across his bones. He smiled when he saw them. He offered a hand swathed in a thick, black rubber glove to Kai. Draven glanced down at it distastefully. Dr Creed chuckled. He removed the gloves. He tucked them into the pocket of his white lab coat. "Dr Creed," he informed Draven, shaking his hand.

"Draven Lockley."

"I have heard of you, Commander Lockley. I would not have expected to see you here, with Kai Vale of all people."

Draven inclined his head. "There is a matter at hand that concerns us both."

Creed lifted his brows. "Are you in disrepair, Kai?"

"No, doctor. We need your help with another matter."

"Ah. Well, I am always pleased to offer my services to you and your cousin."

Draven was not listening to their exchange. He was eyeing the apparatus sceptically. "What exactly do you do here, Dr Creed?"

"Whatever is required of me, for a price." Creed looked at him in interest. "What is it you need of me today, Commander?"

Draven looked at Kai. She turned to Creed to reply. "Have you heard of a man

166

with no face? An assassin?"

Creed hesitated. He glanced cagily about. "Yes, I have heard of such a man. But I did not think he was real. If such a man existed, he would be an abomination. No engineer would do such a thing to a man. That sort of man would not be a man at all."

"He isn't a man, but he is real."

"Is he?" His voice was soft. He was silent a long moment in deliberation. When he looked back at them, his expression was blank. "Why have you come to me? I have nothing to do with him."

"No, we do not suspect that you do," Draven replied stiffly. "However, you do have something we need."

Creed narrowed his eyes. "What is it?"

"Something to stop him. Something to defuse the Abyss."

"Ah." He looked at Kai.

"It is a request from Her Majesty, the Queen," Kai said. "She requires it."

Creed exhaled heavily, but he nodded. "Do you have such a thing?" Draven asked firmly.

Creed's gaze snapped back to him. He nodded shortly. He disappeared behind a curtain they hadn't known was there until the shiny fabric, the exact shade as the walls around them, rippled like liquid. Draven glanced at Kai. Her face was stoic. She did not speak as they awaited the doctor's return. Her breath was slightly short. He stepped closer to her.

Creed appeared around the curtain once more. It rippled for a moment. When it stopped moving, it was as if it had disappeared. Draven blinked. He was unable to find the crease again. Creed looked at him reproachfully. Draven turned his attention to the long, metal rod in the doctor's hand. "What is it?" Draven asked.

Creed held it out to him. "Electricity."

"Electricity?"

Kai took a step back. Creed's eyes slid to her before he turned back to Draven. "It is the opposite of Abyssium. Abyss is of the sea, it is of the sky."

"But what does it do?"

Creed held up the wand. "It is concentrated lightning."

"But what is it for?"

"It burns out the Abyss." Draven raised his eyebrows in interest and reached for it. Kai gave it a wary look. The doctor frowned sternly at Draven. "Do not handle it lightly, Commander. It is fatal to a man. It would burn them up, too. It is for machines, not people."

Draven's expression was grim. "This is not a man. He is a construct."

Creed hesitated. He glanced at Kai. She nodded reluctantly. The doctor placed the wand into Draven's hands. Draven tucked it away in his jacket. "Handle it carefully. If you miss, if you hit Kai or any other human, they will die."

Draven glanced at Kai grimly. "I can assure you, Doctor, I would never allow that to happen."

Draven turned. The doctor placed a hand lightly on his arm. "I will need it back, if you would be so obliging. It is one of a kind. Such a thing is not so easy to come by."

Kai raised her eyebrows. "Where did you get it?"

The doctor hesitated. "From the lands outside the Abyssal zones. A place where I may never again venture. It is irreplaceable. I ask that you treat it with great care."

Draven bowed to him. "Dr Creed, I assure you, I will do everything in my power to see it is returned safely to your hands."

Kai offered him her hand to shake. "My old friend, our Queen will be most grateful for your contribution to her safety."

Dr Creed smirked. "Yes, the Queen has much for which to be grateful to me by now."

Kai inclined her head. "I will see that you receive appropriate compensation."

Now he smiled. "I ask only that I am allowed to continue my work, as you well know."

"You will have all you require, Doctor. I shall see you again soon."

"Let us hope that that is true, Kai. Please, take care. You must make absolutely certain to remain out of the way of the lightning. There is nothing I can do for you if you are struck."

* * *

It was dark and silent outside the Queen's palace. Draven alighted from the flyer, offering his arm to Kai. She hesitated, eyeing the silver wand tucked in

168

his belt. He rolled his eyes and gripped her waist. He lifted her off the deck and deposited her soundly on the ground. She glared at him. When she saw his arch expression, she smiled slightly. "I never would have taken you for timid, Kaia."

She scowled at him. "Timid! I am merely concerned that the thing you're carrying around on your belt could turn me into a smouldering pile of ash."

He raised an eyebrow. "How about what I'm carrying around under my belt?"

"Your innuendo will not distract me from the death stick you're wielding as if it were nothing more than an ornamental baton."

He chuckled and wrapped an arm around her shoulders. "Come now, Kaia, do you really think I would allow you near it if it could hurt you?"

A throat cleared. A figure materialised from the darkness before them. "Abraham," Kai greeted when she recognised him. His posture was rigid, and his expression was grim as he approached them swiftly. "Has something happened?"

He relaxed slightly. "No. The King and Queen are quite safe, as when you left them. The palace is peaceful, for the moment. It will fall to pieces and chaos soon enough, I shouldn't wonder."

Kai breathed a soft sigh of relief. "We must speak to Jila at once."

Abraham inclined his head. He turned smartly on his heel to stride beside them towards Jila's chambers. "Of course. Have you learned something?"

"Yes. The man with no face is Abyssal."

Abraham lifted a dark, bushy eyebrow. "This is something we did not already know?"

"Of course we knew. He could be nothing else." She sighed then recited Ptolemy's tale. "He is a legend among assassins. He is reached at the boundaries of the world."

Abraham looked interested. "The boundaries of the world?"

"The island at the edge of the sea," Draven added.

"Even the assassins fear him," Kai put in. "He is unstoppable."

"That's dramatic. If he's unstoppable, how do you intend to deal with him?"

Kai and Draven glanced at each other. They did not answer as they reached Jila's chambers. The Lezan guards nodded to Draven and stepped instantly aside. Kai scowled. She did not point out that they might not be who they appeared at all and thus should not be so readily permitted entry. She was quite sure she was herself, and almost equally sure Draven was not the changing man. Still, a bit of caution might be the thing.

"Commander, the King and Queen have not ventured from the room. They are perfectly safe, I can assure you," Lieutenant Rhames informed them curtly.

Draven inclined his head. "Has anyone approached?"

"If they had, he probably wouldn't still be standing here, and the King and Queen would be nothing more than memories," Kai muttered.

They ignored her. "No, Commander. It has been all peace and quiet."

"Allow us to enter, if you please, Lieutenant."

He hesitated. Kai rolled her eyes. At least now someone was behaving with a bit of sense. The Lieutenant nodded. He opened the door to bow them inside. When they strode into the audience chamber, Silas and Jila were sitting with their heads together on the divan, murmuring in low voices. They looked up as they heard the footsteps approach and rose in unison to greet the arrivals.

"Ah, you have returned," Silas said. He nodded to them as they bowed in greeting. "Have you discovered anything that might be of use?"

"Yes, much," Draven replied. "We believe we may have--"

He trailed off, spinning in surprise. Abraham strode forwards, shoving blithely past him. The major-domo had moved so quickly and silently, no one had seen or sensed the shift until he was upon the King. A knife shot out from the sleeve of his charcoal grey suit. He swung his arm in a tight, efficient arch. Blood spurted instantly from the yawning slash in Silas' belly and pooled at his feet on the floor before anyone else had even moved.

"Silas!" Jila shrieked. She lunged towards him. The King clung to her. His eyes rolled towards her in shock as they dropped together to the floor.

Draven spun. He yanked the wand from his belt. Abraham was already nearly to the door, moving so quickly he was a strange, shifting blur. Kai was nearly as fast. She seized the treacherous major-domo's shoulder. Draven fired the wand at him. Silver light crackled through the air. The hairs on the back of his arm stood straight up.

"Kai, don't touch him!" Draven shouted. It was too late. She collapsed beside the impostor on the floor. Her long, pale hair smoked slightly. He cursed viciously. He spun on his heel and dropped to the floor beside his sovereign.

Silas groped his hand towards his Commander. Draven moved to relieve Queen Jila of the King's weight. Jila bent over Silas. Her hands were soaked in his blood. "Silas! No!" she said in a desperate, commanding tone. She pressed her hands to the wound. They did little to ebb the flow of his blood across the gleaming scarlet carpet.

Silas rolled stricken eyes to Draven. "My King," Draven said in a low, wavering voice. "I am sorry."

The King opened his mouth as if he intended to speak. His head lolled forwards. His entire body slackened. Draven cupped his cheek gently, tilting Silas' face back to look at him. The King's eyes were glazed and blank. Silas saw nothing more. A single tear slid from the corner of Draven's eye. He did not wipe it away. He looked up at the Queen. His voice cracked as he spoke.

"I'm sorry, My Queen, he is gone."

Jila pressed her face to Silas' neck. Her shoulders shook violently with her sobs. Draven left her alone, staring in shocked silence at the King's still face. After a long moment, Jila's head snapped up. The expression in her dark eyes was glacial and unwavering. "We can do nothing more for him now."

He watched her rise and wipe Silas' blood on the folds of her skirt. He looked at her in surprise. Jila pushed past him towards Kai and her major-domo. Draven slid carefully out from under Silas' limp form. The King's assassin no longer looked anything like the Queen's once steadfast and trustworthy major-domo. In his place was a thin, fragile and wan-looking old man with a deeply lined face. He smelled of burning hair and flesh.

Draven leaned over him. He snapped shackles upon his wrists and ankles. It seemed hardly as if the feeble man could offer resistance. He could not be sure, however, how long Dr Creed's bolt would pacify him. He shouted tersely for Rhames, who rushed into the room. Rhames paused to look upon the scene in aghast silence. His mouth dropped open. "Take him to the dungeon," Draven barked. "If he wakes, if he moves, hit him with this."

Lieutenant Rhames took the wand gingerly from his Commander's hand. He nodded curtly. "Silas?"

"He's dead. Watch the prisoner constantly. Call me immediately if something changes. Do not let him out of your sight!"

"Yes, sir." Lieutenant Rhames lifted the diminutive man without effort. The assassin's brittle bones rattled. Draven did not pause to see if his second had followed his orders. He moved immediately to Kai's side.

"Kai?" Jila asked in a low voice.

Draven lifted the pale woman into his lap. He brushed her singed hair from her face. It was white as marble, still as a statue, but as he leaned over her, he felt her breath upon his cheek. He checked her pulse. It was still strong. He sighed heavily in relief. It had not killed her. Whatever damage it might have done, she was still alive. She looked like a pale, fragile porcelain doll in his arms. He drew his finger lightly down her cheek.

"Is she all right?" Jila's voice was hushed. Her features were stony.

"She is alive. I don't know if…I don't know if she will wake."

Jila lifted her chin defiantly. "She will wake. I will not allow her not to."

Draven smiled slightly. He stood, bringing Kai in his arms. "This has gone too far, My Queen."

"Yes," she agreed firmly. "It has."

"We have him now. We will end this."

"How will you prove he was sent by the Duke?"

Draven peered down at Kai's still, peaceful face, then back up at the Queen. His dark eyes were bright. His expression was rigid. "I will find a way. There is nothing else left in the world for me to do." His breath hitched. "How will we tell Queen Leona? She will be beside herself."

Jila's jaw set. "I will deal with Leona. You take care of my cousin. She is very important to me."

"I swear to you, Your Majesty, I will do all in my power. She is important to me, as well."

"I do not doubt that, Commander. I trust you will care for her accordingly." Jila took a deep breath and straightened her shoulders. "Enough sentiment. We've enough to be getting on with."

CHAPTER SIXTEEN

"*R*ai. Kaia!"

Her eyelids fluttered slightly. She became aware that she was lying on her back, ensconced in the familiar softness of her bed. Her eyes stung. Her head throbbed. She whimpered softly, squeezing her eyes shut against the faint, red light burning behind her lids. She wanted nothing more than to lay perfectly still until the darkness took her once again, far, far away from the pain of her sudden awakening. Why did her entire body ache all the way to her bones?

"Kaia."

His voice was gallingly authoritative. Her brow furrowed. He chuckled low in his throat. There was a slightly hysterical edge to his voice. Her eyes flew open. "I will wake up when I am good and ready, Draven."

He exhaled heavily in relief and caught her face abruptly in her hands. He kissed her soundly on the mouth. "You're all right. Are you all right?"

She batted him away. She sat up gingerly. "I feel all right. Well, not really. My entire body hurts. Even my teeth hurt. You activated me?"

"Yes. Proceeding deactivating you, which I assure you I did not intend to do. Hurts how?"

"I'll be fine. But Creed said the lightning was fatal."

"Yes. But you were only touching the old man; it didn't strike you directly."

"The old man?"

"The man with no face." His jaw set rigidly. "He is only an old man now. He is nothing."

"I don't understand what you're saying."

"He has a face. And he has a name, if we can get it from him."

She raised her eyebrows. "You got him this time?"

"Yes. He's in the dungeon."

"Is he going to come back from the bolt like I did?"

"Not if I can help it."

She hesitated. "Silas?" she asked softly.

Draven looked away. "He's gone."

"I'm sorry, Draven."

"Yes. I am sorry, too." He lowered his head. His breath hitched. "I loved him, you know. He was a friend. I was loyal to him." He closed his eyes. "And he died in my arms."

She lifted her hand, cradling his cheek in her palm. He opened his eyes to look at her in surprise. "What do we do now?" she asked. There was a dark, sick feeling in her stomach. She didn't like it. There were a lot of things going on inside her that she didn't like.

"Your cousin is safe for now. We have our man. We have to find out who sent him. And we will bring whomever he is to justice for killing my King."

Kai nodded. She rolled resolutely out of bed. "I am ready."

"You should rest."

"No. I'm ready. I will help you. I will not let your master die in vain." Draven scowled. Finally, he nodded. She asked, "Do you think he will talk?"

"It is not, at this time, a matter of whether or not he will talk. He may never wake up."

"He's not dead, is he?"

"No. By all accounts, he seems quite fit for a man of his age."

"He's old?"

"Very." He sighed, turning away from her. "Everything may be lost."

"Not lost. We have him. It's over."

"At what cost?"

She sighed. She moved forwards to touch his shoulder. He spun towards her, startling her. He folded her into his arms and rested his chin on the top of her head. "He will wake," she said firmly. "And when he does, he will talk. We will convince him there is no other option."

He chuckled wryly. "How?"

She smirked. "I will find a way. I always do. I can be extremely persuasive when the situation requires it."

He did not sound at all amused when he replied, "That alarms me a bit."

174

"It should."

* * *

Lieutenant Rhames awaited them outside the door to the Queen's dungeon. "Rhames?" Draven asked brusquely.

"He's awake."

Kai and Draven glanced at each other. "Has he shown any sign of regaining his Abyssal abilities?" Draven asked.

Rhames shook his head. "No. He seems like any other man. Older. Weaker. Crazier. But otherwise quite normal."

"Is he talking?"

Rhames hesitated. "He's talking."

"What is he saying?" Kai asked keenly.

Rhames shook his head. "It's mostly nonsense. He's completely taken by the Abyssium madness. We could only make out a couple words. He's extremely disoriented, and he doesn't seem to know who he is or how he got here." Draven frowned. Kai sighed in frustration. Rhames added, "He certainly doesn't remember what happened or what has been going on with the attempts against the Queen and...Silas' murder."

"What is he saying?" Kai demanded.

"It sounds like a name."

"A name? His name?"

"There's no way to know. I've never heard it before."

"Well?" Kai asked impatiently. "What is it?"

"Enyo Fane. Does it mean anything to you?"

Draven glanced at Kai. She shook her head. "No," she replied. "I've never heard it before. Are you sure that's what he's saying?"

"Come hear for yourself."

It was astonishing that the frightened, mad and pitiful old man huddled in the corner of the cell could be the legendary deadly Abyssal assassin, the stuff of wee assassins' nightmares. Kai and Draven exchanged a doubtful, worried frown. They returned their attention to the disoriented prisoner. He rocked agitatedly on his haunches. "Do you think he's faking it?" Kai asked quietly.

Draven hesitated. He shook his head. "I don't know. I don't think so. It could be this is who he is without the Abyss." He stepped towards the bars. He addressed the old man in a carrying, authoritative voice. "Who are you?"

The old man lifted his head, but his wild, blue eyes did not seem to see them at all. He appeared only distantly aware that he was not alone in the cell. He muttered quietly to himself. They leaned forwards to hear what he said. Rhames sighed. "He hasn't moved, and that is all we can get out of him. It's nonsense."

Draven sighed, but he directed his question to the old man. "Do you remember anything?"

The old man didn't look at him. "Enyo. Fane."

Kai and Draven looked at each other unhappily. They reared back when the old man shot to his feet. He threw himself against the bars. His expression was mad and eerily feral. "Enyo Fane!" he repeated.

Draven stepped forwards to peer into his unblinking eyes. "All right. We'll find out who Enyo Fane is. We'll find out who you are."

"Enyo Fane." His eyes suddenly filled. Tears streaked down his cheeks. They dripped down his trembling chin.

Kai spun away from him abruptly. She fluttered her fingers over her brow. Draven glanced at the weeping prisoner, then he sighed and turned to Kai. "Kai?"

She shook her head. Her tone was angry when she spoke. "He's just a sad, barmy old man. Can it really be him who did all this?" She glanced over her shoulder. Her long, pale hair concealed her face and hid her expression from him. "The Abyss changes you. It makes you something not quite right."

He laid his hands gently on her shoulders. "Kaia, you're not like him."

She turned to him. Her face was utterly blank. "Can you be so sure I won't be someday?"

He didn't hesitate. "Yes."

Her lips twitched at this. Her expression softened slightly. Then she squared her shoulders and turned to Rhames. "We need Abraham."

"Abraham?" Rhames asked, startled, as if the name meant nothing to him.

"If anyone can find out what that name means, it's him."

Draven looked at his soldier sternly. "Have we located the major-domo?"

176

Rhames blinked. "Yes, sir. He was discovered in his chambers."

Kai looked alarmed for a split second. Draven suspected she was remembering the state of the Baron Omari on the occasion when they had discovered him in his bed. "Is he all right?"

"Yes. He's alive. He was merely stunned." Rhames frowned slightly. "We are uncertain why he was not killed."

They considered this a moment. "Perhaps he had no need to kill him," Draven mused.

"But he killed Gregori. The need can't have been greater?" Kai replied.

"Well, we assume he killed Gregori. Perhaps he simply chose the identity of someone already dead. Maybe it was your Assassins' Guild who did him."

"It doesn't matter now. We need to see Abraham."

"Is he coherent?" Draven asked his soldier.

Rhames inclined his head. "He should be. There was no lasting damage."

Kai nodded and seized Draven's hand. "There's no more time to waste."

* * *

Abraham's ruddy features were ghastly pale. He looked as if he'd recently been sick. He was otherwise unharmed. He sat up in the four-poster bed in his chambers when Kai and Draven entered unannounced. He sighed, pressing his hand to his forehead. "I suppose you want to hear my version of events, as well?" he asked wearily.

"No," Kai replied shortly. "We can extrapolate. Abe, we need your assistance and your particular expertise."

Abraham arched an eyebrow. "Already? I've not even had a night's sleep after being stunned and impersonated in order to assassinate the King of a foreign country, not to mention questioned endlessly regarding my part in the matter, which I assure you is none at all. Can you not come back in the morning?"

"Feeling grumpy, are you?" Kai asked with a wry smirk.

"Need I repeat the events of this evening for your understanding?"

Draven's expression was arctic. "No. No need. I lost my King tonight, and you are the one who can help us find out the identity of the man responsible."

Abraham's face fell. He nodded. "Of course. Forgive me. What can I do?"

"Enyo Fane," Kai said. "Does it mean anything to you?"

Abraham frowned. He shook his head. "No. But it will within the hour."

"I knew you wouldn't fail us, Abraham."

"Yes, well, when I have fulfilled my duty to King, Queen and country, I will expect you will not fail in ensuring me a very long night's sleep. My head is simply killing me."

* * *

The night sky glittered through the domed glass in Jila's audience chambers. The meagre torchlight set their grim, silent faces in eerie shadow. Tragedy hung in the air around them, shrouding the room in darkness and the hush of mourning. After a long, terrible moment, Jila lifted her red, weary eyes to Draven. Her soft, toneless voice rent the stillness. It startled her companions. "I have spoken to your Queen."

Draven's back stiffened. He inclined his head. He seemed to have nothing to offer in response or was simply too choked with grief to speak.

Jila sighed. "She is most aggrieved. The loss of her husband is a terrible tragedy, but she does not blame Varuna for the murder. She is anxious to bring the Duke to justice." Draven responded now with a deep, weary sigh. "She is coming to claim his body." Her eyes were sharp. Her expression narrowed. "And I intended to have the answers she is seeking when she arrives."

Draven glanced at Kai, who remained firmly tacit, and nodded. "We will have your answers, My Queen."

"I have the utmost confidence, Commander."

A soft, metallic tinkle signalled an arrival outside the audience chambers, and the sombre party exchanged anxious glances. Kai rose to open the door. She allowed a staunch and composed Abraham inside. His colour had improved. As he strode inside, clutching a dossier tightly to his chest, his dark eyes glinted in triumph.

Jila stood, striding to meet him. He bowed to her. She reached out to press his hand in hers. "Abraham, dear friend, are you well?"

He inclined his head. "I am much improved, Your Highness. Thank you."

She smiled wanly and gestured towards the audience chairs. "Come. Sit. Have you learned something?"

He nodded and perched on the edge of a chair across from the Queen. He laid

178

the dossier on the table between them. "It is most shocking, my Queen, I assure you," he told her, but his expression was almost gleeful. "But I believe in it you shall find the confirmation of the Duke's treachery you seek."

The party looked around at each other again, their expressions fixed and anxious. "You have discovered what the name means?" Kai asked after a long silence.

Abraham inclined his head. "Yes. It is his name."

"Truly?"

"His mind is so addled by the Abyss, it is likely all he remembers of his past."

"Who is he?" Jila demanded. Kai snatched the dossier from the table before she could reach it. Jila did not protest or scold her cousin. Her eyes were fixed upon her major-domo.

"Enyo Fane is Duke Julian's grandfather."

Stunned silence fell upon them all. "His grandfather?" Jila asked finally in a low, shocked voice. "How is that possible? I thought he was killed many years ago, when I was still a child."

"He was," Abraham replied gravely. "Or, he nearly was. He was attacked by an angry mob during the peasant uprising twenty years ago and injured mortally. His grandson took him to Yuri Gage."

Draven frowned. "I don't know that name."

Kai's teeth clenched. "He is an Abyssal engineer. Or he was, many years ago. He is dead now. He died in prison, where he was sent for conducting horrifying experiments with the Abyss."

"Julian's grandfather was one of them," Abraham added.

"So he survived," Jila said. Her major-domo nodded.

"Yes. When he awoke, he was changed, as you saw him before he lost the Abyss. He was not the man he once was; he was taken with the madness. He needed more and more Abyss just to survive until he was incurably dependent upon it."

Jila's expression was horrified. "And Julian employed him as an assassin?" When Abraham nodded, she looked uneasy. "Are you certain it is him, in our dungeon?"

"It can only be him."

Draven frowned thoughtfully. "How were you able to learn all of this?" he demanded bluntly.

A smirk twisted Abraham's characteristically bland features. "I have a network of spies and informants that would dumbfound you, Commander."

Draven lifted a single eyebrow. "That unsettles me."

Abraham nodded. His tone was completely serious when he replied, "It should."

Jila sighed and shook her head ruefully. "It is not enough to conclusively implicate Julian in the plot."

Kai scowled. "What more do you want, cousin? The man is his grandfather."

"Your Majesty is right," Draven put in, avoiding Kai's glare. "Though he is Julian's kin--or was before he became what he is now--Ptolemy said he could be hired by anyone with enough Abyss. We still cannot prove it was Julian. If we accuse him without evidence, it could result in a grave diplomatic disaster."

Jila rose regally to her feet. "Thank you for understanding my position, Commander. I look forward to what you are able to learn. Myself, I shall wait here for Queen Leona. She will need a strong companion to assist her through the terrible days to come."

"Yes, Your Majesty."

CHAPTER SEVENTEEN

Cnyo Fane huddled on the dirt floor of his tiny, dank cell. His arms curled around his body and his eyes squeezed tightly shut as if to protect himself from the onslaught of the madness. His low, rumbling mutters, the foam gathered in the corners of his mouth, suggested it was creeping upon him as steadily as the night. Watching him, Kai sighed deeply, leaning her forehead against the bars. "He is the walking dead. Without Abyss, he doesn't even know what his own name means."

Draven sighed, pausing beside her to stare at the once venerated, regal and dignified sovereign. He did not strain to listen to the man's continuous stream of senseless words. Apart from incomprehensible, they were useless to the investigation. "The only way to learn what he knows is to reactivate the Abyss?" His voice was low with a terrible resignation. "It is too great a risk. Even a moment of return to his former abilities and he will be lost to us forever."

"If we survived it," Kai replied dully.

"I fear electrifying him one more time would result in total paralysis or death."

Kai straightened, peering at him with raised eyebrows. "There may be a way, Draven. We may be able to regain his memories without reactivating the Abyss."

Draven frowned. "How?"

"He is stricken with the madness."

"Yes. Clearly." His tone was slightly impatient.

"But Dr Creed might be of further help."

Draven sighed deeply. "Are you certain? I am not entirely pleased with the solution he presented at the last."

"It functioned exactly as he suggested it would."

"You nearly died."

"That was hardly Creed's fault; his instrument was flawless. It was the wielding of it that was faulty." He opened his mouth to respond. His brow furrowed guiltily. She held up her hand. "It could hardly be construed as your fault when I was the one who touched him, rendering myself a target as well. In any case, I'm fit. And Creed's skill may be our only recourse at this time."

Draven sighed deeply. His jaw was rigid as he considered. He was not keen on Abyssal engineers. Their solutions hardly ever seemed to be worth the trouble they ultimately caused. Finally, he drew his communicator from his pocket and flipped it open.

"Rhames."

"Rhames, go into the city and find Dr Creed straight away. Abraham will direct you."

Rhames paused uncertainly, but his voice was brisk when he replied, "Yes, Commander. Of course."

Draven snapped the small, brass compact closed and looked sternly at Kai. "I hope you are right in thinking he can help."

Kai swivelled her gaze from him. She peered morosely down at the trembling old man. She sighed deeply. "As do I, Draven. If he cannot...we may never find the answers Jila seeks." She looked up at him. Her dark blue eyes were shadowed. "And I may someday end up just like him."

* * *

"Is this him? The man with no face?" Dr Creed's voice was hushed. The fascination on his face might have been reverence or revulsion.

"He was," Kai told him in a subdued voice. "You knew about him, then. What Yuri Gage did."

Creed glanced briefly at her. "The underworld is full of rumours. It is hard to keep secrets such as that from people such as I." He stared thoughtfully at Fane. "I admit, I did not truly believe it. If not for your word, I might not believe it still."

Draven did not share the engineer's fascination. He frowned. "He has no memory of what happened to him."

Dr Creed exhaled heavily through his nose. "Perhaps that is best. He is no longer a threat to us."

"We need his memories," Kai told him sharply. "We need him to tell us for whom he is working and to what purpose."

Creed frowned. "You want me to bring him back?"

"Without Abyss," Draven added sternly.

"I see." Creed's expression was thoughtful for a long moment. He glanced at them. "I believe I have a solution."

"Excellent. Carry on, then."

Creed smirked. "This might be a bit delicate. I will need to return to my lab."

* * *

Fane didn't struggle as Kai lifted him into Creed's crude, stiff-backed wooden chair. He twitched slightly as Creed strapped his wrists to the arms of the rigid seat. He did not protest or flail as his ankles were similarly secured. Kai stepped back to join Draven beside the Queens Jila and Leona. Silas' widow had arrived in mourning shrouds by airship moments before. She had been eager to see her husband's killer directly.

The Queens and their guard watched silently. Leona's expression was torn between murderous fury and uneasy scepticism. She seemed uncertain that the man they had captured could truly have perpetrated her husband's shocking and violent end. Kai certainly did not blame her. She might not have believed it herself, had she not seen of what the man had once been capable.

Leona cringed as Creed yanked tightly on the leather restraints. The old man's bones crackled ominously. "Is that strictly necessary?" Leona asked sharply. "There is nothing left of him. He is just an old man. He can hardly stand, let alone fight us all off."

Creed looked up at her mildly. "It is best not to take any chances." He turned back to the patient. He forced a leather bit between the old man's teeth.

Kai watched the doctor with uncanny concentration. She moved away from Draven to circle behind the patient. She laid her hands on his bony, trembling shoulders. Fane's eyes rolled backwards, showing the whites. He did not spit out the bit. He seemed thoroughly unaware of his surroundings and the proceedings. If he did know what was happening to him, he did not protest.

Creed adhered two small, white square pads to Fane's temples. They were brilliantly white against his ashen skin. The doctor attached two thin copper wires to either side.

"What are those?" Jila asked, leaning forwards in interest. "What is this device of yours, Creed?"

The dingus did not appear to be anything particularly exceptional. The wires he'd connected to the pads on the prisoner's temples terminated at the top of a small, smooth and shining brass ball. A gauge atop its centre bore incomprehensible symbols and squiggles. The needle inside spun indecisively, as if it were awaiting instructions. The ball rested upon a flat bottom. Creed placed it delicately on the floor at Fane's feet. "It is of my own design," he explained. "It will emit a brief, powerful pulse of energy directly into his brain, ideally stimulating the areas that contain his memories."

The looks of scepticism on their faces were identical. "Is it dangerous?" Draven asked.

Creed shrugged indifferently. "You might want to keep your distance. I've never actually employed it before. It may simply fry him and turn his brain to jelly."

Kai lifted her hands deliberately from Fane's shoulders, taking a step back. "Is it electricity again?"

Creed smirked slightly. He shook his head. "No. It's Abyssal." He lifted an eyebrow at her. "Still, it's probably best you don't touch him."

Jila sighed deeply. "Is there no other way?"

Creed peered down at the old man. "Not of which I am capable, my Queen. This man's brain is addled by the Abyss. He has the madness. No one has developed a conclusive cure yet. But this might temporarily bring him back to himself." He looked up at her. His blue eyes burned with sudden intensity. "If it works, My Queen, it could put us on the path towards a cure for the madness."

Draven frowned. "A better solution would be not putting it into your body in the first place," he barked.

Creed smirked. "Ah. A purist."

"I merely believe a human being should remain human. When you start modifying people with dangerous substances we barely understand, these are the results you achieve."

Jila cleared her throat pointedly. "Gentlemen, if I may interject, this is hardly an appropriate venue for such a debate. You may take it to the pub when we're through here. Can we focus on the task at hand, please?"

"Forgive us, my Queen," Creed replied briskly. He bowed respectfully to her. He crouched down in front of the patient and pressed a small rivet on the apparatus. It hummed ominously to life. He lifted his eyes to Jila. "My Queen?"

Jila hesitated. Her eyes darted to Leona, as if looking for her support. "If he dies, we've lost everything. My Queen?"

Leona was silent a moment, then she squared her shoulders and nodded resolutely. "I want the answer to who is responsible for my husband's murder. Please. I am willing to try anything. Get on with it."

Jila inclined her head to Creed. He took a deep, excited breath and pressed the slight indentation on the top of the ball. The needle inside the gauge jumped. The ball hummed in crescendo. The old man jerked violently with the sudden, intense pulse. His teeth bared and clenched against the leather bit. His eyes bulged. They were as blue as the sea and wild with shock.

After a long, terrible moment, Fane's body went limp. He was completely still. Kai glanced at Draven over the top of Fane's head. Her expression was rapt with horror. Creed cursed under his breath. He looked bleakly up at the Queens. "Forgive me, my Queens."

Jila took a step forwards. Her tone was sharp. "Is he dead? Did it fail?"

Leona's breath escaped in a soft, anguished sigh. Kai stepped towards the patient. She bent down in front of him. She seemed hesitant to touch him, but she leaned close to him with narrow eyes. "He's not dead," she announced.

"What?" Creed asked. He sounded startled.

"He isn't dead. He's still alive. He's breathing. It's shallow, but he is definitely alive."

They waited a moment. The atmosphere was anxious and charged. "Should I pulse him again?" Creed asked finally.

"No," Draven replied harshly. "Just wait."

Kai was the first to notice the old man's finger twitch as she crouched before him. She reared back sharply, rising to her feet beside Draven. He glanced down at her. He looked amused, despite the tension in the air. Fane stirred more definably. His head lolled from side to side. Creed jumped back from him. "We've got a live one." His voice sounded almost gleeful. The others glared at him.

Finally, the old man lifted his head. His eyes rolled languidly around the room then darted between them all. His voice was timorous when he spoke. "Where am I?"

"You are in Varuna," Kai replied curtly. "In a dungeon."

"A dungeon," he replied in a rapid whisper. His eyes darted wildly around for a long, crazed moment. Then his body went rigid. He squeezed his closed his eyes tightly. His features contracted as if he were experiencing great pain.

Leona scowled, stepping forwards. "Has he passed out?"

Kai leaned down to examine his face. A single tear streaked down his cheek. "He's still awake," she announced. "Give him a moment."

After several long, harrowing moments, Fane opened his eyes. They were shining with tears. He did not bother to blink them away. "Where is my grandson?"

"In Tyr."

"So many terrible things..."

"What do you mean?" Draven asked sharply, bending down so he was eye to eye with the old man.

"I've done so many terrible things."

"Do you remember?"

His voice was an anguished whisper. "All of them. I remember them all. The horror of them." He looked up at them in supplication. "Please, send me back into the Abyss."

"It's gone," Kai told him. "There's no going back."

Fane shook his head violently. "I cannot live, not like this."

"Fane, who sent you to kill me?"

He looked at Jila in confusion, as though he barely recognised her. "Queen Jila?" She inclined her head. His mouth twitched slightly into a grimace. "You are exceedingly difficult to kill. It is most impressive."

He did not sound angry or impressed. He sounded merely weary and resigned. "Who sent you?" Jila barked.

"He isn't my grandson. As surely as I, he is mad with Abyss."

"Duke Julian?" Draven prompted. "He sent you to assassinate Queen Jila?"

"He is a monster. A construct. He is no man. He is no blood of mine." Tears streaked unconstrained down his lined, eroded face.

Jila and Leona exchanged a long, significant look. "Commander," Jila said sharply. "I want his confession recorded."

Draven nodded and flipped open his communicator. He jabbed briskly at the buttons. He placed the small, brass compact beside Fane's chair. "Enyo Fane, did your grandson, Duke Julian of Tyr, send you to kill Queen Jila?" he asked in a clear, carrying voice.

Fane's eyes rolled to Draven. "I was not myself. I am a monster."

"Not anymore," Leona said harshly. "You are only a broken man. Tell us what we must know!"

Fane dropped his head. "So many people, so many faces, so many dead."

"Did Julian send you to kill me?" Jila repeated relentlessly.

"You. The King, the assassin, the man in the hotel, others before you, so many others..."

They had nearly forgotten about the other murders, so embroiled had they been in the intrigue that had followed his escape from the Sulis River bridge. Kai demanded, "Why did you kill them? Was the Tyran working for Julian, too?"

Fane blinked at her in confusion for a moment. Tears leaked from his eyes. "Not a Tyran. He was a Varunian."

"Who was he?"

"The instrument through which my master spoke to me. He will not face me himself."

"Why did you hire Wick to kill the Queen? Why not do it yourself?"

"He was never meant to succeed. I was to follow."

"It was deception? You hired him to mislead us? To turn our attention to our own people? Why did you kill the Varunian?"

"He was afraid. He wanted out. He was no longer needed. He was eliminated. Another life. So many others...men, women, children..." The lucidity with which he had answered her questions seemed on a rapid decline.

"Damnit."

"Monster. I'm a monster."

"So it was Julian who sent you," Jila repeated, as if she could scarcely believe her ears.

"He gives me what I need. I repay him."

"He gives you Abyss to sustain you while you murder people for him?" Leona asked disgustedly.

A sob tore from Fane's throat. "So many terrible things. I have done so many terrible things. We are both monsters." He looked up at Kai, as if he could sense that she was the same as he. "Kill me. Please. I cannot live with what I've done. All the things...they haunt me. Their faces, their screams, their fear. They haunt me."

Kai stepped back from him. Her expression was guarded and uneasy. Draven caught her shoulders as she backed into him. She recoiled from him as if his touch had burned her. Leona advanced upon the old man. Her expression was terrible in its icy fury. "Leona," Jila said softly.

Leona's lip curled. "He murdered my husband. I will gladly give him what he wants."

Jila reached for the Queen. She touched her shoulder lightly. "He is only an old man. He will die anyway, soon enough." Anger flashed in Leona's eyes. She shrugged off Jila's hand as if it were a loathsome insect. "Leona. Do not let Julian turn you into him. Don't take that path. Please. You'll never come back."

Jila's voice was low and cold. The anger drained as suddenly from Leona's face as the tears began. Jila stepped towards her swiftly, folding her into her arms. She led the weeping queen away from the cell, murmuring soft, soothing words in her ear. Jila paused. She glanced over her shoulder at Draven and Kai. "I will send someone to him," she promised evenly. "He will have what he asks for."

Draven exhaled heavily. "What will you do with what we know?"

Jila considered. She looked down at Leona, who lifted her head. She looked abruptly, eerily calm. "Julian will pay for what he's done," Leona said levelly. "But we will behave as civilised people, not vigilantes. We will present the evidence at his own Parliament. And if they decide to execute him, I will be there to watch. And I will find my peace." She turned her firm gaze to Jila. "And if they refuse to hold him accountable, there will be war."

CHAPTER EIGHTEEN

*T*he Parliament of Tyr's tribunal chamber was large and impressive, carved of polished marble and trimmed in ornately engraved gold. Brilliantly coloured and eerily realistic murals covered every wall. They depicted fantastic scenes of the knights, dukes and princes of Tyr engaged in heroic and likely utterly imagined feats. The murals could scarcely be viewed, however, for on this day, the ascending pews were filled with spectators from floor to ceiling.

The Parliament senators sat in a half-circle before the congregation, dressed in elegant robes of silver and gold. Their majesty was overshadowed by the Queens Jila and Leona. The Queens sat facing them from the complainant's table in their finest gowns. Their expressions were imposing. They looked stately, imperious and utterly terrible.

"Kill me. Please. I cannot live with what I've done. All the things...they haunt me. Their faces, their screams, their fear. They haunt me."

The old man's feeble, heartrending voice resounded through the echoing chamber. It trailed off in the endless, awful silence that followed. The congregation had caught their breathes at once, as though in anticipation of an unspeakable tragedy. Sitting with his solicitors at the table beside that which represented the nations of Leza and Varuna, Julian's face was curiously blank. There was nothing in his toxic blue eyes. He might not have even been there or aware at all of the proceedings. His solicitors were equally stone-faced. They practically vibrated with apprehension.

The silent, lingering, shaken moment passed. Expressions of varied fury, repulsion and consternation crept across the faces of Tyr's Parliament members. The Senate Leader rose laboriously to his feet. His posture was stiff. His face was inscrutable. When he opened his mouth to speak, the congregation took a collective breath in anticipation of his words.

"Queen Jila, Queen Leona." He bowed briefly to them. They inclined their heads majestically in unison. "The Parliament has heard your case. Your Grace, Duke Julian, do you have anything to say in this matter?"

His solicitors began immediately to whisper urgently to each other. Julian merely raised his chin with an arrogant, relaxed expression, as though he believed steadfastly in his people's favour. "I need not defend myself from such ridiculous, outlandish charges," he announced haughtily. "It is clearly an attempt by the Queens to discredit me."

The Senate Leader's mouth thinned in displeasure. "And discredit you, they have done."

Julian blinked. Jila rose to her feet. "Your Honours, we must have your assurances this monstrous behaviour will stop immediately and will never again be repeated. Queen Leona and I have elected to present this matter to you for a verdict rather than declaring war and punishing your country for the sins of your sovereign." She straightened her back. She looked around at the Senators with a severe glint in her eyes. "We trust that you will make the honourable decision. We need not remind you that we have the might of both our nations of Varuna and Leza behind us."

The room was quiet as the implicit threat lingered in the stillness. The Senators glanced at each other. Their faces were hard, still and unreadable. The Senate Leader at last inclined his head. "Your Majesty, this matter will be handled accordingly, to the satisfaction of the council." He turned his attention to Julian. His eyes were like cold, grey steel. "You are the Duke of this great country, Julian, but you are not above the law. When you were given the crown, you swore to uphold the honours and virtue of your fathers and our nation, yet you have squandered your power on folly, arrogance and greed."

Julian blinked up at him with huge, electric blue eyes. The congregation waited breathlessly.

"You are a disgrace to our nation. You may be our ruler, but you must submit yourself to the mercy and judgment of the court." He took a deep breath. "We rule that you will be permanently exiled from Tyr to the furthest reaches of the continent, to the nations beyond the Abyssium zone. You will have no access to Abyss or any Abyssal machines. You will have a constant guard to ensure you remain as far from Tyr as possible. Your exile begins the moment you exit this court, and there you will remain until your final days."

The Senate Leader rapped his gavel on the bureau before him. The noise echoed through the chamber in the astonished silence of the spectators. Then a sound like the buzzing of bees filled the chamber as the crowd began murmuring incredulously. The sound built into an eruption of jeers and exclamations. Julian's eerily smooth face was motionless. His eyes were wide with amazement, as though the words had scarcely begun to penetrate his awareness.

The triumphant Queens exchanged a glance. They stood as one. They inclined their heads gracefully to the council. "Your Honours," Leona announced. Her voice carried effortlessly over the noise of the crowd, who hushed at once to hear her words. "We are satisfied with the court's decision, and we will provide any aid needed in the wake of your country's flux to instate a new regime that will better suit the ideals of the nations of the Abyssium zone."

The Senate Leader sighed heavily, but he bowed to the sovereigns. "Thank you, My Queens. We are in your service henceforth."

Leona spun to the assembly. She raised a hand to point at the incredulous Duke. "Remove this traitor at once!"

* * *

There was no expression on her face as Kai watched Duke Julian's removal from Parliament. The once massive and powerful Duke was diminished, in title and structure. He had been utterly crushed with the loss of his Abyss. He was nothing more than a meagre, wretched man. He was no longer a monster. He no longer possessed the means to satiate his rapaciousness and greed. He pleaded for the return of his power, alternately red-faced and enraged, beseeching and howling.

His anguished cries were in vain. His struggles came to nothing, shackled as he was. Chains wrapped about him from ankles to throat. The Abyssal guards who had been once devoted to his service bundled him unceremoniously into a dingy, metal cage on the back of an open wagon. It was hardly as grand as his oldest, shoddiest carriage. With the sharp snap of the driver's reigns, the horses were off. Julian's wails faded into the darkening night like the memory of a terrible dream.

"He will never be able to cause harm to anyone ever again," Draven said in a quiet voice beside her. Kai looked up at him sharply. Her eyes blazed with cold fury. He reared slightly back from her, caught out. "Kaia?"

"He did so much harm." Her voice was low, husky and deceptively restrained. "He killed so many people and destroyed so many families. He turned his own grandfather into an Abyssium mad atrocity. He deserves so much worse."

Draven sighed. "It was right to present the case to his people and allow them to decide his fate. It was justice."

She spun to him. Her eyes were wild. Her voice was harsh as she spat, "Justice? Where is the justice in a life of leisure, under constant guard and without pain?"

"He will be cut off from Abyss. It is the greatest punishment he may receive."

"It is nothing! One can live without it. You do."

Draven seized her shoulders. "Kaia, his people have made their choice. Jila and Leona are satisfied. We have avoided war. Justice is done."

She jerked away from him. "Not for me."

"There is nothing more to be done."

Her expression was so cold, he took a step back from her. "There may be something."

Draven stared intently into her eyes. He saw nothing of his fiery, passionate woman, his shaft of moonlight in the dark. He saw only the Abyss, the very depths of the sea, and intense, simmering hate. "No, Kaia," he said urgently. "No. I know what you are thinking, but no. I will not let you do this. I will not let you lose your soul for that man."

"He is no man."

"And all the less reason to allow you to lose yourself for him. He is no threat to us anymore. This life, the exile and lack of riches and Abyss in his life are a fate worse than death for him." He stepped towards her again. His expression was determined. His tone was supplicating. "Please accept it."

She turned her head from him. The rigidity of her jaw, the glint in her eyes assured him she had remained unmoved. Her blue eyes glowed. It was as though he could see in their depths all the misery the Duke had caused. He saw the dead bodies, her Queen's face, Leona's shattered expression, and the old man's broken figure and heart-wrenching sobs as he pleaded for death. As she looked steadily back at him, he saw nothing but pain and horror and despair. "I'm sorry, Draven," she whispered. "I must."

"Please, Kaia," he said. For a moment, she held his eyes. She considered his anguish and desperation. "Please. For me. Don't do this. Do not carry out this vengeance. It is not for you to do! Do not give up everything." He broke off. He caught her shoulders and drew her towards him. "If you do, you will lose me."

She held his unflinching eyes. For an ephemeral instant, she wavered. A single tear streaked down her cheek. "I'm sorry, Draven. I can't. I can't let him live. I can't let this go on."

"Kai--"

"You knew what I was before this began. You knew how this would end."

"Kaia, it doesn't have to. Not like this. You don't have to let this be who you are!"

"Don't fool yourself, Draven. It has always been who I am."

He released her. There was a terrible regret on his face as he stepped away. He turned slowly away from her. His shoulders hitched almost imperceptibly. She watched him go silently. She did not bother to dash away the tears that flowed freely over her cheeks. The vengeful spirit of her wrath lingered within her even as he drew further away from her. She did not call him back. She lifted her chin. She swiped away the tears. She turned to walk the other way.

She did not turn back.

* * *

The curtains rustled softly. It might have been a whisper or a breath or a phantom in the shadows. Julian bolted upright in the tiny, uncomfortable bed. Sweat prickled on his flesh and ran into his eyes. It stung. Then she was above him. She raised a long, sharp knife to his throat. He knew her face. He knew her dark blue eyes and her long, silver hair instantly.

He had not seen the merciless, wrathful look in her glowing eyes before. Somehow it suited her. She was more beautiful in her terribleness. She was an avenging angel set upon him from the world above. He did not struggle or fight or plead with her. Instead, he looked resigned and almost relieved, as if the moment he had anticipated had finally arrived.

"How did you get past my guards?" he asked in a soft, relaxed voice. She said nothing. She glared down at him with those brilliant, livid eyes. He smiled slightly. "Never mind. It doesn't matter, not now. I should have known it would be you who would be the one to end me. It was you who started all this."

Her eyes glittered. They sparked with spite and rage and malice. "You did all this!" she hissed. "You hurt so many people. You ruined so many lives!"

His reply startled her, not because of the words but because of the sincerity and the pain infused in every syllable. "Yes. I did."

She did not allow him to catch her out. "You were greedy and foolish and depraved."

"Yes. I was all of those things. And more. Things more terrible still." He sounded heartbroken, but she felt no pity and no mercy. "I was the worst sort of man."

"You were no man at all! Now you are nothing."

"I deserve to die." He took a shallow, shuddering breath. "I caused so much destruction." He tilted his head back. He exposed his throat to her. "I am ready. Kill me. End it."

She released a low, feral growl, like a hungry animal scenting fresh blood. Her hand moved quickly, so quickly he saw only a blur in the pale moonlight. There was no pain, no fear. When she drew back from him, a single globule of blood dripped from the tip of her blade. A tiny rivulet trickled down his neck into the collar of his fine silk pyjamas.

He looked up at her in surprise. He reached to his neck to touch the thin dribble. The was no anger in her face now, no rage, malice or murder. She simply looked pityingly at him. It was worse than any other expression he had ever seen on her face. "Why?" he whispered. "Feel no qualm. It would be a mercy. Your conscience is clear. End my misery, please."

She drew away from him. She lifted herself off his trembling body. She stood beside the bed. She peered down at him with that same awful pity. "No."

"What?"

"No, I won't kill you. You deserve nothing. No mercy. You deserve a fate worse than death." For a moment, her lips curved into the shadow of a smile. "I will not tarnish my own soul for you. I will not allow you to destroy me as well."

She turned away from him. He sat up. He reached desperately for her. "No, Luna, please don't go!" She paused. She did not turn her head to look at him. "Please. Kill me. You would be doing the world a great service."

"No," she said. Her back was stiff and straight and immovable. "I would not. You deserve this. You will live a long life. And you will suffer. As long as that life lasts, I hope you suffer. You are nothing now. You will never be anything more."

And then she was gone, as though she had never been there at all, as though she had been merely the softest whisper of fabric or curtain or the faintest breath of air.

* * *

The palace grounds had been transformed into a spectacular, dazzling festival in celebration of Queen Leona's ascension to the throne. The traditional time of mourning for King Silas had ended. Now it seemed as though the entire kingdom had turned out for the gala. The atmosphere was charged. The Lezan people were keen with faith that their new Queen would lead them with as much strength, insight and compassion as her beloved husband.

Lively music, joyous shouts and merry laughter filled the air as the people danced around Draven. They drank the favourite local wine. They venerated the Queen's name and pounded him on the back in congratulations. Leona had awarded him the highest commendation of the kingdom for his part in the undoing of Duke Julian. The honour meant nothing to him. It was little recompense for what had been lost in the course.

He felt no sense of pride, no glory, no sentiment of accomplishment. There was only a yawning, empty, ripping blackness in his chest. His beloved King, his dear friend, was gone. His time of mourning for his monarch had only begun. He could not cast off the vestiges of grief so easily as the others. He could not lose himself in spirit and revelry and hope for the future. There were too many deaths to remember. Too much had been lost. He was a shadow among the jovial crowd. He did not belong there.

He did not start when a familiar, calloused hand clapped him upon the shoulder. "You look glum, my friend," Colonel Grimes said. "Why the dreary countenance? We have a new Queen, the Duke of Tyr has been brought to justice, and you are a national hero. This should be cause for merriment, not melancholy."

Draven ignored the glass Darius raised to him, as if in salute. "I have no leaning towards merriment tonight, Colonel," Draven replied flatly.

Darius smirked. He handed Draven the wine. Draven gulped it down in one swallow without tasting it. "You look like a man sick with mislaid love, my friend," he told him in a voice uncharacteristically gentle with compassion. "Is there no getting her back?"

Draven looked away. His lip curled into a sneer. "I was not thinking of her."

"My friend, I have never seen a sorrier man, and nothing makes a man sorry like a capricious woman. What's happened between you two, then? Has she gone off?"

"She is gone forever."

Darius' eyebrows lifted. "Not dead, I hope?"

"No. Not dead. But she is nothing to me all the same. She is lost."

Darius looked amused. "They are never lost, not completely."

"She made her own choices. She chose retribution. She chose to become a monster." His voice was quiet and cold.

Darius smirked. "So dramatic, always, you young men in love. It is as if

195

the weight of the world is upon your shoulders." He sighed in what Draven considered inappropriate pleasure. "All is not lost, my friend. Sometimes, out of the darkest hour, there is a moonbeam."

Draven scowled at the absurdity. Darius slipped away into the crowd before he had a chance to properly retort. He looked around for him. He opened his mouth to rebuke the unsolicited sentiments. Instead, his eyes caught movement in the crowd. A gleaming, incandescent shape glided towards him. She wore silver to match her hair. Surely it could not be her. She could be only a spectre, a terrible vision wrung from his deepest misery. In his memories, she had never looked quite so luminous as she did amidst the revellers now.

Then she was in front of him. She materialised out of the throng as though she had flashed down from above. She might have been an angel or a ghost. She might have been a devil. She was smiling guilelessly. He did not think he had ever seen her face so bright or so unguarded. She was an apparition, surely. She could be nothing else. She did not disappear in a puff of smoke. When she reached for his hand, her touch was warm and solid and irrefutably real.

He looked down at her. His brow furrowed, and he took a step back. He recoiled from her touch. "Why are you here, Kai?" Though his tone was so cold his breath might have frozen the air, there was no expression in his face. He looked at her as though he did not know her. He looked at her as though the sight of her did not lance through him the way her knife had pierced the Duke's eager throat.

He did not freeze the warmth in her dark blue eyes. Her smile did not waver. "I came for you, Draven."

"No. You chose your path. You chose hate and vengeance."

She shook her head. Her eyes glittered fondly up at him. "If I am hate and vengeance, are you love and forgiveness?"

His scowl darkened. "I don't understand you."

"Can you forgive me?"

He turned his head from her. He crossed his arms over his chest to ward her off. "You killed a man, Kai. You gave everything up. You gave me up."

"I was wrong. I made a mistake."

"It is too late now for that! You cannot simply come back and plead forgiveness. You knew what it meant if you did this. You knew it was the end."

Her voice was light when she asked, "Is it?"

He paused. There was something in her tone that drew his eyes back to her. There was no malice. There was no scorching hate in her dark blue eyes. It was as though they were lit from within. It was as though the darkness he had seen flash within her so many times had been illuminated. He shook his head. "I warned you what your actions would bring."

"I heard what you said. All of it." When his mouth tightened, she stepped closer to him. This time, he stared warily down at her. He did not pull away. "He's not dead."

Draven blinked. "What?"

"The Duke. He isn't dead. I didn't kill him." Draven opened his mouth in surprise. She did not allow him to speak. "My blade was at this throat. I drew his blood, and he begged for death, but I did not kill him. He begged me to end his suffering, and he would have had me give up everything for him. And then I realised it was not a mercy, not to anyone but him, and he did not deserve my mercy. He is nothing." She raised her eyebrows. Her expression was so soft and tender, it seemed utterly alien upon her pale, shimmering face. "He is not worth losing you."

Draven's wary expression did not falter, despite her speech. "He is alive?"

"Yes, he is very much alive, and I expect he will be for a very long time."

"You still chose him, Kai! You chose vengeance. You let me walk away, and you did not call me back. You think you can come now and turn it around? How am I to even know he is alive?"

She smiled. "You know. You can see it, can't you? I did let you walk away, but I came back. I was wrong, and I came back. I am spoilt, Draven. I have given lives away. I have never understood the impact of my actions. But as I held his life in my hands, it became clear."

Draven sighed. He lowered his head. He turned away from her without speaking.

Kai stepped forward. She seized his arm with unexpected desperation. "Please, Draven," she said urgently. "I chose you, in the end. I did."

He threw off her arm. He spun towards her. She took a timid step back, but he caught her up. He grasped her face in his hands. He crushed her against him, and he kissed her. It might have been the first time or the last. When he drew back from her, he laughed. It was as if a light had spread across his sculpted face. "The Duke is alive."

"Yes. I never thought those words would be cheerful ones, but he deserves to live. He deserves his agony." She smiled. She wrapped her arms around his waist. She pressed her face against his chest. His heart thumped steadily, rhythmically against her cheek. "May he live out the rest of his very long life in anguish and despair."

Draven chuckled. "Never before have such sentiments sounded so appealing. You must be rubbing off on me."

She lifted her head to smile at him. "I think, perhaps, it would be best if you did the rubbing off on me. There are many aspects of my personality that would not suit you in the least."

"You do me a disservice. I would, in fact, make a very good brigand."

"You certainly would not. You, Commander, are far too keen on propriety and decent behaviour. I reckon things will be a bit dodgy off the ground."

He laughed. "You may be right about that. Perhaps we should discuss some brass tacks."

"I never was one for brass tacks. Suppose we just sort it out as we go along?"

"I suppose it's too much to hope you'll consider a more legitimate line of work?"

"If by legitimate you mean legal, I will give it due consideration. I would not, however, hold out any great hope for that."

He nodded. "I can learn to live with that."

"I don't suppose you'd consider a less scrupulous line of work?"

"No."

"Right. Well, I suppose there are worse things a man can possess than integrity."

"If that's the case, why you do make it sound so distasteful?"

THE END

ABOUT THE AUTHOR

Stella Drexler is the author of Hex Breaker available from SynergeBooks, CHANT and Angel of the Abyss from DC Press, and the upcoming Nightmare Island Series from Writers-Exchange, as well as several other novels, comics, short stories, essays and shopping lists. She lives in the moment with Mr. Drexler and their Helper Monkey, Casanova. In between working on new books or spending time tamping out the occasional fire, Stella can often be found exploring, adventuring, eating, drinking, dancing, singing, shopping, laughing, sighing, smiling, and otherwise enjoying herself.

Read Stella's Blog at:

www.stelladrexler.wordpress.com

For more titles by Stella visit:

www.dcpressbooks.org